Cottage
on the
Hill

ALSO BY EMMA DAVIES

Letting in Light
Turn Towards the Sun
Lucy's Little Village Book Club
The Little Cottage on the Hill

Emma Davies

Summer at the Little Cottage on the Hill

Bookouture

Published by Bookouture in 2018

An imprint of StoryFire Ltd.

Carmelite House
50 Victoria Embankment
London EC4Y 0DZ

www.bookouture.com

ISBN: 978-1-78681-388-6
eBook ISBN: 978-1-78681-387-9

Thank you for the music.

Chapter 1

Isobel picked up the bow, laid it against the strings of her violin, and began to play. Deliberately elongated, the notes carved through the air around her, filling every corner of the room and bouncing softly on the whitewashed walls before returning back to her, the perfect sound ringing out clear and true. She had no need to check the score, nor think about the tricky technicalities the piece presented – she knew that the music was being played flawlessly. What concerned her today was the quality of the sound she was producing.

She stilled the bow, listening intently as the last note died away, then lowered her violin with a nod of satisfaction. She looked around the space that was to be her home for the next six weeks and congratulated herself on her choice. This little cottage on a hill would do very nicely indeed.

Tucking her long dark hair behind her ears, she placed her instrument on the coffee table in front of her and took in the rest of her surroundings. The living room was a perfect rectangle, with one wall covered in what looked like pages from old magazines, reminding Isobel of the vibrant floral images from the farm's website. Definitely vintage, but still beautiful, they gave the room a wonderfully historical look without feeling like she was in a museum. The furniture was minimal: the desk she had requested, a low bookcase, a wingback armchair beside the fireplace and a squishy-looking sofa opposite it. None of it matched, but it suited the cosy charm of the room, and to Isobel it was perfectly acceptable. She had no need for luxury; she was here to work.

Anxious about finding anywhere at such short notice – it was already well into the holiday season and everything she'd looked at was booked up – it was purely by chance that Isobel happened across the Joy's Acre website; something about it had caught her eye. It was clearly a new endeavour, evident by the availability of only one finished cottage on the site and clearer still from the effusive welcome that she had received; gushing and tinged with anxiety. Still, it hardly mattered. What was important was that the cottage was available, and that they were happy to accommodate her practising day and night. With no other guests and work still being undertaken on site, any noise she might make was not considered to be an issue. Just so long as they understood that she was not here to play for *them*, everything would be fine. She needed absolute privacy while she worked, and no interruptions.

Aside from unpacking her violin to check the acoustics, the only other thing she had done since entering the cottage an hour ago had been to set up her laptop on the desk, together with her small keyboard and two speakers without which she was dead in the water. Her handbag lay abandoned on the kitchen table, and her bags, dumped in the narrow hallway when she'd entered, were untouched. They were of little consequence to her right now, she could sort out the rest of her things later.

She wandered through to the kitchen, glancing at the array of newly installed fittings, and picked up the kettle, taking it over to the sink to fill and wondering in which bag she had packed her teabags. She checked her watch while she waited for the water to boil and drifted back to the desk in the other room. Sitting down in front of the computer, she clicked on the icon to load the program she used to compose her music. Ten minutes later, she had completely forgotten about making tea.

Isobel often had little concept of time when she was working, so it could have been anything between half an hour and four hours later when she looked up again. Frowning, she cocked her head to one side to listen out for what might have interrupted her thoughts. Hearing nothing, she lowered her gaze to the screen once more. No, there it was again. This time she took off her headphones and looked around her, jumping out of her skin as she saw a man's face pressed up against the window to her left, his hand raised to tap on the glass. Composing herself, she raised a hand in acknowledgement to his beaming face and got up and went through into the hallway with a sigh. Stepping over her bags, she opened the door.

'Hi,' said the man, his smile growing even wider. It was the same chap who had helped her carry in her belongings. She gave a brief smile, but remained silent.

'I'm interrupting… sorry, but I just wanted to check that everything was okay…? With the cottage?' he added, taking in her bemused expression.

Isobel stared at him, searching her brain for the piece of information she required. She'd been in such a hurry to get rid of him earlier that she hadn't really listened to what he'd been saying.

'I'm sorry,' she said. 'But I've forgotten your name. You did tell me, didn't you?' She lifted a hand to her lips, the huge jet ring she wore on her right hand flashing in the sunlight.

The man nodded. 'It's Tom,' he replied. 'I'm the thatcher.'

'Of course… And the others…' She peered at Tom. 'Are… Trixie?' She raised her eyes, looking for confirmation. 'She's the one who cooks, yes? The one with pink hair, and the other lady was Clara, I think?'

Tom nodded. 'The gardener,' he supplied. The two of them looked at one another. 'And then there's Seth, the owner of the farm, and Maddie, who helps run the place. Maddie will be the one you've been corresponding with. You'll get to meet her a bit later on, I expect.'

Isobel was beginning to feel a little uncomfortable.

'Sorry, what was it you wanted again?'

He gestured to the hallway behind her. 'Just to see if everything is okay – did you manage to get things up and running?' He was trying to look past her.

'Yes, fine. It doesn't take me long to set up and the acoustics are actually better than I thought.' She registered the slight frown. 'Oh. That wasn't what you meant.'

Tom gave a nervous smile. 'It was actually, but really I'm supposed to be asking if the cottage is to your liking. And whether you have enough towels and pillows, that kind of thing.'

Isobel looked about her. She hadn't even been upstairs yet; what could she possibly be expected to say? The silence grew again.

'I'm a musician too,' began Tom tentatively.

Isobel's heart sank. She had heard that so many times in the past from people who thought it would give them an instant connection with her. And they always, always, wanted to talk about it; they wanted her to ask what kind of music they played, or worse, what kind of music they wrote. Then, once she'd done that, they wanted to know all about her too… Seriously, sometimes the conversation could go on for quite a few minutes.

She gave a tight smile. 'I thought you said you were a thatcher?'

Tom scratched his head. 'Well, yes, that too. But that's just the day job… I play in a band, out of hours, like…'

It was hot standing on the doorstep, and Isobel ducked her face away from the sun.

'How lovely,' she said, suspecting she sounded trite, but not caring. She took a step backwards and pasted on a smile. 'Please could you let the owners know that the cottage is wonderful. I'm sure I'll have everything I need, and so they mustn't worry about me. I'm here to work as I think you know, so...'

'Right. Absolutely,' replied Tom, finally taking the hint. 'And thanks... we're all a bit, well, nervous, I guess. This is a new venture for us so we're just hoping we've got everything covered.' He peered down the hallway, trying to see past her. 'Have you had a chance yet to see what you'd like for dinner? I left the list on the kitchen table... although it's only a guide of course, Trixie is happy to cook something else if there's anything in particular you'd rather have.'

With another sigh, she motioned for Tom to come in, grimacing as she stepped over her discarded bags once more.

'I've been a bit busy...' she muttered. The list on the kitchen table was right beside her handbag, but Isobel hadn't even noticed it was there. She picked it up, scanning the lines. 'Oh yes, the chicken sounds lovely.' She handed the list back to Tom. 'And whatever's easiest for dessert, I really don't mind.' She probably wouldn't eat it anyway.

'And what time would you like it?'

Isobel scanned the kitchen looking for a clock. 'What time is it now?' she asked.

'A little after four.'

'Well then, seven o'clock would suit me. Would that be all right with the cook?'

'I'll let Trixie know, I'm sure it will be fine.' The conversation was becoming more and more stilted by the minute.

'I'm sorry,' she said again, glancing at the laptop. 'I have a deadline…'

'Oh, right… yes of course. I'll let myself out, but do let us know if you need anything else, won't you…? Or if anything is not to your liking…' He was already backing down the hallway.

Isobel nodded, forcing a smile. She waited until Tom had reached the front door then she turned and walked back into the living room. Sitting down at the desk again, she replaced the headphones over her ears, sighed with relief and carried on as if the interruption had never even taken place.

★

'It was awful,' said Tom, 'I felt like a kid trying to make friends in the playground. *Oh, please will you like me, please?*'

Clara flashed him a sympathetic smile. 'Tom, I'm sure it wasn't as bad as you think.'

'Oh, it was. She's altogether more gorgeous up close, with the biggest brown eyes… but she kept looking at me like I was some irritating insect buzzing around her.' He rested his head in his hands and groaned. 'And then when I mentioned I was a musician as well, she practically shut the door in my face. You could see it was the last thing she wanted to talk about.'

Clara sat back on her heels and tucked a stray strand of her long blonde hair behind her ears. She'd been weeding and her muddy hands left a streak of dirt across her face, which Tom politely ignored.

'She's here to work, Tom, don't forget that. All that matters is she *is* here, and paid up for six whole weeks.'

'I know.' He turned his head back towards the cottage, the roof of which he had finished thatching only a few weeks ago. 'I guess I thought…' He trailed off. 'It doesn't matter.'

But Clara was far too perceptive to let his comment go. 'That you might have found a kindred spirit?'

Tom rolled his eyes. 'Is that what we're calling them these days?'

'I was trying to be polite.' Clara grinned. 'She is very attractive.'

'Ah well, you can't blame a man for trying… But you know one of these days my luck will turn and I will find my one true love… In the meantime I have a hot date with destiny, courtesy of Tinder.'

'Is that really her name?'

'Oh, very funny.' Tom grimaced. 'No, her name is Angie.'

'Right, well you've checked Isobel's okay now. She's a grown woman and I'm sure she'll come and ask if there's anything she needs. I'll be out here for a bit yet anyway – I swore to myself I'd get this bed finished today, so I'll keep an eye out for her. Now, go on, off you go, you've got a roof to finish.' She swivelled her eyes past Tom towards the second cottage on the plot. 'It's very quiet, perhaps I'll hear her music out here while I work.'

'Headphones,' said Tom with finality. 'Whatever she plays, I'm not sure any of us are going to get to listen to it.' He gave Clara a wry smile. 'Laters,' he said, already walking away, before suddenly calling out. 'Oh, and tell Trixie madam wants chicken for her tea.'

★

At first Tom didn't even notice the sound of music. The soft notes seemed to blend with the evening air perfectly, the melody drifting up high to where he was sitting on the roof and mingling with birdsong and the rustle of leaves from the willow tree that sat just behind the house. It wasn't until his ears tuned into the pattern of sound that he realised someone was playing. Isobel. He stopped what he was doing, holding his breath so that he might hear better.

He played the violin himself, not well, but enough to get by if he needed to. But he had never, ever, managed to play it like this. He sat up straighter, craning his neck for a better view of Isobel's cottage, and then swung his leg over the ridge, and then again so that he faced the other way. The piece was not one he recognised, but then it had been a long time since he last played classical music. It was slow and measured, lilting as if riding the thermals of warm air as the notes swooped up and down the scale. Then, suddenly, it stopped.

Seconds later it started again, slightly faster this time and played with more force, the final notes of each section elongated, played vibrato. Every now and again he lost the sound as the breeze carried it away and part of him longed to climb down and listen properly, but the other part knew that somehow it would break the spell. And so he sat, entranced, as Isobel played her violin, the same piece over and over again, but each time with slight variation of speed, or tone or technique.

The sun had been high in the sky all day, the fields that Tom could see from his vantage point on the roof turning golden in the light. Joy's Acre sat high on top of a large hill, and its slope and the view of the village beyond spreading out before him was ever-changing depending on the weather or time of day. Tom was so attuned to the sun's passing that he scarcely had need for a watch. The colours would deepen and intensify as the day drew on, reaching full saturation just after dinnertime, before the light became slightly hazy and the colours wispy as the sun began to set.

A beeping sound broke Tom from his reverie and he refocused his attention, swearing under his breath. He pulled his phone from his pocket, grimacing as he realised the time. Angie was in the pub waiting for him, and had been for twenty minutes by the time she had texted.

Tom pushed the phone back into the pocket of his jeans and closed his eyes, feeling the heat gradually dissipate from the day. Of course, what he *should* do was climb down from the roof. The pub was in the village and he could be there in ten minutes, but even as the thought crossed his mind, Tom realised he wasn't going to go. He should never have made the date in the first place, but he had made it more out of habit than anything, believing as he always did that it would make him feel better. It rarely did, and it was time he stopped putting himself and his dates through this charade.

He sent a brief text saying that his car had broken down, and that his phone battery was about to die. He'd bought himself some time, that was all, and would explain things properly to Angie later. He didn't want to think about anything now; all he wanted was to listen to the music and let it return him to the way he had felt moments earlier.

By the time Isobel had finished playing, and Tom finally climbed wearily from the roof, he was astonished to find that another hour and a half had passed.

Chapter 2

The bedroom window had been wide open all night, but still Isobel lay drenched in sweat. Her eyelids flew open, breaking the stranglehold of the images in her head, a vision that was always the same; an utter darkness which slowly, insidiously, revealed pinpoints of light like the eyes of maddened beasts baying for her blood. She would try to run but her legs were rooted to the spot, just as she tried to cover her ears to block out the sound of cackling laughter and the cold, cold whisper of ugly words against her cheek. The cotton sheet had twisted around her legs, pinning them together, and the duvet had ridden up so that she felt as if she was suffocating beneath it. She clawed it away from her face.

Isobel had hoped that the change of scenery might make a difference, and that her nightmares wouldn't find her here, but it would seem that it made not one ounce of difference *where* she was, the dreams followed her because of *who* she was.

She threw back the covers and sat up, pulling at the hair that had stuck to her bare back and trying to waft a little air onto her neck while she waited for her pulse to stop racing. Eventually, when she felt calmer, she stood and crossed to the window, her gaze extending out across the garden, the curves of her naked body thrown into soft relief by moonlight. Of course, there was no sign of the thatcher now. He had eventually climbed down from the roof when she had finished playing and she'd watched him make his way across the garden in the rapidly dimming light.

She was surprised she had noticed him at all; he had been sitting so still when she had glanced out of the living room window the evening before. She often walked as she played – it helped her loosen up – and, initially, she'd thought he must be engaged in his own work, but some half hour later she realised he was still there and that, in fact, he was listening to her play.

It was the most extraordinary feeling. She was certain that he couldn't see her – the evening sunlight reflecting on the window made sure of that – and it was likely therefore that he was unaware she had seen him. But his presence intrigued her; there was something very intimate about it, and she found herself playing to him, drawing strength from her invisibility, becoming more and more immersed in her music until she found the perfect stillness deep inside of her and knew that she could have played forever. It had been years since she had felt even a glimmer of that, and as she'd played the final few bars of music, tears had run freely down her face. She shivered suddenly at the memory of that short release. In the end though it had made no difference; the nightmare had come again just as it had on so many nights before.

Her feet padded through the thick rug by the bed and she made her way carefully out of the bedroom, navigating the stairs and the hallway until she reached the kitchen. She collected a glass of water, and took it through to the living room. It was tempting to play the piece again, just one more time to clear her head, and she almost took up her violin, stopping at the last moment and taking a long drink of water instead. She held the cold glass against her cheek and breathed deeply. There would be time to work tomorrow, and the day after, she reminded herself, and here without all the interruptions of home she could focus, and she could heal.

The bed felt cool and inviting as she slipped back into it, and she drew the covers back over her. This time she slept.

★

Tom switched off his phone and groaned as he rolled over. It was only eight o'clock, and a third text message from Angie had just pinged onto his phone. It was his own fault; what he should have done last night was tell her that he had simply changed his mind about their date. Instead, after listening to Isobel play, he had embellished his earlier text about a broken-down car, saying that his phone had died on him when he'd rung the local garage and he'd had to wait to be towed home. He'd even suggested she drop him a line so they could rearrange, but he really hadn't expected her to, assuming that he wouldn't hear from her again. He composed another apologetic reply, but this time made it clear that he was calling it a day; nothing to do with her, his fault entirely, and sent it before he could change his mind. Then he stared at his phone, biting his lip as his finger hovered over his Tinder app. He pressed delete. He really couldn't do this any more.

His wake-up call had come a couple of weeks ago. A gig with the band had turned into a late-night drinking session and he had woken up the next morning beside a girl whose name he didn't even know, or certainly couldn't remember. He would be the first to admit that from the outside his morals looked questionable, but that was low even for him. The trouble was, it was too easy. He was good-looking and there was something about being in a band that made him seem even more desirable. A succession of shallow relationships and one night stands were the perfect bandage for the hurt he felt inside, and so he had continued to play the role of handsome cad with an eye for the ladies for as long as he could. Even at Joy's Acre, among friends, he went along with the charade.

He had already made up his mind to clean up his act, and last night something about the music he had heard had reinforced that feeling. It had been too beautiful a moment to be sullied by what would in all likelihood have been a one night stand. Isobel had not even known that he was listening to her, and that had made the music even more poignant; she had played for no other reason than because she could – for the sheer joy of the music, the sense of being at one with an instrument, and the knowledge that she could create magic from a collection of strings bound over a wooden box. Tom understood what it was to play, but he had never been able to *really* play as Isobel had, and for some reason it had moved him greatly.

He squinted one eye at the clock and gave another moan. It was time to get up. In fact, if he didn't get a shift on, he would be late. He tutted as he caught sight of a piece of paper by his bed. It was a request for a quote on a re-roof; he had meant to contact the customer yesterday, but by the time he got home, he had clean forgotten. He picked up the note and took it downstairs, placing it by the kettle while he searched for a clean mug. He found one which didn't look too bad, swirled it under the hot water tap just to be on the safe side, added two spoonfuls of coffee and waited for the kettle to boil.

Grabbing a clean tee shirt from a pile on the kitchen table, he returned upstairs to shower, but by the time he had washed, groomed the stubble on his chin to just the length he liked it and hunted for his wallet, he was so late he had to run from the house, both his coffee and the note from a potential customer forgotten.

Work for the day was already well underway when he arrived at Joy's Acre, and he gave a cheery wave to Trixie as he passed by the kitchen window. With any luck, she would be out with bacon sandwiches shortly, and if it was a real red-letter day, she would also have made some of her cheese and onion muffins.

He peered up at the sky, but it was already set into a cloudless blue. There were hours of work ahead of him yet and having the pink-haired ex-barmaid on site to cook for them all was an absolute godsend. She hadn't been with them long, in fact, she had joined them not long after Maddie had been employed to whip Joy's Acre into shape before they all went bust. Maddie had discovered Trixie in a local pub, and it had only taken one sample of her exquisite cooking for Maddie to offer her a job. Trixie had jumped at the chance to come to live and work at Joy's Acre and had become an instant part of the team.

As he rounded the corner of the main house, the large barn at the far end of the site came into view. Its big double doors were wide open, the figures of Seth and Maddie silhouetted against the sunlight in the doorway. He made his way across the garden to them.

Beside the barn were three more cottages, almost identical to the one that Isobel was now staying in. Tom's current job was to re-thatch the first of these, with numbers two and three following as soon after as they could manage, but the barn was also a massive project, and would in time provide somewhere for Clara and Trixie to live as well as a communal space for guests to use. However, knowing quite how to achieve all this on a tight budget was proving to be tricky, and most of Seth's time was occupied by his effort to keep costs to a minimum.

Tom smiled a greeting. 'Another gorgeous day,' he remarked.

Maddie looked at her watch. 'And you're on time too.' But she was grinning, just teasing him. 'So, did Angie not turn out to be the woman of your dreams? Or was she just very gentle with you? Usually when you've had a hot date you look a tad bleary-eyed the next morning.'

Tom returned the grin. He was well used to having his love life ridiculed, and to be fair, he asked for most of it. But it was part of his character at Joy's Acre and if he gave them no reason to think differently he couldn't really complain. Besides, he enjoyed the banter... up to a point.

'I'll have you know I slept alone last night,' he retorted.

Maddie raised her eyebrows. 'Stood you up, did she?'

Tom just laughed. There was no point in making a big deal of it. 'Something like that. Or maybe it's time to turn over a new leaf. So, yes, I'm as fresh as a daisy this morning and ready to crack on...' He pulled a face. 'But I could do with some more spars if you've got a spare hour to make some today.'

Seth rolled his eyes. 'I love how he asks you now, and not me, but it's my own fault, I suppose.'

The spars were big 'staples' that held the straw tight to the roof as it was thatched, each made from a length of birch twig, twisted and bent along its length. There was a distinct knack to making them and now that Seth had taught Maddie how to do it, she was even better and faster than he was.

Maddie grinned, but nodded. 'No problem, Tom. We're just trying to decide what's next for the barn.'

Tom looked around him at the huge empty space where there was still an awful lot of work to be done. He pulled a face. 'Rather you than me.'

'Yeah, we need a big magic wand at the very least.'

Tom held out his hands to show they were empty. 'Sorry, no can do. But I'll get on with my roof as quickly as I can, that way at least we can finish off the cottage and get it ready for occupation. It would mean a bit more income coming in which would help, surely?'

Seth nodded. 'How are things going, Tom? Are we still on schedule?'

'As long as the weather holds we are. I'm trying to get as many hours in as possible right now, but at least the days are long, which helps.' He stopped, thinking for a minute, wondering how best to phrase his next statement. 'I'll get going in a minute, but I just thought I ought to remind you about the wedding at the end of the month. It'll be here before I know it and I'm going to need a bit of time with the band, for rehearsals and stuff. I just wanted to check that you're still okay with it? The timing is crazy, I know, but…'

Seth sighed. 'Tom, it's fine. Your gig has been booked for ages and you can't let them down. Besides, I never want Joy's Acre to feel like somewhere we all have to clock-on and clock-off. Everyone here more than pulls their weight, so there's plenty of room for give and take.'

Tom smiled. That was exactly what he'd expected Seth to say, but Tom was also well aware that he hadn't always pulled his weight in the past, and being a very old friend of Seth's had meant that he'd got away with plenty that he shouldn't have. Seth joined in with the banter about his timekeeping, his love life, his frequent visits to the pub and resultant hangovers – it was all part of the friendship they shared. But in fact only Seth knew the real reason for Tom's wayward behaviour and cut him slack accordingly, even though it never really helped him address the problem. Perhaps not even Seth truly understood what Tom needed.

Tom glanced at his watch. 'Right then, I best get going. No hurry with the spars, Maddie, I've enough to be going on with. Just whenever you can fit them in.'

He walked back out into the sunshine, smiling at the thought of another day doing what he loved most.

★

Heights had never bothered Tom. As a child, he had climbed every tree in his village, thrilled by the view from up in the air, and the sense of freedom he gained; so different from the atmosphere on the ground where he felt stifled and confined. Airborne, he could see what others couldn't see, he could hear what others couldn't hear, and best of all, because he was alone in his little eyries in the sky, no one, especially his parents, could tell him what to do.

They had been deeply disappointed in his decision to become a thatcher and not a doctor, or a solicitor, or banker. But for Tom, who had a deep love of the outdoors and craftsmanship, it represented the perfect career.

He scaled his ladder quickly and surveyed his kingdom before checking over his work from the previous day. His gaze turned automatically to the cottage next door. There were no signs of life from within, but Tom hoped that at least he might get the opportunity to say hello. What he must not do, however, was make any reference to Isobel's playing; it had been private, a performance just for her benefit, and if she knew he had been listening, he doubted he would ever hear her play again.

Chapter 3

The morning had not been a good one. Isobel was a creature of habit and when she had gone back to bed in the small hours of the morning, she had expected to wake at her usual time. Instead, she had fallen into a deep sleep which, on waking, left her groggy and at least an hour and a half behind schedule. Her days were always the same. She worked between nine and twelve and then stopped for a half-hour break. Another three hours would take her until half past three when she would again stop for thirty minutes. Restarting at four in the afternoon meant that she could fit in another three hours before dinner at seven. That was nine hours' work a day, which was not as much as she had been used to in the past – things had been very different then, and she had been considerably younger. Today, however, even after showering and binding her hair into a plait rather than drying it, the time was still a quarter past ten when she switched on her computer. To make matters worse, around lunchtime, just as she was getting into the swing of things, there was an unexpected knock at the door.

A tall, dark-haired woman dressed in simple, unfussy clothes held out her hand expectantly.

'Welcome to Joy's Acre,' she said. 'I'm Maddie.'

Isobel took her hand and gave it a brief squeeze. 'Thank you,' she said, unsure whether she was supposed to say anything else. 'I'm Isobel,' she added, as an afterthought. 'Isobel Hardcastle.'

'And our first guest.' Maddie blushed. 'I'm sorry, we've probably all been fussing over you, rather.'

'Not at all,' Isobel lied. 'Although you honestly shouldn't worry. I'm very capable of asking if I need anything, and I really don't require much. I'm here to work after all, so…' She was beginning to sound like a broken record. 'I'm sure everything will be fine.'

She smiled at Maddie, hoping she would take the hint. Now that she had stopped working, she could feel a headache forming and if she didn't get back to her desk soon and work through it, she would never get rid of it.

'Right,' said Maddie. 'Excellent… well, I'll just…' She paused. 'The thing is we're just about to have lunch. Out here on the lawn. It's such a beautiful day and it seemed too good an opportunity to miss…' She took a slight step back and Isobel could see a long table had been brought out to the garden, a bright yellow tablecloth covering it. 'You're very welcome to have your lunch here of course, but we wondered if you might like to join us?'

Isobel checked her watch, aware that things were already being ferried back and forth outside. Her heart sank. They had probably thought this would be a lovely surprise for her – both a way of breaking the ice, and of giving her a little special treatment as their first guest. It was the very last thing she wanted to do. She still wasn't very good with people and, besides, the sequence of notes she had been working on was still there in her head; the solution to the problem that had been nagging her, just inches away, if only she could carry on for a few more minutes… But even as the thought flitted through her head she knew the notes were fading.

'I hadn't even realised the time, but what a lovely idea,' she said. 'Although you really shouldn't have gone to so much trouble. I hope that wasn't for my benefit alone?'

Maddie looked slightly uncomfortable. 'Guilty as charged,' she said with a grin. 'But, I'll be honest with you – downtime has been a little hard to come by lately and once we'd decided to have a picnic everyone got ridiculously excited. Trixie has made enough food for an army.' She gave Isobel a cautious look. 'Although, of course if you're busy feel free to say no, we really shouldn't presume…'

Isobel shook her head. 'No, it's fine, how could I possibly refuse such wonderful hospitality?' *It would be much the easiest thing*, thought Isobel. If she said yes to them now then they might leave her alone. Whereas, if she refused today's invitation, this cajoling could go on for days. Far better to pretend to be sociable now and join in. Then, as soon as they saw she was happy and settled she'd be left alone to get on with things. 'What time would you like me?' she asked. 'I might just go and freshen up a bit,' she added.

'Perhaps in fifteen minutes or so. Would that suit you?' Maddie glanced behind her. 'I'll just go and give Trixie a hand to carry the last few bits. Come whenever you're ready.'

Isobel nodded that she would and closed the door, sighing as she walked up the stairs. She needn't stay for long, just half an hour so that they wouldn't think her rude.

She examined herself in the bedroom mirror. Her hair would probably still be wet if she removed it from its braid, and so she decided to leave it, smoothing the ends away from her face, and peering at her reflection. She wore no make-up but her skin was clear and creamy, her cheeks and lips naturally blushed pink, and her brown eyes huge beneath perfectly arched and plucked brows. A slight widow's peak sitting slightly left of centre was the only thing that marred the symmetry, but other than that, were it not for the slightly stern expression she habitually wore, she would be considered beautiful by most people she met. Isobel had no time for vanity, however, and she picked up a tube of sun cream that lay on top of the dressing table and began to rub some into the back of her neck where she felt the tension in the muscles, digging her fingers in harder.

★

A bacon sandwich had duly arrived shortly after Tom had turned up for work, but by lunchtime he was starving again. He was also gasping for a drink. It was hot, thirsty work up on the roof and the sight of Maddie waving at him from down below was a welcome one.

'Food is ready!' she called up. 'Come on, Trixie's rustled up a feast.'

Tom replied with a broad grin. He waved and gave a thumbs up, swiping his hand across his face to wipe away the perspiration. He turned his tanned face to the sun, checking its position in the sky and realising it would be a long time yet before dusk. Just as well – a huge expanse of roof lay beside him and he would need to put in another long day's work to make any real headway. He rubbed his eyes and began to stow his materials where they wouldn't fall, before shinning down the ladder.

Everyone else was already seated around the table when Tom arrived. There were only two places left, but rather than sit at the head of the table where he would feel conspicuous, he chose the place immediately to its right. Since Trixie had arrived at Joy's Acre they always stopped for lunch and, even though this was often just sandwiches, the bread was always freshly made and Trixie made sure she came up with some great combinations for fillings. It was a perfect break for all of them, busy as they were with different things in different places, and the opportunity to come together and share aspects of their day was something they all treasured and were rapidly getting used to. He could see that Trixie and Clara already had their heads bent together, no doubt discussing menus for the days ahead dependent on what was ready to harvest in the garden, but they both looked up when he arrived, smiling a greeting. It made him feel as if he belonged.

And Maddie was right, Trixie had indeed prepared a feast. The table was groaning with food, both savoury and sweet. Big bowls of colourful salads jostled for room with two types of quiche, sandwiches, triangles of homemade pizza and a huge jug of lemonade. If he had his way he would have made straight for the Victoria sponge which Trixie often made, the best cake he had ever tasted. However, the manners drilled into him as a child dictated that pudding (or dessert as his mum called it) was left for the second course. He was so intent on filling his plate that he hardly noticed the place beside him had become occupied until the conversation stilled.

He looked up, practically choking on the cherry tomato he had just popped into his mouth. He had no idea that Isobel would be joining them for lunch. He put his plate down, chewing quickly.

'Isobel!' exclaimed Maddie. 'Welcome to Joy's Acre… again!'

'Yes, welcome,' echoed Seth, raising an imaginary glass to her.

There was a smattering of laughter around the table, and Isobel herself smiled, dipping her head in acknowledgement.

'Thanks,' she said, looking shyly back at the many faces turned towards her. 'It's beautiful here. I'm so glad you had room for me.'

She glanced around the table looking unnerved at the array of food in front of her.

'I know,' said Trixie, grinning. 'Once you get me going, there's little hope of stopping me. But if I know this lot, it'll all get eaten, and sooner than you'd think.'

Tom looked down at his own plate which was heaped with food. It seemed rather extravagant now.

'I need to keep my strength up,' he said, hoping that Isobel didn't think he was a complete pig.

To his embarrassment, Clara groaned. 'Oh Tom, don't. At least spare us the details of your love life while we're eating, please.' She rolled her eyes at everyone around the table and was rewarded by a gale of laughter from Maddie.

He couldn't even look at Isobel. And to his even greater embarrassment, he felt his cheeks burn bright red. He would normally have retaliated with a cheeky comment, but not today. Not when the most beautiful woman on the planet was sitting next to him. Instead, he said nothing and was just about to sink his teeth into a sandwich when he realised that Isobel was still sitting, unmoving. He cleared his throat.

'Can I pass you something?' he asked, hoping he didn't have tomato juice down his shirt.

Her eyes were roaming the table, considering the options. 'Perhaps just some of the salad,' she replied. 'Thank you… And a slice of the quiche.'

He waited while she helped herself from the bowls and plates he offered up, refusing most of the options. He watched her small neat fingers as she did so. Even her hands were beautiful; slim, with long fingers, and the way she held them…

'Well it's very exciting having a musician here, Isobel,' said Seth. 'You said in your emails that you were working on a project, so presumably that means composing, does it?'

Isobel paused, looking at Seth intently for a moment, before her expression softened slightly. 'Yes,' she said. 'Something I've been writing for a little while, but which became… delayed. Now I've been given an opportunity to finish it, but I have a rather tight deadline for its delivery.'

Seth held up the jug of lemonade and a spare glass towards her. She nodded, and once poured he passed her drink along the table.

'That must be difficult,' he said. 'Working to a deadline, I mean. I imagine it must be hard being creative on tap?'

Isobel gave a slight smile. 'It can be, on occasion, but you just have to put the hours in and get it done. Same as most things.' She looked down at her lap momentarily before raising her head once more, this time giving Seth a slightly bigger smile. 'That sounded rather pompous, sorry... but I'm afraid I'm not very good at conversation. Too many hours spent practising on my own.'

She didn't look particularly sorry, thought Tom, entranced by the way the coil of her plait snaked its way around the curve of her long neck. If anything she looked wary.

He cleared his throat, conscious that he was staring at her. 'Is that how you got to be so good?' he asked, cringing as he suddenly realised his mistake. 'I mean, you must be if you put in that much practice...'

Isobel stared at him, eyes narrowed, and he thought for one moment she was going to challenge his comment.

'Yes,' she said, after a second, 'although actually, I haven't played in a long time, not properly. These days I mostly compose.'

'For what though?' asked Clara. 'Which instrument?'

'The violin. Although the piece I'm working on now is for a string quartet, so there are four of us, two violins, a viola and a cello.'

Clara sighed. 'How on earth do you even begin to do that?'

'It's complicated,' she replied. 'Hence why I need to be here for six weeks.'

'And we're already keeping you from your work,' said Maddie. 'But it is lovely to have you here.'

Isobel dipped her head again. 'It makes a nice change for me,' she said carefully. 'I don't live too far away, but I had no idea this place even existed, and it's a beautiful spot. The view from my bedroom is lovely.' She turned to include Seth in the conversation as well. 'Have you had this place a long time?' she asked, finally picking up a piece of quiche, and taking a small bite.

'Me?' replied Seth. 'Well, yes I've been here a while… The house belonged to my wife's family.'

Isobel looked at Maddie, clearly confused. She frowned gently. 'But I thought…' she said, looking at Maddie. 'Oh, I'm sorry…' A pink flush crept up her neck.

Seth exchanged a glance with Maddie and gave a shy smile. 'No, we're not married,' he explained, leaning towards her, 'but you didn't get it entirely wrong. Maddie and I are, well…'

'Love's young dream,' sighed Clara, and then giggled. 'It's a recent thing,' she added, 'and they're still stupidly embarrassed about it, even though the rest of us could see it way before they did.' She grinned happily, crunching on a stick of celery.

'I should explain,' began Seth, clearing his throat. 'My wife died six years ago, Isobel—' He put out a hand as hers fluttered to her throat. 'No, don't worry, it's fine… She inherited the farm from her grandfather, so we came to live here intending to renovate it and bring it back to life.' He pulled a face. 'She became ill not long after we moved in though, and after her death I'm afraid it took me rather longer than I anticipated to make our dream come true… In fact, it took Maddie here to finally spur me into action and the result is the cottage you're staying in now. The rest is rather a long story, but Tom and I go way back, and Clara is another friend, who very kindly came to rescue my garden from the wild.'

'I've only been here since the spring myself, Isobel,' added Maddie, 'and Trixie even less time than that. But there are plans afoot to open the rest of the cottages for accommodation in due course, and in time to return the land to traditional farming. The site has a rather interesting history actually.'

'I saw that,' nodded Isobel. 'On your website, I think.' She frowned. 'In fact that's how I found you in the first place.' She stared into middle distance. 'I Googled places for artists to stay, meaning somewhere more like a retreat I suppose, but then I found you. I probably wouldn't have paid it much attention if your website hadn't been so appealing. I thought the colours were beautiful.'

It seemed an odd thing to say, thought Tom, seeing as Isobel was wearing a black tee shirt and a long black flowing skirt in the same dark palette she had also worn the day before. But he nodded at Maddie anyway, who beamed with pride.

'Way to go, Mads,' he said, grinning.

Maddie returned his smile. 'I designed the website,' she explained. 'So that makes me very happy to hear. But more than that, we rather hoped that the story of our artist in residence would be a draw for people, even if she is in spirit form.'

'Not that she's haunting us,' put in Seth quickly. 'But her husband built Joy's Acre for her, not only as a grand gesture of love, but as a kind of sanctuary, a place where she could paint undisturbed. I suppose, in its own way, putting this place back together has given us all a little of that. When you're here, sometimes it's easy to forget that the real world outside the gates exists at all.'

Now it was Isobel's turn to pull a face. 'Well that would suit me fine just at the moment,' she said, opening her mouth to say something else, but then thinking better of it. 'This is gorgeous quiche, Trixie,' she said instead, although she'd hardly eaten anything. 'I'm sorry, I'm not a very adventurous eater, I'm afraid, but this is all lovely.'

Trixie just laughed, her spiky hair glowing a vivid magenta in the sunlight. 'Quiche, adventurous? You're really not, are you. Don't you worry though, by the time you leave here you'll be a connoisseur of the kitchen garden, and all it has to offer. Even if that is courgette one hundred and one different ways...' She caught sight of Isobel's expression. 'Don't worry, I'm not about to inflict that on you!'

The conversation continued for a while longer as plates were steadily cleared and glasses emptied, refilled and emptied again, but Tom remained uncharacteristically quiet. With Isobel sitting at his side at the head of the table, it meant that whenever she spoke her eyes were fixed on someone else and she looked straight past him. It gave him ample opportunity to study her, while looking to the others as if he was turned to her out of polite interest. The more he looked, the more he was struck by something he couldn't quite put his finger on. It had caught his attention yesterday, but he hadn't thought a great deal of it, having spent so little time with her. But there was definitely something about her mannerisms that seemed familiar, and yet he was certain they had never met before. Try as he might he couldn't work out who she reminded him of, but it tugged mysteriously at something deep in his past...

Chapter 4

There were still plenty of hours left in the day but Tom was struggling. The picnic at lunch had been a lovely idea, but it had been too long a break and he had eaten far too much. Now he was feeling incredibly sleepy and the heat of the afternoon wasn't helping in the slightest. He climbed his ladder wearily, willing his legs to respond. Hoping he would find a cooling breeze up high to make him feel more alert, he was dismayed when he reached roof height to find the sun's rays even more relentless.

He glanced over to the cottage on the opposite side of the garden. Isobel had been the first to leave the table, thanking everyone politely, but explaining that she really had better get back to work. He had watched her as she walked barefoot up the path, acutely aware of the way she swayed as she walked.

If he had been sensible, he would have gone back to work himself at that point, but that had always been his trouble; he never knew when to stop. Instead he had stayed talking to Clara and Trixie about their plans to try and expand the business potential of the gardens at Joy's Acre. So far, their forays into selling its produce had been very successful and they were keen to build on the great start they had made. It was always interesting talking to them, but often left him feeling rather inadequate by comparison. They had energy and drive in spades, not traits Tom was renowned for…

Sighing, he took up his tools and began to work. Fifteen minutes later, he put them down again and climbed back down the ladder. His vision was swimming in and out of focus in the heat and he couldn't concentrate. There was only one thing for it.

Picking his way through the garden, he took the path that led behind the cottage where Isobel was staying and opened the gate at the far end into the fields beyond. A beautiful willow tree lay just the other side and was a particular favourite spot of his. He crossed into the dappled shade and sat down, leaning his back against the trunk, and within minutes he was asleep.

★

Isobel tutted and pulled the headphones from her ears, banging them down onto the desk. She had worked solidly for the last hour and it was all utter rubbish, she might as well delete every note. The break had done her no good at all and it had snapped her concentration so that she completely lost the flow of what she had been doing. What was worse was that she'd known this would be the case when she had accepted the invitation. She should have just stuck to her guns and had lunch like she usually did, alone.

Her last thought made her tut again, all the more angrily. Being on her own was what had caused all the trouble in the first place, but how on earth was she supposed to spend more time with people when all they did was cause her problems? She shivered despite the heat of the afternoon, and rose from the desk. She could feel herself beginning to panic, and knew that there was only one thing that would soothe her. She picked up her violin from the coffee table, feeling its familiar weight in her hand, and walked out the room.

She knew what she would play; it was what she always played when she needed something comforting, and the one piece she had never played in public. This piece was hers, and she hugged the thought of it to her as she followed the path from the cottage, not really caring where she was going.

Her arrival at Joy's Acre had been rather rushed, her desire to leave home overriding all thoughts about where she was going and what she would find when she got there. But the view from her bedroom window had shown her what lay beyond the gate behind her cottage, and although she had scarcely given it any thought before now, it was the perfect solution.

The long grass tickled her legs as she walked, one hand lifting her skirt clear from the patch of brambles that lay beside the gate. She walked onward until she was far enough into the field to be clear of the hedgerow and then she stopped and lifted her face to the sky. Her arms hung limply by her sides, her violin dangling from her left hand as she breathed deeply, listening to the sounds around her.

Far in the distance came the drone of an aeroplane, and nearer to home a fat bumblebee buzzed around the clover heads that wafted lazily in the breeze. Every now and again the wind stirred the longer grasses into a rustling sigh, and the air filled with expectant birdsong. Slowly, Isobel lifted her violin, raised her bow, and began to play.

The first note soared out into the space around her and she felt her breathing calm and slow, allowing her to reach deep inside for the dizzying rush of energy that came next. Her bow flew across the strings in a blur of movement, raising notes in perfect accord. Her movements were automatic, instinctive, driven from years of playing, and she had no need to think about how she was *playing*, more about how she was *feeling* – it was this that directed her bow. It was a piece of music that never sounded exactly the same no matter how many times she played it, because it was hers, to mould and to shape at her whim, always following the melody but never bound by tempo or style. She found the music from within, and it played her, just as much as she played it.

After five minutes or so, Isobel slowed the pace and allowed her mood to slow with it, feeling the calm that now nestled inside her, filling the space inside her head. She slowed the music still further, extending each note until it had almost died away before playing the next, listening as the sound rang out across the field. She smiled, building the tempo back up to the pace she had originally written it, and she followed the slower section for a while, feeling the sun on her face, relaxed and at peace. She could still feel the music; she hadn't lost it after all.

Eventually, she stilled her bow and opened her eyes, gradually letting her surroundings seep back into her consciousness. The fields and trees and grasses were just as they had been before; it was she who was different. She stood for a moment more, and inhaled a deep breath before turning to make her way back to the cottage.

She had taken only a couple of steps when she stopped dead, the breath catching in her throat as she caught sight of Tom. She realised immediately why she hadn't seen him at first. He was sitting with his back leaning against the curve of the willow tree and the angle had meant that he was hidden from view as she had walked into the field. It was only now, as she faced in the other direction, that he came plainly into sight.

He scrambled to his feet, running a hand through his hair to tidy it.

'I'm so sorry,' he stuttered. 'I didn't know what to do. I couldn't leave, it would have… you would have…' He ground to a halt. 'I was asleep.' He stared at the ground about a foot in front of her.

She felt her anger began to rise. He had ruined everything, he—

'That was private.' She glared at him. 'You had no right to listen to it.'

The smile fell from his face. 'Well, what was I supposed to do? If I got up or moved I would have disturbed your playing. I didn't think you'd want that so I—'

'Carried on spying on me!'

'No,' he said, his voice low. 'I sat as still as I could, trying not to sneeze, or scratch or even breathe, so that you could have the privacy you needed. If you hadn't seen me, you would have been none the wiser.'

'But I *did* see you.'

'And *you* interrupted my sleep.'

She gave a scathing laugh. 'Well who sleeps like that in the middle of the day anyway? You're like a child.'

He visibly swallowed. 'One that knows when it's no longer safe to continue working at heights in this heat. Or perhaps that never occurred to you?'

She bit back the comment she was about to make. It was a valid point, but it made no difference. That piece of music was intensely private, and no one, but no one was ever allowed to hear her play it. She cast about for something else to say, but he beat her to it.

'I don't think I've ever heard anything like that before in my life,' he said. 'It was incredible, truly incredible.'

He was standing, hands hanging limply by his side, head tilted slightly to the left. She could tell that he meant it, but she would be damned if she would acknowledge his compliment, not when he had made her feel so exposed.

The heat began to rise up her neck. 'Been to many classical concerts, have you?'

It was meant to be a sarcastic remark, designed to throw him off his stride. But to her surprise his expression didn't alter.

'Yes, actually.'

'Yeah… like I believe that.' It was an automatic retaliation. The words shot out of her mouth before she could stop them, but Tom looked like he'd been slapped.

She felt dreadful. Her sudden anger left her as quickly as it had arrived and in its place was shame. Tom hadn't meant any harm, he'd simply been unlucky enough to be in the wrong place at the wrong time and, she realised, he'd been trying to be nice to her.

The thought that he was actually a fan of classical concerts intrigued her, and she had an urge to find out more. She held his look, toying with the idea that had just come into her head. It was probably unwise but she was going to do it anyway. She sighed, and invited him back to the house for a cup of tea.

★

Tom was about to refuse when he suddenly remembered who Isobel was – a guest at Joy's Acre. And while he didn't think he'd been particularly rude, he had managed to upset her, quite comprehensively. Ordinarily in this sort of situation he would have made a polite excuse and left Isobel to calm down, but so far her stay with them wasn't going at all well. After all, lunch hadn't exactly been a success; despite everyone's best efforts, Isobel had barely eaten a thing and, although she had been polite enough, the conversation had seemed forced. It had been clear she wished she was somewhere else.

Reluctantly he accepted her invitation. At least if they had a chat, there would be an opportunity to improve the situation – it could hardly get worse. He indicated to Isobel that she should lead the way and was just following her back up the path when he heard an excited squeal.

'Uncle Tom!'

Tom's mouth dropped open in surprise. 'Oh my God, Lily!'

He ran down the path just as a small child came full pelt across the garden, shot past Isobel, and threw herself into his arms. He gave her an enormous hug, lifting her up and spinning her round before slowly putting her back down on the ground. He straightened, giving Isobel an apologetic glance before turning back towards the garden. A young woman was walking towards them.

He held out his arms once more. 'Kate,' was all he said, before pulling her in close and holding onto her for some time. He closed his eyes as a wave of emotion washed over him, and it was some moments before he could even speak. To cover his embarrassment, he picked up Lily again, pushing his face into the side of her neck, knowing that his stubble would tickle her and make her squirm. 'Look at you,' he said to her laughing face. 'You're huge! How did you get to be so big?'

And then he turned back to Isobel, feeling awkward. 'This is my niece, Lily,' he said. 'Who I haven't seen in absolutely *ages*. And my sister-in-law, Kate.'

Isobel smiled, looking equally ill at ease. 'Pleased to meet you,' she said politely. There was a pause for a moment. 'I'll go back inside,' she said. 'Perhaps I'll see you later.'

He nodded. It wasn't great timing. But given what had just happened between them, perhaps it was for the best. It would give Isobel a chance to calm down a little before they spoke. Besides which there were things he needed to say to Kate, without an audience.

He smiled at Kate, feeling a silence begin to grow. He knew that both of them were waiting until Isobel was out of earshot, and it was Kate who spoke first.

'Blimey, Tom, who on earth was that gorgeous creature? I hope we didn't arrive in the middle of something…? Although, I am pleased to see you're keeping yourself occupied.' There was a twinkle in her eye.

Tom groaned. 'Oh, don't,' he said. 'It's bad enough that I haven't seen you for forever, without looking like the total womaniser you always take me for. No, Isobel is just a guest. She's staying here in one of the cottages.'

Kate laughed. 'Yeah, right, pull the other one, Tom. No one can look like that without you taking an interest. I bet she's not *just* anything.'

He ignored her. 'Don't take any notice of Mummy,' he said to Lily, 'she's being very rude,' and he stuck out his tongue before lowering the child to the ground once more.

He looked up at his sister-in-law, a million questions on his lips. She looked well, he thought, certainly better than the last time he had seen her, although to be fair that was some time ago. He tried to remember when it was, ashamed when he realised that it must be well over six months ago. It was before Christmas so…

'How are you, Tom?' she asked suddenly.

He dropped his head. It should be him asking her, not the other way around. 'I'm okay,' he said. 'Busy. There's plenty here to be going on with, and after that I'm hoping to make a real go of the business.'

'That wasn't really what I meant.'

Her sparkling blue eyes were turned on him, fixing him to the spot.

'No, I know…' He ruffled Lily's hair. 'But, yeah, I'm okay. Off the booze… most of the time.' He thought back to a couple of weeks ago when that had certainly not been the case. 'I still get the odd moments, but you know, they're getting fewer and farther between.'

He drew in a breath. 'Anyway, what about you? You're looking well, really well in fact.' And she was. The sun had brought golden highlights to her already blonde hair, and her face was glowing with health. 'It's so lovely to see you.'

She nodded, smiling, and looked across to Lily, fidgeting slightly with a bracelet on her slender arm. It was clear that she wasn't going to answer his question.

'Lily has something to tell you, and well, we've haven't seen you in a long time so…'

Lily beamed. 'I've been learning to play, Uncle Tom,' she said. 'Just like you. Only the flute, not the banjo, because they don't teach that at school. But Mummy says when I'm older maybe I can learn that too.'

He looked up to see the proud expression on Kate's face. 'And she's doing really well, Tom. Nothing to do with us—' Her hand went to her mouth as she faltered a little. 'She just came out with it one day, saying that she wanted to learn an instrument like her uncle.'

'But that's brilliant, Lily, well done you,' he said, dropping to his haunches so that he was closer to her height. He looked up at Kate, but she avoided his gaze, just as he knew she would. He should say something really but it was hard to know what. Instead he focused his attention on his niece. 'So, what have you learnt? Can you play any tunes yet?'

She nodded, blonde curls bobbing with the vigorous movement. 'Lots!' she said. 'And that's why we came, Uncle Tom. 'Cause I'm going to be playing in the end-of-term concert, and Mummy wondered whether you'd like to come.'

'I would love to,' he said, looking up at Kate again. 'When is it?'

'Next Friday,' she said. 'At four o'clock.' She was biting her lip.

'Then I'll be there. Just try and stop me.'

Lily threw her arms around his neck again, and he pulled her in close, deliberately trying to catch Kate's eye. She mouthed 'Thank you' at him. He would ask her, he decided, but perhaps not yet.

'And Lily finishes school that day for the summer so we wondered if you'd like to come back with us afterwards and stay for tea? I know it's short notice, but we can have a catch-up then.'

Tom smiled. Of course, now was not the time to ask her about the thing she was trying hard not to mention. The thing which was making her eyes sparkle and had removed the tired pallor from her skin. She had it all planned, after all. There would be a proper civilised occasion to have a talk about how she was, and what was happening in her life. It would be a much better opportunity than now, with a snatched, unprepared-for conversation when he was supposed to be at a work.

'Will Adam be coming, Mummy? Tom can meet him if he is.'

Tom saw Kate's eyes flutter closed as her daughter innocently gave the game away, and he had to smile to himself; out of the mouth of babes, indeed.

'I'm not sure, sweetheart.' She looked at her watch as Tom straightened up. There was a pause for a few moments and then, 'Actually, we ought to be going now, Lily.' She couldn't quite meet his eye.

'Right, well, come on then, scamp,' he said to Lily. 'Give me another hug to be going on with, and I will see you on Friday.' He waggled a finger at her. 'And don't forget to practise!'

'I won't!'

She kissed his cheek before running off ahead of her mum. Tom watched her fondly, the innocence of her youth utterly beguiling. He waited until she was a little distance away, before turning back to Kate and gently taking her arm. He caught the other one and pulled her round to face him so he could softly drop a kiss on her forehead.

'I'm happy for you, Kate, I really am. I never expected you to stay on your own forever.'

She blushed. 'I know, it's just that—'

'Just nothing,' he interrupted. 'Be happy, Kate, that's all I want.'

Her eyes began to glisten. 'Thanks, Tom. I know I should have told you, but…'

He held a finger to her lips. 'There's never a right time, except the one we have now. That's all you really need to know.' He stared into the distance. 'And Lily is an absolute credit to you. Look at her, she's happy, carefree, excited by learning new things, everything a child should be. It's the right thing for her too.'

'It's early days, Tom. Who knows whether it will work out.'

He linked arms with her as they began to walk down the path. 'Who knows indeed. But you can have enormous fun trying to find out.'

Tom walked Kate and Lily out to the car, waiting until Lily was settled inside and safely buckled into her seatbelt, before leaning in to give her another kiss. He stood back and watched as the car reversed before pulling forwards again and making its way slowly down the drive. He waved the whole time, intermittently blowing kisses at Lily, and keeping the smile on his face until he was sure they were out of sight. Then he stood for a moment, his face falling, before retracing his steps back into the main garden.

He had known that this day would come. Never quite sure when, but knowing that it would. Kate was too young, too vibrant a woman to be on her own, and he was certainly no substitute for a father figure in Lily's life. His niece needed the security and love from two parents, but even though he knew it was the right thing for them both, he felt the hurt wriggle its way down inside him that little bit deeper. Not that he would ever let Kate see that, of course, and he *was* genuinely happy for her, but it was another chapter over, another sign that things were moving forward and leaving the past behind. And he really wasn't sure that he was ready for that.

Chapter 5

Tom paused before knocking on Isobel's door. He wasn't in the mood for tortured conversation, but he supposed he ought to get it over and done with. For all their sakes, it wouldn't do to leave their very first guest quite as irate as she had been earlier. And he had quite enough to be thinking about already without getting into trouble with Seth as well. Or Maddie, for that matter. She could be quite the force to reckon with.

The door opened almost immediately and, in the split second before Isobel smiled back at him, Tom was caught by another flash of recognition, which went almost as quickly as it had come.

It was a small smile but it was a start. She pulled the door wider.

'I saw you coming,' she said. 'So the kettle's on.' She turned and walked back down the hallway.

Tom trailed after her. 'I should apologise,' he said. 'For being so rude earlier. It was one of those awkward situations,' he added. 'Not awkward between you and me, but between me and my sister-in-law, and I felt like you got caught up in the middle of it, so I'm sorry. Kate and I haven't seen each other in ages, and I'm supposed to be Lily's godfather, but I'm doing a terrible job. Kate's on her own now you see, and I always feel rather guilty when I first see them and never know what to say.'

He was rambling now. 'Sorry,' he said again.

'Oh, I rather thought you were going to apologise for listening in on my practice earlier.'

Something deflated inside of Tom. This wasn't going to be as easy as he'd hoped.

'Well, yes of course, I apologise for that too, but…' He should have stopped right there, but the 'but' had just slipped out.

'But?' Her two eyebrows were arched in perfect symmetry.

He squirmed. 'But, in my defence, I didn't actually ruin your playing. It wasn't my fault you took up position where you did, and I was asleep when you walked into the field. If I'd have been awake, I would have alerted you to my presence before you even started. In any case you still played beautifully.'

He groaned inwardly. *Oh, just shut up Tom, don't dig the hole any bigger than it needs to be.*

She turned her back on him, reaching up into a cupboard and taking down two mugs.

'I hadn't even noticed,' she replied. 'Any awkwardness with your niece, I mean. But then I don't have much experience with children. I'm an only child so no siblings to procreate, and I certainly don't have any of my own. In any case, Lily seemed to be very fond of you, so you can't be doing too bad a job.'

Tom shrugged. 'That's young children for you. They're happy to enjoy the present and she doesn't seem to bear a grudge about the length of time that goes by between my visits.'

'So why don't you visit? Do they live too far away?'

He shook his head. 'About five minutes from here. I practically have to drive past the house on my way home. It's pathetic. I should see far more of them than I do.'

'I'm sure you have your reasons.' She pulled out a box of teabags from the same cupboard. 'I only drink fruit tea when I'm working,' she added. 'Do you want one of those… or coffee, I suppose? Someone left some here.'

Tom winced. That 'someone' had been Maddie, who had carefully put together a welcome pack of necessities for their guest. He'd had teeth pulled that were more enjoyable than this conversation.

'Coffee would be perfect, thanks. Milk and two sugars.'

'I suppose you always think because they live just up the road that you can visit them any time, and I imagine you always convince yourself you'll do just that. But then, somehow… you never do.'

'Something like that,' muttered Tom, wishing she would bloody well hurry up with his drink.

She swung around, tilting her head at him. 'I suppose you think I'm being critical?' she said. 'I'm not. I just know how time flies by, without us ever realising how much of it has passed… and I know what families are like too. I suppose we love them really, but it's never as straightforward as that, is it?'

Tom looked up sharply from where he was picking at a callus on the inside of his thumb.

'No,' he said slowly, a surprised expression on his face. 'It's not.'

She set a mug down in front of him. 'So, what did they come for today then? If you haven't seen them for so long.'

Tom was certainly not about to tell her the real reason. 'Lily has started music lessons at school,' he said instead. 'There's an end-of-term concert on Friday and they've invited me to go and watch.'

'Oh? Which instrument?'

'Well I would imagine it will be a variety, but Lily will be playing the flute.'

She nodded, taking her own seat, a slight wistful expression crossing her face. 'I always wanted to play the flute as a child. Far more romantic than the violin, or so I thought at the time, hard to remember why really. The concerts I do remember though. Endless numbers of them – Easter, summer, Christmas, harvest festival. Any excuse to be shown off…'

She pulled at the string of the teabag still floating in her drink, dunking it up and down. The sweet sickly smell was making Tom feel slightly queasy. 'That all stopped after a while though. I moved on to bigger things. It's years since I've been to that sort of concert.'

Tom had the distinct impression that she wasn't really talking to him, just speaking out loud.

'You could come if you liked?' The words were out of his mouth before he had a chance to rein them in. That caught her attention.

'Oh, I don't think so. Why would you possibly want me there?'

Good question.

'Well, trip down memory lane and all that? I'm sure Kate and Lily wouldn't mind. Think about it. It's not until Friday anyway. You don't have to give me your answer now.'

She dipped her head in acknowledgement. 'Memory lane isn't somewhere I'm hugely keen to go, but I will consider it, thank you.'

It was clear that enough had been said on the subject. She took a sip of her tea.

'I'm sure you will have told me, but I'm sorry, I can't remember what you said you play yourself?'

'Selective memory?'

'Very.' She gave a slight smile. 'And I probably made that obvious.'

Tom ignored the comment. 'I've never actually told you what I play.'

There were sudden creases at the corners of her eyes. 'So?' she asked.

'Guitar, ukulele, banjo, violin – very badly – and accordion.'

She stared at him. 'Really?'

'Really. I play in a folk band, pubs mostly.' He shrugged at her expression. 'Yes, I'm one of *those* musicians…'

'Oh, I didn't mean—' Her hand fluttered to her throat.

'Oh, yes you did! Don't try and deny it.' But he smiled back.

'I heard it said somewhere that folk music gets everyone in the end, but…'

'You'd rather be ritually disembowelled?'

'I didn't actually say that.'

Tom grinned. 'It's okay. I won't take it personally.'

'But yet you've been to more than one classical recital by the sound of it. How come?'

'Middle-class parents with aspirations,' he said. 'Ones who thought that if their layabout son was going to become a musician then he should at least be one of note, and not some two-chord-nobody in a *band*.'

Isobel was about to pick up her mug again, but she stopped midway, stiffening.

'How old were you?' she asked.

'Mid-teens, I guess. Young enough that they were still paying for my music lessons anyway.'

'So did you fulfil their dreams for you?'

'Nope. Despite their ambitions I still ended up playing in a band, although that came much later of course, just after I gave up on trying to find a respectable career and became a thatcher instead. That *really* pissed them off.'

'Good for you.'

Tom looked surprised. 'Really?' he said. 'Good for you? Most people look vaguely affronted when I tell them things like that.'

She dropped her eyes as she finally placed her mug back on the table. 'Thatching suits you, that's all. I can't see you as a doctor or a banker.' She paused for a moment. 'So what did you play back then, as a child?'

He smiled, watching her from across the table.

She groaned, cupping her head in a hand. 'Violin, of course. How could it be anything else?'

'Well, you did ask… And it's now my least favourite instrument, to play I mean,' he corrected himself. 'I could *listen* to it all day.' He saw her blush slightly as he realised what he'd said. 'Much though it pains me to say it, I think being taken to all those concerts time and time again as a child must have rubbed off on me. It was twenty or so years ago, and although at the time I tried to deny that I enjoyed them, the music sort of snuck up on me in my old age.'

Isobel snorted. 'You're just scared to admit you like classical music because it doesn't really fit your image.'

Tom looked taken aback. 'Do I *have* an image?' he asked.

'Yeah, you know that whole—' She stopped suddenly, looking down at her hands.

'Seriously though,' he said. 'My parents and I had rather a falling-out. And while that led to my rebelling against playing the instrument of their choice, I hope I know enough about the violin to hear when it's being played exceptionally well, and I haven't heard anyone play to your standard for a very long time.'

Isobel dipped her head, blushing. 'Thank you,' she said. 'I've played since I was a child too, from a very early age, so I get what that whole parental pressure thing feels like.'

Tom lifted his head and was about to say something when she suddenly picked up her mug and drained the contents; a very obvious full stop if ever he saw one.

He glanced at his watch. 'I should get back to work,' he said.

She nodded gratefully. 'Yes, me too. Lots to do.'

The conversation felt suddenly awkward again. 'Well, thanks for the coffee – hopefully the forty winks and the caffeine will have done the trick. I'm going to be in all sorts of trouble if I don't get a few more hours in today. Deadlines and all that.'

'Tell me about it. Far too much slacking going on today, although at least I wasn't asleep on the job.'

'I wasn't asleep on the job, chance would have been a fine thing. Some bloody woman was playing the violin, sounded like a cat being strangled.'

Chapter 6

Tom woke with a start and lurched from the chair, groaning when he caught sight of the clock on the wall. His head was still reeling and he had to grasp the side of the table to stop from falling, kicking the bottle at his feet as he did so. It skittered across the floor, spinning. Staggering to the sink, he filled a mug with water, and drained it in one long series of swallows. Belching loudly as he finished, he wiped a hand across the back of his mouth.

Swaying slightly, he tried to muster himself for the journey upstairs. He needed to get to bed, and soon, or Seth would have his guts for garters. He let go of the sink and began to pick his way across the room, holding onto the bannisters in a well-worn routine when he reached the stairs. And then he began to climb.

His last thought as he crashed onto the bed was of Isobel.

★

Not nearly enough hours later, Tom gritted his teeth and flicked the shower onto cold, flinching as the icy water cascaded over him. He stood for as long as he could bear it before turning the shower back to its original setting, almost slumping against the wall in relief. Two minutes later he did it again. After quarter of an hour of alternating between hot and cold water, Tom decided things were as good as they were going to get and turned off the water, wrapping a towel around his waist.

He had sworn to himself over and over that he was never going to do this again. It was too easy to hide behind the comforting numbness that booze brought rather than face up to the things which tormented him and so, two weeks ago, he had removed every bottle of alcohol he had from the house. Except that last night, as he'd sat at the kitchen table replaying thoughts of his meeting with Kate, he had remembered the present he'd been given by a grateful couple whose wedding he had played at recently. The bottle of whisky they had brought him back from their honeymoon was still in the boot of his car, and it had taunted him endlessly until he had gone to fetch it. Even then, he hadn't opened it straight away. He had sat looking at it, telling himself that it was not the answer, but as the night wore on, the quietness had seeped into the corners of his mind and he knew he had nowhere to hide. He vividly remembered the feeling of release his first drink had given him, but not the last.

So far that morning he had managed to avoid every mirror in the house, but as he collected his car keys from the hall table half an hour later, he accidentally glanced at his reflection. He stared at himself for a couple of minutes, trying to find the image of a person he recognised behind the dark shadows under his eyes and the heavier than usual beard line.

Seth was already waiting for him when he arrived at Joy's Acre. Not in an obvious way of course, he was too good a friend for that, but nonetheless Tom spotted him loitering in the garden as he neared the cottage he was working on.

'Morning,' said Seth, coming over. 'Everything okay?'

Tom ignored his question. 'I know, I'm late, I'm sorry.'

'No problem. It's just I said I'd give you a hand this morning, that's all, but I'm only free until one o'clock.'

Tom looked at his watch. It was a little after ten; he'd already lost two hours' work. 'I remember, and like I said, I'm sorry.' He glanced up at the ladder in front of him. 'Still, I'm here now, so let's get on, shall we?… And yeah, before you ask, I'm fine to be doing this.'

Seth raised an eyebrow, but Tom looked away and started to climb.

It was a good ten minutes before Seth spoke again. 'The thatch is looking good, are you happy with how things are going?'

'Happy enough,' muttered Tom. 'Just not enough bloody hours in the day.' He was well aware that this would probably invite comment, but even if his work pattern wasn't always regular, he'd been putting the time in one way or another, and the thatch was progressing well.

Seth was about to answer when Tom suddenly held up his hand to prevent him from saying anything further. He was listening. The opening bars of a Tchaikovsky violin concerto were wafting across the garden.

After a few more seconds he turned to look back at Seth, waiting for the inevitable comment about his timekeeping. Instead he was surprised to see an amused expression on Seth's face. He frowned, his brain slow to process what he was seeing, but eventually the penny dropped.

'And no, it's not what you're thinking, so you can take that smirk off your face. I am categorically not interested in Isobel.' He turned back to the task in hand, well aware that Seth was staring at him. 'I like her music, that's all.'

The warning note to Tom's voice would have been enough to put most people off pursuing the conversation, but he and Seth went too far back for that.

'You like her music,' Seth intoned. 'And you're sure that's all…? You haven't noticed her stunning looks then? Those deep dark eyes you could drown in…'

Tom looked up, glaring. 'Drop it, Seth,' he warned. 'Yes, I've noticed the way she looks. I've also noticed the way she talks to people; the woman nearly bit my head clean off yesterday when I'd done nothing wrong. Besides which, do you really think someone like Isobel would ever be interested in someone like me? She's nice to look at, but that's it.'

'And?'

Tom couldn't respond. Seth knew him too well and behind the supposedly glib comment was a very well-aimed hook designed to draw him out the water like a fish wriggling on a line.

The two men stared at one another for a moment, but Tom wasn't about to be drawn in. 'I need to work,' he said instead.

Seth sighed. 'Fair enough… And so, on to matters of a more practical nature: have you had any breakfast?'

Tom shook his head. 'Didn't seem like a very good idea first thing…'

'And now?'

'Yeah, okay.' Tom knew he was referring to a bacon sandwich, and he watched while Seth took off his kneelers and made his way back down the ladder. He inhaled a deep breath and picked up his mallet, forcing all thoughts from his brain beyond the straw he was working with.

He felt better after he'd eaten and the two of them worked solidly for an hour or so with little need for conversation. The music continued, but for the most part Tom was able to block it out. It was only when he stopped to assess the section he'd been working on that the melody swam back into his consciousness. He wiped a hand over his face; the heat was already building.

'Jesus, she doesn't ever bloody shut up, does she?' Seth had done the same as him, pausing for a moment to wipe the sweat from his face, and he was now staring over at Isobel's cottage. 'The same thing, over and over. Doesn't she know anything else?'

Tom looked up. 'She's practising, that's what you do. It's the second movement she's having trouble with, not that she is really, I mean she's playing it pretty much flawlessly from what I can tell, but she's obviously not happy.'

Just as he said it, a raucous screech rang out, the sound of strings being tortured in anger.

'Ouch…' said Tom. 'Told you she wasn't happy.'

Almost immediately the music started up again, from the beginning this time.

'She's got stamina,' said Seth, 'I'll give her that.'

The same thing was just occurring to Tom, and he wondered if that was the real reason why he had never continued playing at that level. 'Yep, she probably does several hours' practice like that every day, and I mean every day, weekends, holidays… every day.'

'So what is she then, some sort of starlet in the music world? Should we have heard of her?'

Tom pulled out his set pin, Seth's words striking a distant chord. He struggled to grasp his thoughts.

'I don't think so… I've never heard of her. She's been playing since she was a child, she told me that yesterday—' He stopped, thinking for a moment before shaking his head and carrying on. 'But that's what you have to do to get that good. I guess she's probably played in orchestras before, that kind of thing. But it's like a muscle, you know, if you don't use it, you lose it.' He replaced the set pin a little distance from where it had sat before so he could measure the depth of the thatch.

'Well, I'm glad you managed to have a chat yesterday. She seemed a bit quiet when we were having lunch and she didn't stay for long, did she?'

Seth was fishing again.

'No, we talked later in the afternoon...' He measured his words carefully. 'I was having a break, and we... came across each other.'

'That's when she took your head off, was it?' Seth let the sentence dangle.

Tom stared at the sheaf of straw in his hands and let out a loud breath. 'Okay, I'd gone to have a kip in the field behind the cottage if you must know. Isobel came in, didn't see me until she was about to leave, and then blew her top because I'd overheard her playing. It wasn't my fault she didn't see me, and honestly, you should have heard her, a right bloody prima donna. Saying I had no right to hear her music – when she was playing in the middle of a field!'

'So that's when she told you about how she played as a child?'

'Not exactly, no...'

Seth remained silent.

'I sort of calmed her down a bit and she invited me back for a cup of tea... Well I could hardly say no, could I? She's our first guest, Seth, I didn't want to leave her angry because of something I'd done, that would have gone down *really* well.'

'I see, so you went to try and make amends, that kind of thing?' There was a slightly amused tone to Seth's voice that Tom didn't like the sound of. He could see exactly where the conversation was headed.

'I agreed to have tea, yes, but it's not what you think. Then Kate and Lily turned up and—'

'Ah...' There was a huge weight behind the word.

Tom sagged against his ladder. 'Kate's got a boyfriend, Seth...'

Seth didn't say anything; he didn't need to.

'And that's fine. I mean, I knew she wouldn't stay on her own forever, and she'd looked really well, gorgeous actually, but it's just that…'

'She's moving on from Matt…?'

'Yeah… I wasn't expecting it now, that's all.'

Seth held a sympathetic hand against Tom's shoulder. 'It had to happen sometime, mate. Your brother's been gone a while, and for Lily's sake as much as anything, perhaps it's for the best.'

Tom's eyes lit up. 'Lily looked so grown up, Seth, so beautiful. You'd hardly have recognised her. And she's been learning the flute – in fact they came to invite me to a concert. She looked really happy.'

'Then that's all you need to think about.'

Tom looked across at him and nodded. 'I know, but…'

Seth held his look and Tom could see him struggling for an opening. He might as well come clean – Seth had pretty much worked it out, after all.

'So, yeah, last night… that's what it was all about. I did what I usually do whenever that subject comes up; I went home, thought about it on repeat, totally screwed myself up, and got completely off my face on cheap whisky. Only in this case it was the best part of a spectacularly fine bottle of Lagavulin. I'd already got rid of all the other booze. I don't know why I do it, Seth. It never helps.'

He wasn't looking for an answer. Seth and he had turned the subject inside out over the last couple of years, less times in the last few months admittedly, but there really wasn't anything to add.

His friend considered his question nonetheless. 'Perhaps,' he said slowly, 'because now you recognise that you're saying goodbye to what's in the past.' He paused for a moment. 'And maybe now is the right time to do exactly that.'

Tom gave a wry smile. 'That's the stupid thing. I already know that. I decided a couple of weeks back to clean up my act. No more booze, no more chasing every girl I see, thinking it will help. It's not a quick fix I need, Seth, no more trying to paper over the cracks. This time I need a proper renovation job.'

Seth suddenly grinned. 'Welcome to Joy's Acre.'

'It's also why I need nothing whatsoever to do with our resident musician.' He groaned. 'Jesus, I even invited her along to Lily's concert after we got talking about parents – that was a really smart move – and then I made it even worse by making some flippant comment about her playing sounding like a strangled cat. What was I thinking? I mean it, Seth, if you so much as catch me looking in her direction, I give you absolute permission to punch my lights out.'

★

Isobel couldn't ignore them for much longer – the missed calls stacking up on her mobile were becoming harder and harder to dismiss. Eventually at five o'clock she made herself a cup of tea and sat down on the sofa to prepare herself. There was nothing they could do about her being here – she was a grown adult, not a child any longer, and all Isobel had to do was stay calm and be firm about her intentions. She picked up her phone and made the call.

'Darling, thank heavens you're all right, where are you?'

Isobel ignored her mother's question. 'I'm absolutely fine, Mum. I just decided to go away for a few days, that's all. Somewhere nice and peaceful where I can work without interruption.'

'But darling, you have all that here. Don't be so ridiculous.'

Isobel drew in a breath. 'You say that. You say it all the time, but you check in on me every five minutes to see how things are going. You ask me constantly if I've done my exercises. You force food down me when I'm not even hungry. I can't think when you're always watching me, it's so claustrophobic.'

There was an intake of breath and an angry silence.

'And where would you be, Isobel, were it not for those things? Tell me that.'

Her mother was gathering herself for an attack, but Isobel had heard it all before.

'No? Shall I tell you? You'd be a nothing, a nobody, just the same as the rest of them, with no talent to speak of beyond some pathetic ninth grade certificate stuck on the fridge door. Don't you realise how special you are, Isobel? Don't you realise the sacrifices we've made on your behalf, just so that you can get where you are today…?'

Isobel held the phone away from her ear, but she could still hear her mother's strident voice.

'…And who would look after you, were it not for us. You can't cope on your own, Isobel, you know that, you never could.' Her voice softened slightly. 'Come home, and we can have a chat about all of this. I know it's only because you're so anxious that you've done this. I know you're not really trying to make us suffer…'

Isobel swallowed. 'Mum, I'm not coming home, do you hear me? I'm writing music, I'm doing my practice, I'm eating well, and I'm not coming home. I'm only phoning now so that you know I'm okay. There's no phone signal at the cottage where I'm staying. In fact, I'm having to stand in the middle of a field to make this call. I won't be ringing again until I'm ready, so there's really no point in trying to contact me.'

'But how long are you going to be away for?'

'Six weeks.' Isobel shut her eyes.

'Six weeks!' her mother shrieked. 'Don't be so absurd. Your composition has to be *finished* in six weeks, or had you forgotten? And this is your only chance, Isobel, your *only* chance. Have I made myself clear? You are to come home straight away and we'll say no more about it. Tell me where you are and I'll come and pick you up before you make an absolute disaster out of the thing.'

'No, Mum. I'm staying here.'

'Then I shall have to see what Dr Mason has to say about it.' Her voice had dropped dangerously low.

'Call him. I doubt he'll be interested, not now I've discharged myself from his list. I'm no longer his patient. I'm no longer anyone's patient...'

'You ungrateful little—'

Isobel disconnected the call.

Chapter 7

Isobel raised both arms above her head and, linking her fingers together, turned her palms to the ceiling, stretching as high as she could. She waggled her head from side to side and then, dropping her arms, began to roll her shoulders in a circle, forwards and backwards. She had the most unbearable headache and her shoulders and neck felt like they were caught in a vice.

She should have left the phone call until this morning, not made it so late in the day when, inevitably, it had led to a night with very little sleep. Isobel had lain there for hours, alternating between bouts of seething anger and anguish bordering on terror. Now she had spent the morning unable to settle to any meaningful work, remnants of the conversation with her mother working their insidious way into all the gaps between her notes. She needed a break and some fresh air.

Opening the front door, she automatically looked across to her right and to the cottage where Tom was working. He had been there first thing, but now there was no sign of him and she frowned; it was the hottest part of the day and he was quite possibly snoozing somewhere in the shade. A gentle breeze blew across the garden and she lifted her hair away from the back of her neck, enjoying the feeling as the current of air tickled her bare skin. She stood on the path for a few moments feeling the soothing warmth of the paving stones underneath her bare toes, before making her way towards the grassed area and the bench that lay there.

'Good morning!'

The friendly greeting came from her left and she turned to see Clara hard at work, digging in one of the beds. She hadn't realised that there was anyone in the garden and her first instinct was to turn away, but the sight of Clara's friendly face made her recognise that being on her own was the last thing she wanted. She waved tentatively.

Clara's long blonde hair was wrapped into a messy bun and piled on top of her head, sagging slightly to one side each time she pushed the fork into the soil. She must be boiling – Isobel had been feeling the heat simply sitting still in the cool of the cottage.

'You must be baking in this weather,' she said. 'Can I get you a glass of water or something from the cottage?'

Clara straightened and indicated an empty plastic water bottle standing on the path a little distance away. 'I actually remembered this morning to bring this out with me,' she said, grinning, 'but I'm afraid it didn't last very long. I'd love some more, if you don't mind?'

Isobel collected the empty bottle, returned to the cottage and filled it with water before taking it back to Clara. She was still digging. Now that Isobel was closer she could see that Clara was not simply turning over the soil, but digging up piles of onions. She handed her the drink, watching as Clara lifted the bottle to her lips and drank almost half of it straight down.

She grinned. 'That's better. You don't realise how thirsty you are until you stop and think about it, do you? Still, I'm not going to complain about the heat, it's going to do wonderful things for my *Allium cepa*s.'

'Your what?'

'*Allium cepa*s,' repeated Clara. 'Or onions to you and me.' She squinted at Isobel. 'I need the sun to dry this lot out, you see, and the longer it stays hot, the better. The drier they get, the better they'll keep, and Trixie will be needing loads of these over the coming months.'

Isobel frowned. 'I never knew that,' she said. 'I thought you just dug them up and then, hey presto, they're ready to use.' She looked around her. 'There's so much to do here, isn't there?'

'There is, but that's what I love – every day brings something different. Once I've got this lot dug up, I'll be pinching out the tips on my tomato plants, feeding my peppers, and if I get that lot done I've got some cabbages to sow for next spring.'

'Blimey, and I thought I had my work cut out for me.'

Clara reached down and pulled free the onions she had just unearthed, shaking the soil from them before placing them to one side. 'Well I couldn't do what you do,' she said. 'I haven't got a creative bone in my body.'

'Most people say that.' Isobel smiled. 'But you'd be surprised; pretty much everyone likes music, and most people can hold a tune and recognise notes with a little instruction. Although, I'll be the first to admit that this doesn't apply to *all* people.'

Clara laughed. 'I think I may well be that exception,' she said. 'But I guess music is like anything – there's lots to learn, but if you get the basics right, you can go from there. Same with gardening. People always tell me they don't know how on earth I remember all the names for things, or how to care for each individual plant's likes and dislikes, but if you're interested in something it's instinctive to want to learn more. Then it just comes with time, until you don't even realise it's become a part of you.'

'I guess so,' replied Isobel, thinking. 'But music is very structured, it has its roots in mathematics, and although there are variations in sound from each particular instrument depending on where you play it, how you play it, and even the instrument itself, by and large you always know what you're going to get out of it.' She stared at the pile of onions beside Clara. 'When I play *I* decide how something is going to sound and that's exactly what I get, but surely when you grow things you can never be that certain of the results. Doesn't mother nature like to stick her oar in from time to time?'

'Oh, that she does. Sometimes I think she's the most incredible woman, hugely generous, with an ability to create something from almost nothing. That's when I'm completely in awe of her.' She paused, thrusting her fork back into the soil and straightening up. 'Of course, at other times I could cheerfully strangle her. Too hot, too cold, too wet, too dry, and then just when you think everything is going to plan she sends vast quantities of some hideous insect to steadily chomp its way through everything you've grown.'

She kicked at the pile of onions beside her and then bent down to pick one up. She grinned. 'And, of course, there are those times when everything goes exactly to plan and yet you still get some little blighter like this.' She held out the onion, which was small and shrivelled and nothing like its perfectly formed counterparts. She shrugged. 'Although, I confess, a part of me likes that too.' She gave an embarrassed smile. 'I tend to root for the underdog.'

Isobel winced, looking at the sad little object in Clara's hand. 'I'm not sure I could cope with that,' she said. 'I like everything to turn out the way I want it to; a little regimented perhaps, and there's always nuances of course, but with music the end result is either right or wrong, and if a note is wrong it's not something either you, or your audience, can put up with.'

Clara watched her for a moment. 'What, even if you've played with all your heart?' she said. 'That doesn't sound very forgiving. I think if I were listening I'd much rather hear someone who played with everything they had, even if they missed a few notes, than someone who played perfectly but without any feeling. Imagine how flat that would sound?'

'I'm not sure I quite understand what you mean.' Isobel was beginning to feel very uncomfortable. 'It's almost as if you're saying that it doesn't matter how good the music is? But if I play incorrectly the music is just wrong, it doesn't sound the same. How can that possibly be what any audience wants?'

'No, I didn't quite mean that,' said Clara, looking a little awkward. 'And obviously someone who plays to your standard would be technically brilliant as well. But when your audience can see and hear when you've invested every little bit of yourself, all your emotion into the music, I imagine it must make the performance feel even more special. Just like me and my vegetables…'

'But I don't… that isn't what I—' And then Isobel stopped because she really didn't know what else to say. She stared at Clara. She wasn't the first person to say these things to her, and every time someone did, Isobel knew deep down they made absolutely perfect sense. That's why it was so hard to understand why she had never been told that when she was younger. All her hours of practice, the playing of the same pieces over and over again, had only ever been about her technique. That was what was important. Each note, perfect. Followed by the next note, in the perfect place, at the perfect time. People never realised how hard it was to achieve that. It was never about emotion. How could it be, when emotion was the thing that got in the way? The thing that made her forget what perfect was? And perfection was what she strived for, that was what they always wanted, and what she'd been taught to deliver.

She could feel an ominous chill sweep through the pit of her stomach but she gave Clara a broad smile. 'Oh yes of course, you're absolutely right.'

'Perhaps that's why I like my garden so much,' added Clara. 'It's full of so many different personalities, just like pieces of music. The sunflowers are so in your face – *look at me, I'm amazing*, they shout. The Michaelmas daisies are so friendly; they always look to me as if they're smiling, nodding their heads gently in the breeze. The peonies are voluptuous, rich and intoxicating, while the roses are much more demure, like shy debutants.'

Isobel looked at the garden around her. She could see all the flowers that Clara was referring to, and yes, the daisy heads were nodding gently and the colours of the peonies were rich in contrast with the roses, except that they were still flowers. Isobel couldn't see how they had personalities of their own – differences admittedly, but that was just down to size, shape and shading. And she couldn't see how it had anything whatsoever to do with music.

It was true that she had favourite pieces to play, some of them fast, some of them slow. Some were technically very difficult, and others less so, and it was usually the case that the more difficult pieces gave her the biggest feeling of accomplishment, but did they really have personalities of their own? She thought for a moment. She supposed they must do. They could certainly change her own mood when she played them, so it stood to reason that her audience would feel the same way when listening to them, but it shocked her to think that she had never been taught to play that way. To her, a good performance was one where she played perfectly, nothing more, nothing less. She had never even given a thought to the moods and emotions of the people listening to her music. The voices of countless critics paraded through her head just as they did during her worst nightmares, and despite the heat of the day, she shivered from the cold inside her.

Isobel had come outside because she thought the break would do her good. It was supposed to give her some respite from the thoughts pressing inside her head, but all it had done was throw up *more* questions. And they were questions to which she had no answers. It wasn't Clara's fault. The garden was lovely, and Isobel could recognise real passion for something when she saw it. On any other occasion, it could have been just the thing she needed, but today, even Clara's easy conversation couldn't take away how she was feeling.

She chatted for a few minutes more, both of them wandering back up the path towards the place where Clara had originally been digging. A check on her watch confirmed that Trixie would soon be appearing with lunch, and both this and the amount of work that Clara still had to do gave her a good excuse to head back to the cottage. She waved goodbye, slightly saddened that she found herself glad to be closing the door behind her once more.

She stood in the centre of the living room for a few moments. Her computer screen was lit up with the random movements of her screensaver, but she knew that as soon as she moved the mouse her work would appear just as she had left it. She picked up her headphones and passed them from hand to hand as she walked back and forth across the room. That morning had seen her begin to flesh out the opening movement of the piece she had been working on, and although progress had been hard going, she had put that down to her general distraction. Now she was beginning to wonder if that was not the real problem at all and if all along she had been trying to convince herself that her composition was good, when she knew deep down that it was not. Now her break in the garden had allowed her to see that she hadn't been distracted at all; she had been deluded. She had been labouring away on something she had known to be flawed. The thought of listening to it again filled her with trepidation. She pulled out her chair and sat down.

Taking a slightly deeper breath, she rested her hand on the mouse and, with a few clicks, set her music playing. She stilled herself, closing her eyes and concentrating on what she could hear: the pattern of notes, the tempo, the rise and fall and fluidity of the sound. It was five minutes long and she listened, scarcely breathing, and instead of interpreting what she heard from the point of view of a musician, she tried to listen as if she was sitting in an auditorium.

Even before the piece was halfway through, she had her answer. She had deliberately written the music to be challenging. It was designed to showcase her skill as a composer and she knew that, when it was eventually played, there were very few musicians apart from her who could do it justice. It was meant to be a piece that would receive a rapturous reception, silencing her critics once and for all. After such a long absence from the music scene people would be clamouring to hear something sublime from her, an original piece of work that transcended all else, and that was what Isobel had been determined to give them. Except she hadn't. The music carried no story, it had no personality and, in contrast to the vibrant colours in Clara's garden, it was dull and lifeless.

Chapter 8

A beautiful perfume hung on the evening air as Isobel made her way to the bench. She didn't recognise the particular scent, but the garden was massed with flowers and it could be any number of them. Dusk was just beginning to fall but at the height of summer the air was still warm, even at this time of night. The longest day was behind them though and Isobel registered a slight sadness that the days were already on the wane. All too soon the dark days of autumn and winter would be upon them, and she really had no idea where she would be by then, or what she would be doing. She sighed.

Clara too, she noticed, had made the most of the long day, waiting until the heat of the sun had gone from the garden before watering the crops and flowers which covered every inch of the space. Isobel had seen her from the window, wandering up and down the paths for the last hour or so, but now she was gone and Isobel could see drops of water glistening on the foliage around her. Part of her had wanted to come out and talk to the friendly gardener again, but she hadn't known what to say, and so she remained inside. Perhaps she might pluck up the courage on another day.

Now, she simply sat and listened to the birdsong. Unusually, her right shoulder was aching, symptomatic of the tension with which she had played during the afternoon. She had set her piece of music to one side and instead gone back to one of her practice pieces, trying to analyse the music, the emotion contained within, but every time she stopped, her thoughts had got the better of her and she had worked herself into a fury, playing far too aggressively which got her nowhere. She had neither played well, nor accomplished what she had set out to do, and now she had wasted a whole day. It was time she could ill afford to lose. To try and soothe her frustration she had taken a long shower after dinner and read for a little while, but now the prospect of a night tossing and turning was ahead of her and she didn't know what to do with herself.

A loud jangling sounded from behind her and, startled, she twisted around. Tom was making his way across the garden, his mobile phone jammed to his ear. From the way he was walking she could tell he had no idea she was sitting there.

'Tom Hollingsworth,' he began.

She tried to slink down further into the seat.

He paused, frowning. 'Ah, hello, yes I did get your message. How can I help…? No, it's not that, I… Perhaps if you tell me now, I can pop out tomorrow and take a look… Oh, right…'

Tom cut off the call, swinging his foot at the path and scuffing it in anger, before storming towards her. 'Bollocks!' he said loudly, mid-stride.

She saw exactly the point he caught sight of her, and for a second she thought he was going to carry on marching straight past, but then he stopped, holding out his phone to direct her attention to it.

'Sorry,' he said. 'I just lost a job. A big one.'

'Oh… I wasn't listening, but I couldn't really help hearing… sorry.'

Tom heaved a sigh. 'No, I think I shouted loudly enough for everyone to hear, not your fault. In fact, absolutely, totally, one hundred percent my fault. I should have called them back days ago, and I forgot, so they've gone elsewhere.'

'Ah.'

'Indeed… a shitty end to a shitty day in fact.' He plonked himself down next to her on the bench, and then immediately scrambled back up again. 'Sorry, you don't need this either, do you?' He made to walk off down the path.

'Tom, wait. What do you mean?'

She saw the hesitation cross his face. 'The Tchaikovsky? I've never heard it played quite like that before… What were you *doing* to it earlier?' His eyes searched her face. 'Although, to give you your due, I admire your commitment. I mean, you murdered it over and over again…'

She could feel the hot flush racing up her neck. How dare he when he had no idea what she was up against? When he didn't have care in the world, just sat on a bloody roof all day in the sun…

'Sorry, I said you didn't need this, and I was right.' He hung his head. 'I'll leave you in peace. Night, Isobel.'

She took in his tired eyes, his hair sticking up on end. Even in the dimming light, she could see his face was far too pale. Isobel dipped her head.

'No, *I'm* sorry. I can see you haven't had a great day either.' She shuffled over on the bench and waited while he retook his seat. They sat in silence for a few seconds.

'Actually, I wasn't trying to murder the *music*…'

'Ah… so *someone* or *something*? An ex-husband perhaps, a jealous boyfriend…?'

'My mother, actually.'

He nodded, considering her words, but remained silent.

'So, you've had a rough day too?'

He rubbed his jawline. 'I wasn't feeling great, that's all. I don't usually feel like work is work, if you know what I mean, but it's been a bit of a hard slog today.'

She turned to face the cottage behind her. 'But it's very late. That's still pretty dedicated, particularly if you weren't feeling well.'

Tom smiled. 'Not dedicated often enough actually, hence the lost job. No, I haven't only just finished. I went for a walk after dinner, a long one, to try to clear my head a bit before I even contemplate heading home.'

'And I'm out here, trying to avoid going back inside…' She shrugged. 'What are we going to do, sit out here all night?'

Tom eyed the bench, and the soft grass that lay in front of it. 'I'll take the floor,' he said.

Isobel returned his wry smile and there was silence for a few moments before Tom spoke again.

'I admire *your* dedication actually,' he said. 'Even though you were frustrated you must have played that piece, what, twenty, thirty times?'

'I never count,' she replied. 'That way madness lies. I just do it until I'm satisfied, or I feel like I've made enough progress.'

'So, what was the problem?'

She stared out across the garden. It probably wasn't wise to be talking about it, but it had been a very long time since she'd been able to share anything.

'Funnily enough it wasn't the Tchaikovsky that was the problem. In fact, it was supposed to be part of the solution… it just didn't work out that way.' She tucked her hair behind her ears. 'The composition I've been working on isn't going well; it's making me panic rather.'

'Because of your deadline?'

She nodded.

'I have a deadline too,' he replied. 'Tricky buggers. The more you think about them the worse it becomes, until it gets so that you can't think of anything else. Then you might as well give up altogether.' He sighed. 'I'm not best qualified to give advice, but if you want mine, I'd try and forget about it for a while. Do something else, go for a walk, anything, but learn to take a break and pace yourself. The chances are you'll still get done what you need to.'

'But what if I don't?'

He gave a sudden smile. 'I see you spotted the fatal flaw in my plan.' He shrugged. 'I told you I wasn't very good at dishing out advice, but to be fair I do think you'll get it done, you seem very…'

'Obsessive?'

He didn't reply straight away.

'I was going to say committed, but if you think you're obsessive, doesn't that tell you something? I do think I could learn a lesson or two from you though,' he said. 'I give up too easily. That job tonight's a prime example. All I had to do was give the folks a call, but I put it off and put it off, telling myself I was too busy and I'd do it the next day, and then of course, I didn't. End result? Quite rightly, they took their business elsewhere.'

'And I probably need to take a leaf out of your book, and learn when to stop. To go for a walk, or something, anything, instead of thrashing my violin.' She pulled a face. 'So, I have four and a bit weeks until the end of the summer, by which time my magnum opus will be ready to be delivered.' She raised her eyebrows. 'And you have until the end of the summer to finish the roof, by which time the Thatcher's Cottage should be ready for occupation. So, perhaps in return for helping you run a tight ship, you might help me achieve a little more balance in my life, get a little perspective on my composition.'

He was about to reply, but then a wary expression flashed over his face. 'Let's just see, shall we? I don't like to make promises I can't keep, Isobel, but I tell you what, think about coming to Lily's concert? It might do you good to get out for a bit and listen to someone else play for a change. I can't guarantee that the music will be up to much, but everyone loves a good kids' concert, don't they?'

The thought made her stomach churn. 'Thank you.' She smiled. 'I'll think about it.'

Chapter 9

'Tom, can you turn back around to face me a little? Lovely though it is, all I'm getting are photos of your bum.'

'And what's wrong with that? I thought you were trying to encourage people to visit…!'

Maddie lowered the camera, laughing. 'I would hope they'll come for the accommodation, rather than just to look at your underwear.'

Tom lifted another bundle of straw, settling it into place. 'So why are you taking pictures of me then? I'm massively photogenic I know, but…'

'They're for the website,' Maddie explained. 'I want to get the details of this cottage on as soon as I can. If everything goes according to plan, we can accept bookings for the end of August, and I don't want to lose out.'

He considered his recent conversation with Isobel before answering. 'Then you'd better pray for good weather,' he replied. 'It's been too fine for too long now. It makes me nervous.'

'And is that the only thing that might put a spanner in the works?'

It was a reasonable question. Tom had been less than reliable on occasion, but the fact that Maddie felt she needed to ask the question still hit home.

'Unless I fall off the roof, yes… and I'm not planning to,' he added, catching sight of her face. 'But in all seriousness, the forecast looks set fair for the time being, but August can be a funny month. I'll do what I can.'

'I know you will, Tom.' Maddie smiled. 'And in the meantime, give me your best *look at me I'm gorgeous* grin and I shall immortalise you on the website.'

He did as he was asked, going along with the banter. He might have opened up to Seth, but no one else at Joy's Acre was aware of the struggles in his past, and for now he was happy to keep it that way. His looks and his love life were the butt of many a joke at Joy's Acre but only Seth knew why Tom never wanted to get close to people, or why the flirting, and the jokes and the series of one night stands presented him with the perfect smokescreen. But he was such an idiot. Only the day before Tom had told Seth he wanted nothing more to do with Isobel, and yet last night he had somehow entangled himself with her in something which had disaster written all over it.

Isobel was beautiful, and she was smart, and he'd seen enough to know that she would get under his skin very easily indeed. And if she did, gradually, bit by bit the truth would come out. And Tom would have to deal with it. The problem was, Isobel's suggestion that they try and help each other out seemed like the perfect answer to the situation they both found themselves in. She was obviously struggling with her composition and he'd spent so many years without any real direction in his life that things were long overdue for change. He turned his attention back to Maddie.

'Not being funny, Mads, but shouldn't you be taking pictures of the inside of the cottage as well? Just in case people want to see more than my blond-haired, blue-eyed good looks.'

Maddie stuck out her tongue. 'Actually, this was my idea,' she said, 'although I'm slightly beginning to regret it now… You know how we decided that each of the cottages was to have a theme, reminiscent of the Victorian farm? Well, this is obviously the Thatcher's Cottage, and as well as having the story behind how Joy's Acre got its name, we thought it would make an interesting angle for the website if we followed the renovation of each cottage through to its completion. We can include our ideas for the furnishing and decoration of the interior as well, just as we have for the Gardener's Cottage where Isobel is staying.'

'And do we have any ideas for the interior?' asked Tom, arching his eyebrows.

'Yes, as a matter of fact we do… I do.'

Tom loved teasing Maddie. 'You're so clever,' he simpered.

'It's my job,' she said pointedly.

'Ah, but is it?' he asked, cocking his head at her.

She smiled then, a beaming smile which lit up her entire face, and even from the roof Tom could see her blush. 'I admit it might be rather more than that now…'

'Well then, I'm glad. No one deserves it more than you do.'

Her relationship with Seth was still in its early days, but Tom had never seen his friend looking happier, well not for a long time anyway. Seth had given Maddie a very hard time when she'd first arrived at the farm. The last few years had been tough for him too, and at first he'd seen her as a meddling interloper, but Maddie had been the bright spark they'd all needed to start to transform Joy's Acre into the vision that Seth had always had for it; and just as she had fallen under its spell, so too had Seth fallen under hers…

Tom stared out across the slope of the fields, bright in the morning sunshine, thinking about Isobel's words from the night before. He was so lucky to be doing the thing he loved, and yet, given the lacklustre way he ran his business, you would scarcely know it.

'Actually, Maddie,' he began. 'I wanted to ask you something myself, about the website, but only if you promise not to laugh.'

She had raised the camera to take another picture but lowered it again at his words. 'Go on,' she said, looking up at him, 'I promise.'

'Well, I've been thinking about this for a while, seeing as I'm getting older and all that, but I wondered whether I ought to have a website myself.' He pulled a face. 'I know, it's a radical idea, and I'll be the first to admit that I'm a shocking businessman, but I probably ought to try and get myself in some sort of shape, at least look like I'm running a proper service and all that.'

Tom didn't expect her to laugh, but he did expect a degree of levity. The downside to always playing the fool was that invariably no one ever took you seriously. To his surprise, however, Maddie glanced at her watch, and then back up at him.

'Have you got time for a break?' she asked. 'I could show you now if you like, the possibilities at least.'

He swallowed, slightly nervous about looking a complete idiot, but perhaps there was no time like the present. He began to unbuckle his knee pads.

'I'll be with you in a jiffy,' he said.

★

By the time Tom had made two coffees and brought them through to the study in the main house, Maddie had already booted up the computer and was staring at a page of search engine results. He placed the mugs down on a piece of paper and pulled up a chair beside her.

'What's that?' he asked.

'I'm just checking out your competition,' she said, clicking on a link. They were rewarded by a page which even Tom could see looked very amateurish. He peered at the screen.

'Aye, Farmer and Sons,' he said. 'I know of them, but I don't hear much about their work. They're over Hereford way, a bit too far maybe for word from folks to reach me here.'

Maddie nodded and clicked the mouse again, returning to the search results.

'What about this one?'

The site was very slick, with moving images which faded in and out across the screen.

'Yeah, they get a lot of business, but they're a national company.' He pointed to the lower edge of the screen. 'See? They have a Shropshire address but they cover most of the Home Counties as well. I hate that kind of thing.'

'But they're successful?'

'Probably, and they have a website with all the bells and whistles on too. I imagine that pulls in the punters.'

'Possibly,' Maddie replied. 'Although, personally I think it's a little too... what's the word? Impersonal perhaps? Showy? Too much design over substance. It doesn't say very much about the people who work for the company, or about the fact that they're local craftsmen, serving local people. If I were looking for a thatcher I think I'd like to know who was going to be working for me, and what sort of affinity they have with the local area.'

Tom shrugged. 'But perhaps that's because you have a level of integrity that most people don't. They just want a job doing reasonably okay for a cheap price.'

'Possibly. But perhaps it's more a question of what they think is available... Maybe, given a choice between cheap and showy, or a local person with a lifetime's knowledge of the buildings around here, a passion for his work, and for the traditions of our countryside, they'd pick that option after all.'

A wry smile crept across Tom's face. 'Okay, you got me,' he said. 'I can already see your little grey cells hard at work.'

'I'm just saying that in a very short space of time I can clearly see where you might pitch your own site. What we've looked at so far has been very uninspiring, but with a little bit of thought you could come up with something that would serve you well in terms of future business.' She gave him a sideways look. 'You know you're okay here until at least the end of the year though, don't you?'

'Yeah, I know. But after that? It's all a bit vague, and while I've always worked on the principle that something will turn up, what if it doesn't? I'd rather not have to resort to bar work again just to keep the wolf from the door. I'm getting too old for that.'

'But what about your music?'

'What about it?'

'Well, isn't there a way you could make more money from that than you do?'

Tom stared at her. 'Have you even heard us play?' he asked. 'Nah, it's just a bit of fun. Me and the boys never meant for it to be anything serious. I mean, not like Isobel, it's a different kettle of fish altogether.'

'Okay.' Maddie turned her attention back to the screen, a slight smile crossing her face. 'So let's concentrate on this for a moment. You could put together something relatively simple with a couple of days' work; that's all it would take.'

Tom shook his head. 'No, Maddie, that's all it would take *you*. I'm completely clueless, remember?'

'So, I'll do it for you. The ideas can still be yours – how you want it look, what you want to say – the rest is just mechanics. One of the most important things you need are some decent photos, and with any luck I may have just taken a few.'

She picked up the camera from the desk. 'Let's have a look, shall we?' She attached a lead from the computer and waited for the pictures to transfer. 'The other thing we should do of course is credit your work here on the Joy's Acre website. Testimonials are another great marketing tool. If you had a website and we linked to it, it would serve us both.'

She took a gulp of her coffee. 'In fact, that's just given me another idea…' She pulled a pad of sticky notes and a pen towards her and scribbled across one of the sheets. 'Right, now let's see what these all look like.'

The photos were not what Tom had been expecting at all. From up on the roof all he had seen was Maddie pointing the camera in his direction and he'd envisaged a series of shots with him smiling away. Instead, without him realising, Maddie had used the zoom to extraordinary effect. In one picture the ends of a sheaf of straw were silhouetted against the bright blue of the sky; another photo showed only his hand in close up as he layered the straw. Even a clump of hazel twigs, as yet unused, which would bind the straw to the roof had been captured, the light and dark patterns of shadow they cast bringing the roof to life. What could have been flat one-dimensional shots had instead brought the very essence and meaning of the craft to life. They showed the roof as a living, breathing, thing and, as Maddie clicked through each of the pictures in turn, the images also showed Tom as master of it.

Maddie turned to smile at him. 'I lied about the photos of your bum.'

'I can see… Maddie, these are brilliant. Seriously, I love the angles you've used and the way you've focused in on the intricacy of the work. They're so different from anything you'd expect to find. And you're going to put all these on the Joy's Acre website?'

'Well yes, some of them. I want to show the story of how we came into being, how we're more than just a group of holiday cottages. I want to develop our name into something that people remember.'

This was not something that Tom had ever considered, even thought about, let alone allow himself to become excited by. But he could feel the flickerings of interest stirring within him.

'Can you show me the site?'

She clicked on another tab, and suddenly there it was. The colours sprang out from the screen; the homepage of Joy's Acre, like a vintage painting in a frame, just as if Joy had painted it herself. He had seen the site when Maddie had first put it together, but he hadn't realised she was still working on it, and he felt a little ashamed that he hadn't even bothered to take a look at it again. He wondered whether anybody else had. He moved his hand to where hers lay over the mouse.

'May I?' he asked.

She slid the mouse towards him, and for the next few moments he clicked from page to page, scrolling and scanning until he had taken in everything before him.

'Have you shown this to anybody else? To Seth, or the girls?'

She looked at him quizzically. 'Well yes of course, you've all seen it.'

'No, I mean recently. Since you've made all these changes.'

'Well there's not really much to show, I've added a few bits, that's all.'

Tom looked at the screen, and then back at Maddie. 'A few bits? This isn't the same site you showed us all those weeks ago, it's bloody brilliant! Where on earth did you get the idea for this?'

'Tom, this is what I do for a living. Well, did do, before I came here.'

'But it's like a scrapbook! It's like sitting down with a book on your lap, and a cup of tea, chatting to an old friend about everything you've been up to.'

He clicked onto the Gardener's Cottage page again. From the moment they had started work on it, Maddie had been taking photos, making little sketches, and scribbling down quotes from things people said. Somehow, she had laid them all out so that they looked like they were pinned onto pages in a notebook. Some of the pictures had even been made to look like they had curling bits of Sellotape across the corners; a tiny detail that brought the whole screen to life.

It was their journey from beginning to end, sharing with anybody who cared to read it their thoughts and their hopes for the little cottage on the hill. By the time anyone had read to the end, there was no way they'd want to stay anywhere else, at which point there was a link to a booking form. It was all incredibly simple, but utterly brilliant.

They were similar pages on the site for the gardens, showing Clara's beautiful planting with its array of flowers and vegetables, jostling side by side for space. Birds darted from seed head to seed head and butterflies sipped nectar from the colourful blooms. Pictures showed seedlings growing into small plants, being transplanted, growing into bigger plants, and finally becoming two burgeoning stems of cherry tomatoes. A further photograph showed those same tomatoes roasted with herbs, olive oil, and pepper, and served on the bruschetta which Trixie had fed them all for lunch one day. There were links too for recipes, and some tips for not only how to grow the vegetables successfully, but how to cook and serve them as well.

Day in, day out, Tom had turned up for work, climbed his ladder to the roof and begun to work his magic with the straw that would soon become a new thatch. But even from his elevated viewpoint, he had somehow never seen the bigger picture, he had never truly understood what he was a part of, and what Maddie and Seth were trying to achieve. Looking at this website was a humbling experience and all the inspiration he would ever need.

'Do you know something, Maddie? I think I'm a teeny little bit in love with you myself.'

Maddie just grinned. 'So, is that a "Yes please, Maddie, I'd love you to make me a website"?'

'Are you sure you have the time? This must have taken you ages.'

'Not really – once you have the theme and if you know what you're doing it doesn't need to take that long. You wouldn't need anything as complicated as the Joy's Acre site anyway, so I can fit it in no problem. Jot down some basic information for me and then we can work through it together.' She paused for just a moment, running her tongue across her lips and grinning cheekily. 'I do just have a condition though…'

'Go on…'

Maddie pulled open a drawer in the desk and took out a largish book. 'I got this from the local library,' she explained. 'And a little bird told me that you're a dab hand at making them, which is good because I'm going to need loads of them to decorate the new cottage.' She grinned at him. 'Do we have a deal?'

Tom groaned. 'How could I possibly refuse,' he said, taking the book from her hands and looking at the elaborately woven corn doll on the cover.

Chapter 10

Tom fidgeted on the hard plastic seat. There wasn't nearly enough space for his long legs between him and the row in front, but he knew it wasn't this that was making him ill at ease. For goodness' sake, why did he have to go and open his big mouth? No more had been said about Lily's end-of-term concert and if he had just kept his mouth shut then everything would have been all right. Instead as he had passed Isobel in the garden this morning, floundering about for something to say, he had asked her if she'd given any more thought to coming along. It wasn't as if he even wanted her to come. The concert would be fine, but then there was the whole conversational minefield of tea afterwards to be got through, when the whole subject of Kate's boyfriend would inevitably come up. It would be hard enough on his own, without having Isobel there as well, someone he barely knew.

And she was clearly having second thoughts about her decision to come. It had taken her an age to decide in the first place, and of course seeing her hesitation he'd felt stupidly duty bound to encourage her in case she took offence. Now, after suffering a near-silent journey to Lily's school, Isobel was sitting bolt upright in her chair and had scarcely said a word. To make matters worse, although he had sent a quick text message to Kate asking if it was okay to bring Isobel along, she had jumped to entirely the wrong conclusion about their relationship. Things were getting more complicated by the minute.

'I don't suppose you've ever done this before, have you?' asked Tom. 'Sat in the audience, I mean.'

'Never. In fact, I don't remember any of it.' She was sitting looking around the room with an expression on her face that Tom couldn't quite fathom. If he had to put a name to it though, he would say she looked scared. Her face was still turned away from his. 'I know I came to concerts like this all the time, but I don't recall playing in them, I only remember the ones…' She stopped suddenly, her hand touching her throat. He could see a pulse beating underneath the delicate pale skin.

'Well, I guess you were only little. I think I'd struggle to remember—'

She turned to him then, an urgent expression on her face. 'No, it's not that, it's…' But once more she ground to a halt, whatever she wanted to say stuck in her throat. She looked around her again, up and down the row where they were sitting, bodies pressed up close on either side. 'I'm sorry Tom, I—'

Her words were cut off as the piercing whine of feedback blared out from a set of loudspeakers on either side of the stage. It was cut off just as quickly. A harassed-looking teacher appeared from the left, quickly climbed onto the stage and disappeared behind the curtain. An expectant hush fell over the audience.

Tom leaned in towards Isobel, but the moment had passed. Her eyes were fixed ahead as she followed the movement of another member of staff up onto the stage. He was aware of Kate's voice on the other side of him.

'That's the Head,' she whispered.

He turned and smiled at her, nodding. The concert was about to begin.

The chat in the room all but ceased, followed by a few final coughs and the rustle of clothing and paper as parents sought to get comfortable for the hour or so ahead. Next to Tom, Isobel sat like a coiled spring. Years of playing had given her perfect deportment, worthy of any Swiss finishing school. She never slouched, and usually her posture was relaxed and elegant. Today she looked stiff, her muscles taut and held ready – for what? Fight or flight? Tom looked away. He had a sudden unbearable desire to hold her hand.

The head teacher was speaking now, welcoming them all, and Tom fixed a grin on his face as he studied the hand-drawn programme he held. First up was a recorder ensemble.

Predictably, the recorders screeched and clashed their way through three minutes of tortured music, but the assembled hall still clapped enthusiastically at the end, hearts warmed by the beaming smiles of the children playing. To Tom it was an adorable mess of bad notes and good intentions; more importantly, as he looked around at the proud faces and broad smiles, he could see that the children playing were somebody's sons and somebody's daughters, and that was all that really mattered.

He couldn't help wondering how Isobel was feeling. His ear was naturally attuned to wrong notes and mistimings but Isobel had more music in her veins than blood. Her professional ear would be thinking about the overall sound, probably even the acoustics in the room, and every wrong note must be making her flinch. She had said she couldn't remember playing in concerts like this, but something was making her uncomfortable, that much was obvious…

After several more performances Tom realised that Lily was just about to walk on stage. He could see her waiting in the wings with two of her classmates, and he swung a glance at Kate, sitting on his left. She turned and gave him a beaming smile, holding up two crossed fingers for good luck. He realised that Isobel would possibly not recognise Lily, and was just leaning across to whisper that she was about to come on, when he saw that Isobel had been following the programme closely and was about to do the same. Their heads touched somewhere over Isobel's left shoulder and, for a moment, had anybody asked, he would have sworn that time was standing still.

They both pulled away but not before he caught the corners of her lips lifting slightly. As Lily walked on stage, he heard a soft sigh catch in Isobel's throat. It seemed as if they both stopped breathing after that, willing Lily to play her heart out and get it just right.

As the final bar of music faded away, spontaneous applause erupted from around him, the loudest of all coming, quite rightly, from Kate. Isobel looked up, startled for a moment, catching Tom's expression before scanning the faces of the people around her, and then, suddenly, her face creased into a broad grin and her hands crashed together as she clapped with enthusiasm.

It wouldn't have mattered if every child had played appallingly. It would still have been the best concert that Tom had ever been to. He couldn't contain his excitement as the crowds gathered at the end of the show.

'You were just brilliant!' he exclaimed, picking up Lily and giving her a huge bear hug. 'And of course the best one there,' he added. He laughed as Kate tried to poke him in the ribs. 'What…? She was, I'm only telling the truth.'

He turned to face Isobel, as she surreptitiously touched a finger to the corner of her eye. He gave her a quizzical look but she avoided his gaze, turning instead to his niece.

'Well done, Lily,' she said, 'that was *so* good. Did you enjoy it?' Lily nodded up and down several times. 'Well then, that's absolutely the best thing. And the only thing that matters.'

Lily struggled from Tom's arms, and he watched her as she ran off to find her friends. The three of them stood awkwardly for a moment until Isobel came forward.

'She did so well,' she commented. 'And it's really hard to keep smiling when you're playing the flute, but somehow she managed to do that and play the right notes. She looked like she was having a ball.'

Kate groaned. 'She's been so excited that it's all we've heard for weeks. I probably shouldn't say this, especially to you, but I'm a little bit glad it's all over. I mean, I'm thrilled that she loves it, but it's rather wearing after a while.' She smiled at Isobel. 'Tom told me that you're a violinist. I hope you don't mind.'

If she did, she didn't show it. 'Not at all… but I'm trying not to think like one today. Actually, it was lovely just listening to the kids. It was so unlike my experience of this kind of thing…' She stopped, smiling shyly. 'Well, that doesn't really matter, but I think you're right, by the way. If Lily continues to enjoy playing then that's wonderful, and I think every child should have the experience if they're able to, but there are so many other things that children need to be doing too. It's good that you're not all over it like a rash.'

'Oh God.' Kate shuddered. 'Like those dreadful pushy parents you see on the television? I couldn't stand that. There has to be a balance, doesn't there? Although…' She tilted her head at Isobel. 'I guess you don't get to be a great musician without commitment?'

'True enough, but there's commitment and then there's obsession. There's also the understanding that children perform better on a diet of encouragement and support rather than an unhealthy fixation with every little mistake.'

Kate gave a nervous laugh, but she nodded. 'Fortunately, I think the people who make those kind of programmes look for the most extreme examples they can find. Most parents are like me, proud, but we just want our kids to be happy at the end of the day, whatever they do.'

Isobel's hand lifted, a gesture Tom was beginning to recognise. 'I'm sorry, I didn't mean to imply—'

Kate touched her arm. 'Don't be daft, I know you didn't, although I'll tell you something for nothing, and no offence, Isobel, but I count myself eternally grateful that Lily didn't want to learn the violin. I've seen some of the home videos of Tom as a child with his brother, and the noise was the most horrendous thing I've ever heard…' She rolled her eyes for good measure.

Tom let out the breath he was holding. 'Oi!' he said, trying to sound indignant. *Bless you, Kate*, he thought as the moment of tension dissolved. 'I wasn't *that* bad.'

'No?' She winked at Isobel. 'He was, you know…'

To his relief Isobel grinned too. 'Well, I haven't heard him play yet, so I've no idea whether he got any better or not.'

'Haven't you?' She turned to Tom. 'What, are you scared she's going to think you're rubbish?' she teased. 'Actually, his band is pretty good. You should go and listen to them play sometime. I'm surprised Tom hasn't asked you.'

It was inevitable, he supposed. Tom could see where the conversation had been going, but he was powerless to do anything about it. He shifted his weight onto the other foot. 'I'm not sure Isobel's all that keen on folk music, are you?'

Before she could answer, Lily came running back over to them, swinging her school bag. 'Mum, can I go back to Caitlin's house… pleeaase? Her mum says it's okay, and I can stay for tea.'

Kate gave them an apologetic look. 'Not today, sweetheart. Tom and Isobel are coming back to ours, remember. Perhaps you can go another day.'

Lily's face fell. 'Oh, but Mum, Caitlin's going to Australia tomorrow to see her granny, and she'll be there nearly the whole of the holiday… If I don't go today, then—'

Tom took a step forward, giving Kate a reassuring look. 'If it makes it any easier, we can come another day, one day in the holidays when you've got nothing else on.'

Kate was in two minds, he could tell. Whether to stick to her guns or acknowledge this was one she could afford to let go. The parent's eternal dilemma. But there was also another reason for her wanting to see them today. She lowered her voice a little, angling her body away from Lily slightly.

'It's just that I thought we could have a chat, you know… about Adam?'

'I know,' he replied. 'But, it's honestly fine.'

Now that he was faced with the possible choice of not having to stay for tea, Tom wasn't entirely sure which option he preferred. He still hadn't quite got to grips with how he felt about Adam, and if he was honest he was not at all comfortable with the idea that Kate thought he and Isobel were an item. He could see an awkward evening ahead of him.

'Well, if you're sure…' said Kate, looking at her daughter, who was practically jumping up and down with excitement. Suddenly, her face cleared.

'I tell you what,' she said, smiling broadly. 'How about we do this properly? Adam is away at the moment, but once he's back, why don't the five of us get together for a meal? I'd love you to meet him.' She paused for a moment. 'I know it's a bit awkward, but hey, it's got to happen sometime.'

Tom's heart sank. That really wasn't what he had in mind. He daren't even look at Isobel. He arranged his face into what he hoped was a suitably enthusiastic expression. This must be so hard for Kate, after all.

'Well, yes, that's a thought...'

She nodded firmly. 'Good,' she said. 'That's settled then. I'll contact you, shall I? Once I've fixed up a date.'

He found himself agreeing. He did sneak a look at Isobel then, only to find that she was smiling too. He couldn't tell whether it was genuine or not.

Lily was tugging on Kate's hand and Tom realised that the room was rapidly clearing. He bent down. 'You have fun, Lily, and I'll see you later, alligator.'

She beamed and kissed his cheek. 'In a while, crocodile... And thanks for coming, Uncle Tom!'

Kate gave them an apologetic look. 'I ought to go and have a word with Caitlin's mum...' she said, already being towed away.

Tom waved her on. 'Yes, sure, no problem. We can find our way out.'

And then there were just the two of them, standing rather awkwardly in an almost empty hall.

'Well... that didn't quite go according to plan.' He hoped that Isobel could see the funny side of it. To his relief she smiled.

'No... but then I don't suppose we can begrudge Lily time with her friends. She is a bit of a star, isn't she?'

Tom looked proudly in the direction in which she'd left.

'She is. An absolute credit to Kate. She's had a tough time, but you'd never know it looking at Lily.'

He was, he realised, immensely proud of Kate too. Her journey had been far harder than Tom's, but although in a way she'd had to carry on for Lily's sake, he doubted that he would have come through the way she had were he in her shoes. He was full of admiration for her.

'Have they been split up for long?' asked Isobel politely. 'Kate and Lily's dad, I mean… your brother.'

A flash of pain passed through Tom. 'Not exactly, no.'

'Oh, I'm sorry. I just assumed…' He could feel her watching him. 'You must feel quite awkward about meeting her new man then, when everything is still quite fresh.'

He turned his face away from her then, staring out across the hall. 'We should go,' he said, steering her into the hallway. He waited until they had left the building, nodding their thanks to the head teacher, who was standing by the door as they passed. They walked to his car in silence.

'It's been two years actually,' he said as he beeped open the car doors. 'But you're right, it's still hard. I often wonder whether it might have been easier if they had split up, just drifted apart like couples do. But they didn't, and I'm not sure how I feel right now. I'm glad for Kate – it's been a long time, too long to have to bring up a child on your own.'

Isobel looked at him over the roof of the car. 'I'm sorry, I'm not sure I follow…'

He took a deep breath. 'Kate's been on her own these last two years,' he said, 'ever since my brother committed suicide.'

Chapter 11

Isobel took a step backwards in shock. 'Oh.' It was clear she had no idea what to say. 'Tom, that's awful, I'm so sorry.'

A wave of shame washed over him. He should never have just come out with it like that. He'd put Isobel in the most awful position.

'No Isobel, I'm sorry…' He walked around the rear of the car so that he was standing next to her, and reached out a tentative hand, which hung in the air between them. 'I shouldn't have come out with it like that,' he said. 'But in all the time since Matt died I've never yet managed to find a way to soften that sentence.'

He looked down at his feet. 'I'm only thirty-two, Isobel, my brother was two years younger than me. Whenever I tell anybody that he died, they automatically think it was through tragic circumstances. More often than not, their first instinct is an accident, or possibly some incurable disease. You always end up having to explain, and there's never an easy way to say that someone took their own life.'

'No, I can see that. But you mustn't apologise; it was my fault, I shouldn't have asked.'

She was staring at his hand, and embarrassed, he suddenly withdrew it, thrusting both hands into the pockets of his jeans. He shrugged.

'You weren't to know,' he said. 'And your question was a natural one to ask. My brother and Kate might just have easily been separated or divorced, it would have been the far more logical explanation given the circumstances.'

'Now you're just trying to make me feel better,' she said.

Tom gave a slight smile. 'And what would be the point of trying to make you feel worse?'

The silence stretched out between them, with him scuffing at the tarmac and her fiddling with the strap on her bag. Tom could bear it no longer. He pulled his hands from his pockets and raised them in a helpless gesture of surrender.

'I tell you what,' he said. 'Neither of us knows what to say right now, and I don't know about you, but I could do with something to eat now that the prospect of tea has disappeared. How about we go out for some food? It's a perfect evening and there's a great place I know along by the riverside. Nothing fancy, just simple well-cooked food, but we could carry on our conversation in a slightly more relaxed setting.'

He looked at her, waiting for her reply, but Isobel looked like her mind was a total blank; a rabbit caught in headlights.

'It's just a bite to eat,' he added, wondering if she thought he was asking her on a date. 'And maybe a wander along the river, but it's no problem if you'd rather not.'

'No, I…' she said quickly, touching a hand to her skirt. 'Thank you. As long as you think I'm suitably dressed?'

Tom looked down at his own worn jeans and tee shirt. 'Perfectly,' he said.

It didn't really occur to Tom what he was doing until they were practically halfway there. Had he fallen into his own trap, without even realising it? Because this was what he did, he took women out for drinks and dinner when he was feeling low – in fact, he was well practised in the art. But this wasn't a date and asking Isobel out had simply been a reaction to his sudden realisation that, for the first time since his brother had died, he had a real urge to talk about Matt; or rather he had an urge to continue talking about him with Isobel, which wasn't quite the same thing. It was an extraordinary feeling, and Tom wasn't quite sure what to make of it.

The Bumble Bee was a tiny place. He had come across it purely by chance one evening while out walking along the river. In fact, its idyllic position was probably the only reason it managed to stay in business. Hidden from the road, and with no discernible signage, the best way to access the pub was from the river itself, and the moorings which ran the whole length of its garden were well used. Despite the perfect evening, there were tables still available in the garden, and Tom led Isobel across to one beside the river's edge. The gentle sway from a weeping willow provided a pleasantly soothing background to their conversation.

Isobel folded her hands underneath her thighs as she took her seat, looking around her.

'It's so beautiful here,' she said. 'I can see why you like it.' She had hardly said a word on the drive over and, it was only now, seeing the beauty of the gardens, the air full of scent from the burgeoning flower beds, that she found her voice. 'The river looks so pretty.'

Tom followed her gaze. The river was lit with rippling gold as the lowering sun caught the surface, mirroring its colour.

'I'll pop and get a couple of menus, shall I?' he asked, anxious to be doing something. She nodded gratefully, and he made his way back into the bar.

At first, he thought she'd done a runner on him. Returning to the table, all he saw were two empty chairs, but then as his eyes scanned the garden anxiously, he realised that she had simply moved to stand beside the river. A swan was moving sedately downstream, a clutch of cygnets swimming close by, and as Tom went to join Isobel the swan steered towards the bank.

'Aren't they beautiful?' she said, eyes still on the water. He could see she was counting. 'There's seven of them, look. Do you think she's hungry?'

'Opportunist perhaps,' replied Tom. 'I would imagine there's fairly rich pickings along this stretch of water, and the boaters are probably a good bet for a slice or two of bread.'

Isobel nodded. 'Do you know, I don't think I've ever fed swans before, or ducks for that matter.'

'You must have.'

She frowned. 'No, I don't think so.' He could see she was about to say something else but then she changed her mind, and held out a hand instead. 'Are those the menus?'

He pulled out one of the large folded cards from under his arm and passed it to her. 'They've got two specials on today as well,' he said. 'Either beef Wellington or mushroom stroganoff if you don't fancy anything else.'

Isobel carried the menu back to the table and began to study it. 'I'm not usually very good with food. It's rare for me to fancy anything, but...' She trailed off, lips moving as she read through the choices.

'Well I'm afraid my problem is exactly the opposite, especially now Trixie's with us,' he said, sitting back down. 'I'm getting far too used to her wonderful cooking. Of course, being outside in the fresh air all day helps as well.'

Isobel looked back up and stared out across the garden. 'You have a very physical job,' she said. 'But you know I am *trying* to take your advice.' She gave a shy smile. 'I think I've been outside more over the last couple of weeks than I probably have in the last six months. I even managed to go for a walk yesterday.'

'And I had a meeting with Maddie,' Tom replied, keen to show that he was keeping up his end of the bargain. 'She's going to put together a website for me so that I can at least try and drum up a bit of custom for the business and get things in order. Sadly, I won't be at Joy's Acre forever. Once the cottages are done I shall move on. Good for you though. I can't imagine working the way you do, even though I'm full of admiration for your work ethic. I'd get cabin fever within a day.'

'Yes, well, it's only just struck me that there is a choice about such things.' Isobel spoke without looking up, and although she had tucked her hair behind her ears to read the menu he still couldn't see the expression on her face clearly. But then he didn't need to; the edge to her voice cut the night air like a knife. She dropped the menu down suddenly. 'Sorry, we didn't come here so that you could listen to me. You were going to tell me about your brother?'

'Was I?' His mouth went suddenly dry. It was easy to think, sitting here in a beautiful garden with a beautiful woman, that they were here for an entirely different reason, and he had to remind himself that they weren't. 'Maybe we should order first?' He bent his head back down to make his own choice.

'Well, I think I'm going to have the crab cakes,' said Isobel.

She was smiling, and Tom was grateful that she hadn't pressed him. He wasn't quite sure what he would have said. He held out a hand for her menu. 'And what would you like to drink?'

'Just some water please, sparkling, if that's okay.'

'Fine, unless you're sure you don't want anything stronger? The local cider is very good.'

'I'm sure, thank you.' Her answer was very final, and Tom wondered whether she didn't drink or just didn't want to drink tonight.

He nodded. 'Back in a sec.'

He desperately wanted a drink. In fact, he desperately wanted more than one drink. It felt like it was the only way he would be able to cope with this evening. But as he approached the bar he realised he couldn't possibly. Not only had he made a promise to himself, but he had driven Isobel here, and although she wasn't drinking, there was no way he could ask her to drive them both back to Joy's Acre. And so, reluctantly, he gave his order for sparkling water for them both.

There hadn't been many occasions when Tom had even felt comfortable talking about Matt, and to do so now without even a drop of alcohol to ease his passage seemed foolhardy in the extreme. He was rapidly beginning to regret asking Isobel here in the first place, and he almost smiled to himself at the absurdity of this statement. Normally he would have given his eye teeth to be in the company of someone as beautiful as her.

From the entrance to the bar Tom had a clear view across the garden to where Isobel was sitting. Her posture was self-conscious and it came again, the weird flash of recognition he had experienced before. There was something about her neck, or her hair, maybe? But the longer he looked at her, the more the odd feeling receded, until his thoughts were reduced to simply observing how ill at ease she looked, as if she wasn't used to being out in public, or alone with a man. It was odd, given how beautiful she was – he would have thought that her past life had been littered with potential suitors queuing up for a chance to get to know her – but he had no desire to make her feel even more uncomfortable. It would be much easier if he were to simply say that he'd rather not discuss his brother just now… Though if he did that there was every possibility that Isobel would think he had got her here under false pretences, and who would blame her?

He placed both glasses on the table with a smile, and sat down, stretching out his legs in front of him. He patted his stomach. 'Hopefully the food won't be too long.'

Isobel picked up a glass. 'Were you very close?' she asked, taking a sip of water.

Tom's heart nearly skipped a beat. He had been trying to appear relaxed, as if he were just enjoying the soft evening air, and hoped that Isobel might follow suit. That way the two of them might have sat companionably for a few moments, giving him a little extra time to decide what to say. Instead, Isobel had jumped right back into the conversation as if he had never been away. He could feel her watching him, and he licked his lips.

The fact of the matter was that, against all odds, he and Matt had been very close. They shouldn't have been really, they were chalk and cheese in many ways. It wasn't until his brother had died that Tom realised quite how alike they were in one very important way, which was how they had both felt about their parents. The only difference had been the way in which they expressed their pain.

He turned to look at Isobel. 'Matt and I were best friends,' he said. 'And had been ever since we were children.'

'So, then I expect it's the guilt that's the worst thing, isn't it? I imagine it must be.' Her eyes were like rich brown cocoa. 'Losing someone so close to you must be awful. I can't even begin to think what that must feel like. Thinking that for all those years you'd known what that person was like, what they were thinking, how they were feeling, so surely you should have seen how unhappy they were. How had things got so bad that you didn't realise until it was too late?' She looked down at the ring on her finger, and turned it slightly before looking back up. 'You must have felt there was some way you should have been able to stop him from taking his life.'

Isobel looked up at him, a gentle expression on her face, and Tom stared at her. Her words were quite blunt, and yet she delivered them in such a way that Tom was certain she understood exactly how he was feeling. Her eyes were warm and soft with sympathy.

In all the years since Matt had died Tom didn't think he had ever heard anyone say these things to him, and yet he had always wished they would. He was fed up with saying thank you to people who had told him they were sorry. Or worse, telling them it was okay when neither of these things was true. He was neither thankful nor okay, and yet he continued to follow this accepted pattern of platitudes.

People always asked him how he was as well, in the special gentle tone that was reserved for people who had experienced a terrible loss. Except that they never really wanted to know the answer, and so he would tell them he was *fine*, you know, *getting there.* He wanted to scream at them. How could he possibly be fine when he was the most fucked up he had ever been in his life and couldn't see how that would ever change?

And the very worst thing was when people tried to commiserate with him by sharing stories of their own family bereavements; a hideous death from cancer, a life cut short by a tragic accident, or the simple comfortable death of an elderly relative. He wasn't interested, and he certainly wasn't about to turn his brother's death into a competitive league table of sorrow.

What he had always wished for was someone to hurl his guilt and anger at. Someone to agree with him that he had failed his brother by being so busy looking the other way, and behaving in a ridiculous way to prove a point to his parents, that he hadn't noticed how screwed up Matt was. Someone to acknowledge that Tom could have saved him, if only he had been paying attention.

He never wanted people to make him feel better. He only wanted his grief to be accepted for the very real thing it was, not glossed over, but instead a thing that it was okay for him to feel and that he could express in any way he chose. And now here was Isobel doing the very things that he had longed for all this time. Not even his sister-in-law, who understood more than most, had done more than just allude to it.

He stared at her, taking in her expression, her calm acceptance of his guilt. Unquestioning. Non-judgemental.

'How can you say that?' he asked, and then stopped himself. *No, that came out wrong.* 'What I mean is, how is it that I've only just met you, I hardly know you and yet you've had the guts to hit the nail right on the head? You've said the things that no one else would even admit might be a possibility. No one else has ever done that before, not even Kate.'

Isobel's expression remained unwavering, as she thought for a moment before speaking again. 'Well, you could have contradicted me, jumped down my throat after my very first sentence. But you didn't, and that in itself says as much as your words ever could.' She gave a slight smile.

Tom shook his head. 'But people don't want to hear about my guilt, and if I even so much as try to talk about it they always tell me I'm being foolish, and that I mustn't think that way, I'm just upset. It's like they want to move on from the subject as quickly as possible, just in case there is a teeny tiny chance I might be right, and then what would they do?'

'Run a mile probably, if my experience is anything to go by. Of course, now I'm going to go and ruin it all by saying that just because you feel guilty doesn't mean that you are guilty, but I assume you know all that. It's probably the question you ask yourself over and over. It's the thing that keeps you up nights, the thing that makes you drink too much, yes, I recognise the signs... And what's worse is that it's a question that will never go away, because the only person who can ever answer it is Matt.'

To his surprise Tom actually chuckled. 'Okay... you're slightly beginning to scare me now. How come you got to be so wise?'

Isobel lifted her glass. 'Oh, that's easy,' she said. 'It's because I'm just as screwed up as you are.'

Chapter 12

It must be the heat that was making her so agitated. But as Isobel paced across the living room floor, she knew that she was just kidding herself. Her distress had nothing to do with the weather. It *was* a hot day, but she was wearing a short cotton shift dress, had bare feet, and her hair was tied up into a loose ponytail that left her neck and shoulders exposed. She wasn't that warm.

She wandered over to the window and stared outside. She could go and have a word with Clara, she supposed, but she wasn't altogether sure she would be able to help, and the same was true for both Maddie and Trixie too. Which left only Tom, and for some reason she was reluctant to go and ask him. It wasn't that they hadn't got on yesterday, they had, but perhaps that in itself was part of the problem. Isobel wasn't at all sure how she felt about Tom. He was probably the only one who would understand her predicament and yet she felt a real need to keep some distance between them. His reputation with women was bad if the various comments made by the others were anything to go by, and that sort of complication was the last thing she needed.

Her laptop made a faint purring noise from behind her, as the fan began to whirr. She could always listen to the music again, but really, how would that help? With an audible tut she walked from the room,

down the hallway and opened the front door. She didn't even know if
he was out there, but almost as soon as she stepped foot in the garden,
she could hear him whistling up on the roof. In fact, he was whistling
the melody from the exact same piece of music she had been listening
to, and she grimaced.

She headed down the path until she was almost at the cottage on
the far side from hers. Almost immediately she heard him call out.

'*Peter and the Wolf!*' he shouted. 'I haven't heard that in years!' He
was waving at her now.

She smiled, raising an arm, but not at all happy about having to
raise her voice. 'Can I ask you something?'

He cupped a hand to his ear, but she certainly wasn't about to
shout any louder, so she stood there awkwardly, not knowing quite
what to do.

'Hang on, I can't hear you… I'll come down.'

Within seconds, it seemed, he had shinned down the ladder.

'Is everything okay?'

'I've been listening to a piece of music—'

'Yes, *Peter and the Wolf,*' supplied Tom, interrupting. 'I could hear
it from the roof.'

She hesitated. 'I'm sorry, I'm supposed to be helping you get the
roof finished, not distracting you.'

'But?'

She bit her lip. 'I wondered if I could ask your opinion on something. Have you got a minute to come inside?'

He nodded, following her into the cottage.

'So, you obviously know the piece of music,' she said as soon as
they were both in the living room.

'Spent many a happy hour as a child freaking myself out listening to it. I knew the story of course, but that didn't stop me from feeling the same way, every single time I listened to it.'

'It scared you?'

'Yes, didn't it scare you? Those big booming notes every time the wolf appeared. Prokofiev was genius, wasn't he?'

'But how old were you when you listened to it?' she asked.

Tom scratched his head. 'Oh, only little. I don't know, about seven or eight perhaps. I know I was learning the violin by then.'

'And did you ever go and see it performed?'

'No. I think I would have liked to, but my parents probably thought it was a bit... simplistic maybe?'

She frowned. 'How so?'

'Well it was written for children, wasn't it? As a vehicle for teaching the instruments of the orchestra, with each character in the story having a different instrument play its theme. I loved the music, but to them it was nothing more than a fairy tale, and as such had little merit in their eyes. I still used to listen to it though. I was just thinking about it actually, up on the roof, how I'd play it on a Sunday afternoon while they were having an afternoon nap. It's funny though, I haven't heard it for years and years and yet I can remember every note as if it were yesterday.'

Isobel watched him intently, an almost fierce expression on her face. She knew she was making him feel uncomfortable, but she didn't care, she had to know if she was right.

'I was forbidden to listen to it as a child,' she said quietly. 'My parents said it made the instruments into caricatures and belittled them. If I listened to it, that's all I would ever play.'

'Ah…' He paused before saying anything else. She knew he didn't get on with his parents, but that didn't give him carte blanche to be openly critical of hers.

'Perhaps I loved it so much for the simple reason that I *was* a child. Prokofiev wrote the music for people of that age and maybe that's why it resonated with me so much – in just the same way that a child's favourite book can hold little value for an adult. I can see that this may be the same kind of situation.'

'But why did you love it so much?' urged Isobel.

'When I was learning to play the violin my parents wanted me to listen to great violin music, and I understand why – it was something they wanted me to aspire to. But at that age, to me that music sounded boring, it was too difficult for me to comprehend and it seemed so far out of my reach. But when I listened to *Peter and the Wolf* I understood that you could have fun with music. You could play with it, and yet it was clever too. The simplest of melodies were so carefully thought out that they instantly gave shape to each of the characters. The music brought them to life, and I realised then how music could tell stories. It was this that inspired me, still does actually.'

He nodded at Isobel. 'That's why I love folk music so much,' he added. 'Much of it is traditional stories handed down from generation to generation. They were stories told around the fireside, different stories for different occasions, and eventually they became set to music.'

Isobel listened quietly while he spoke, but her thoughts were spinning far beyond what he was saying, back to her childhood. She was horrified to feel tears suddenly welling in her eyes.

'I knew they were wrong,' she said. 'I knew it.'

She blinked hard, turning her head away, and moved off across the room. 'Shall I make us a drink?'

'A coffee would be great, thanks,' he replied, following her into the kitchen. He was watching her, she could feel it. *Damn.*

'I was thinking that I might go for a walk later this evening,' she began, changing the subject. 'When it cools down a bit. Are there any footpaths at the back of the house? I need to follow something, my sense of direction is terrible.'

'No, I'm afraid not. But you really can't get lost, just count the fields. There's a beautiful spot two fields over where a tract of woodland acts as a divider between the next. If you go in the evening you'll get to hear the nightingales sing, and that is music of a very special kind.'

She concentrated on spooning coffee into a mug for Tom. 'I hate to tell you, but I'd be hard pressed to know what one of those sounds like, but thank you, it sounds lovely. I might not even get there at all, it all depends on how I get on this afternoon. I thought I'd had a good few days working on my composition, but in fact, it turns out they weren't that good after all. I have some serious headway to make.'

'So where does the Prokofiev come in?'

'Could you play something for me?' she asked, ignoring his question. 'One of your stories?'

There was silence for a moment as he considered the question.

'I could… but it will have to be some other time, I'm afraid. I don't have any of my instruments with me.'

'Well, that's no problem. You've seen the set-up I have in the living room. Someone with your knowledge would have no problem understanding its capabilities. I have pretty much any instrument imaginable at my disposal.'

He hesitated. 'It's not quite the same though, is it?… I'm not really used to playing like that… I kind of need the instrument in my hands to just jam it up.'

'Keyboard then?' she suggested. 'I'm sure you must play.'

He shifted his weight from one foot to the other.

'You're not being shy, are you?' she asked. 'Or perhaps it's that you're too modest...?'

Tom ran his fingers through his hair. 'Isobel, I'm sorry. It doesn't much matter whether it's shyness or modesty, because I'm still not going to play for you. Not here, not like this.' He paused, softening his expression. 'I'm used to playing for other people, but in bars, at weddings or at birthday parties where people are relaxed and have had a few drinks. And I play with the band, I don't play on my own, like this, it's too... intimate.'

'Oh.' She was taken aback. She really hadn't considered that he would refuse.

He gave an uneasy shrug. 'I'm sorry, but there you go. If you want to come and see me play, you can come to the pub with me one evening, listen to me and the boys.' He gave a slight smile. 'You'd be very welcome to do that.'

'No, well in fact you couldn't stop me, could you? It being a public place and all that.'

His eyes blazed in response, but she held his look defiantly for a second, before dropping her gaze. She really shouldn't have said that. What on earth was wrong with her? She could see his jaw clamp together. The silence grew loud.

'Isobel, what's wrong...?'

She looked up sharply, a query on her face. 'Nothing's wrong, I—'

He took a step closer. 'Yes there is...' He heaved a sigh. 'Listen, yesterday I bared my soul to you. You might not have realised it, but that was a big thing for me. I shared things with you I've never shared with anyone, and right now I'm struggling to understand why, when today you're acting like nothing's happened.' He was becoming angry now. 'You made me feel better about Matt than I have in a very long time, because you seemed to understand what I've been going through, and when I asked you how come, you said you're screwed up too!'

He gave her a very obvious once-over. 'And from where I'm standing now I think I'd have to agree with you. So, I'll ask you again… What's the matter, Isobel?'

His eyes were still locked on hers, the blueness of them filled with a gentle kindness, and something else, something she'd never expected to see: warmth. A ripple of emotion ran through her. She swallowed and licked her lips.

'I don't know,' she said, beginning to tremble.

She turned her face to the wall, but within two strides Tom was by her side, his hands holding her arms, gently tugging at her as if he wanted her to let go of something. She clung onto her resolve until the last moment, until, finally surrendering, her tears came in a fierce rush of emotion that almost took the legs out from under her. She clung to Tom as a small child might, almost unaware of her surroundings save for an overwhelming need for comfort.

It was a strange feeling for her. Tom's arms and chest were hard, which somewhat took her by surprise, but the hand that came up behind her head to hold it against his shoulder felt gentle, as his fingers moved over her glossy hair in slow motion. It was the most wonderful sensation. And for the first time that Isobel could remember she let herself relax, giving in to the pressure of his arms which were willing her to do so. She was utterly unable to speak, aware only of his soft voice in her ear, telling her that everything would be all right.

Oh, how she wanted to believe him. To believe that she had a future doing the thing she loved the most. But her violin was a cruel mistress, bestowing her gifts on the one hand and taking away with the other. She had given herself completely to her playing of it, but at what cost?

In truth, it was a question on which Isobel did not require enlightenment. She had been well aware of the answer for years, but the real question was how she was ever going to overcome it. And it was this that was causing her to cling to Tom now.

With this understanding came another: that whatever happened in the next few minutes would be crucial for them both. Isobel was beginning to feel hugely embarrassed and awkward after her outburst. She had trusted Tom with her innermost feelings and unwittingly placed a huge responsibility upon him. Slowly, she began to pull away.

His shirt was damp, a darkened patch over one shoulder, but he swiftly unrolled one of his sleeves until the worn material of the cuff hung down over his hand. He pulled it down further, gripping the edge of it between his thumb and forefinger and then, using the heel of his hand, swiftly wiped away Isobel's tears. Not unkindly, but rather more matter-of-factly.

'Don't you dare apologise,' he said. 'I'm not particularly fond of this shirt anyway,' he added. 'So it really doesn't matter that you've ruined it.'

Her mouth opened in surprise, unsure of what response to make until she caught sight of the grin he had very firmly fixed to his face. She lifted a hand to her mouth.

'Oh God,' she said. 'That was awful.' But she was smiling between her fingers.

'What was?' he asked. 'Your crying buckets all over me… or the fact that in doing so you have covered me with snot.' He held up a hand. 'No wait, actually neither of these were awful – the shirt will be good as new come wash day, and, if anything, you seemed to rather enjoy the impromptu howling session.'

She snorted suddenly as she laughed, which made her laugh even harder. 'Could this actually get any worse?' she asked. 'Apart from covering you in bodily fluids, I bet I look a right state.'

'You look hideous. For goodness' sake, woman, pull yourself together.'

She wiped under her eyes, still amused, but sobering slightly now. She laid a hand on his arm.

'Thank you,' she said, and she knew Tom understood her perfectly. There was no need to say any more.

He turned and scooped up the two mugs from where she had left them on the table.

'I'll finish making these,' he said. 'You go through there and do those things you women do to compose yourself. I won't be a minute.'

She did as she was told and by the time he returned Isobel was sitting back at her desk, having blown her nose and dabbed at her face so that pretty much all traces of her earlier tears had gone. He laid her tea beside her and then went to sit in the armchair opposite her. He blew across the surface of his coffee.

'So, I think we might have established that there is in fact a little something that's bothering you. Are you going to tell me what it is, because I'm sure you do know… or would you rather I leave?'

'No!' Her reply was instantaneous, and then softer: 'No,' she said, 'please don't go.'

He waited for her to speak as she struggled to find a place to start.

'This is really difficult,' she began.

He took a sip of his coffee. 'So, start with the Prokofiev. I'm not sure what that's got to do with anything, but it obviously has, so…' He let the sentence dangle.

Isobel wriggled on her chair, taking a breath.

'I have a composition to write, you know that. And it has to be special, very special. You don't need to know why, but it's very important to me, and…' She threw up her hands, searching for the right words. 'Well, put bluntly, what I've written is shite. I mean utter shite, totally, spectacularly, comprehensively—'

'I get the picture…'

She smiled, and then swallowed. 'I can't do emotion, Tom – in my music, I mean. I never have been able to. When I play, it's accomplished, more than that… perfect, always, but I'm like a machine. I have no soul when I play.'

He was about to contradict her but she held up her hand. 'And when I compose it's flat, lifeless. It has no colour, no story, passion, nothing. I've been listening to *Peter and the Wolf* because of the story-telling aspect of the music, how every instrument has its own character, and I understand it… I just can't *do* it…' She trailed off, dropping her head.

A frown hit Tom's face before he could stop it.

'See!' she said. 'I knew you'd think I was stupid.'

'Isobel, I don't!' He reached out a hand to lightly touch her arm. 'Not everyone wears their heart on their sleeve, and that's fine… But I am perhaps a little curious…' He waited to see how his response would be received before continuing. 'For me, music is *all* about emotion… When I play at my best it's like every part of me becomes every part of the music. There's an utter connectedness that binds it and drives it. I guess I thought it was the same for everyone else.'

'It is. Everyone except me.'

He was about to contradict her. It was the kind of thing you said when you were in a slump, struggling with a piece of music which try as you might wouldn't go where you wanted it to. But then he realised that she was serious. Absolutely so.

He thought for a minute. 'Okay… so let me hear you play.' He nodded towards her violin which lay beside her mug of tea. 'Something you've written though, not a piece by another composer. Play me what you were working on this morning.'

'But it isn't completed yet. I couldn't possibly play you that.'

He raised his eyebrows, and his meaning was crystal clear.

She took up her violin, lifting it to her chin, and readying her bow. Almost immediately she began to play.

The piece lasted around eight minutes or so, and Tom listened without speaking until the end, watching her carefully. At the end of that time he waited for a few more seconds before nodding briefly.

'Play it again,' he said. 'Once more with feeling, as they say.' He grinned.

This time, as she played, Tom closed his eyes and, when she had finished, he continued sitting, not moving a muscle until the sound completely died away. Slowly he lifted his head and his eyes found hers.

He nodded. 'So, what's it about?' he asked. 'What's the story here?'

'That's just it,' she said, trying to keep her lip from trembling again. 'I don't think it has one.'

He nodded, reaching forward to pick up his mug, and then drained its contents in one almost continuous movement. 'Do you know what I think?'

She moved her head, just a fraction.

'I think that *you*, Isobel Hardcastle, need to live a little, and that once you have, you will find the thing inside of you that so desperately needs to be communicated will come tumbling out so fast that you won't be able to stop it.'

And with that he got up, replaced his mug on the table and dropped a light kiss on her forehead before walking from the room.

Chapter 13

Tom had put in a solid afternoon's work following his visit with Isobel, and by the end of the day had made good progress – good enough that he felt able to return home straight after dinner rather than squeeze in a few extra hours. Since then he had changed the sheets on his bed, put on a load of washing, and given the kitchen and bathroom a thorough clean, both tasks long overdue. Now though, as he sat at the kitchen table idling with the day's post, there was nothing much else to occupy his brain, and his head filled with the thoughts he had been trying so hard to keep at bay ever since he had held Isobel in his arms.

Tom was torn; she was one of the most beautiful and intriguing women he had ever encountered, yet her need for him felt driven by comfort, the sort a daughter might look for from a father. He knew deep down that had he sought to offer anything else it would have been a huge mistake, and the fact that he hadn't wanted to was a surprise, even to himself. He couldn't remember the last time he had held a woman that close and not woken up beside her the next morning. Isobel was different, or he was different, but the realisation that all he wanted to do was make her feel better was perhaps one of the most pivotal moments of his life, so far.

But what did he do now? Over the last few years all the women he had met had been a distraction. He wasn't proud of it, but the lifestyle he had led had kept him from dwelling on his grief and all-consuming guilt over his brother's death. Previously he had feared that allowing anyone to come close would mean he had to share his innermost demons, but now Isobel, with her calm and accepting manner, had drawn from him things he had never shared with anyone else. He had stared his guilt full in the face while in her presence, and all he felt now was a peaceful release. So where did that leave him? And where did it leave Isobel and her demons?

The book Maddie had given him was still on the table where he had left it, and he pulled it towards him, opening it at a random page. He had been making corn dollies for years, although he preferred to call them 'cornucopias', which he reckoned had a slightly less 'girly' slant to it.

When he was an apprentice thatcher it had been a way of passing the time in between jobs and most of the trainees did it, the methods and traditional designs passed down from family to family, region by region. Originally corn dollies were made to thank the gods for a successful harvest and crafted by the local village women as fertility symbols. The dollies would be kept inside until the following year and then 'offered' back to the field come planting time to ensure another good year. And a good harvest not only meant plentiful wheat for bread, but also plentiful straw for thatching.

There were one or two designs that Tom favoured and, over the years, he had made so many he could practically make them with his eyes shut. He wasn't sure exactly what Maddie would want to use in the cottage he was currently re-thatching, but he suspected it would be something which showed more skill or had a more elaborate pattern than some of the simpler designs. Leafing through the pages, he waited for something to catch his eye – what would be really good was if he could find something he could tie in with the story of Joy's Acre.

He peered closely at one of the pages for a moment, thinking. In a way, everyone at Joy's Acre had their own individual stories – Trixie and Clara, Maddie and Seth, and him too – but put them all together and they made up one big story, the story of Joy's Acre itself. And, just like a single blade of straw, on its own it made little impact, but put it together with similar pieces and you could create something much stronger, like a roof, for example. And just like Joy's Acre, his roofs were the sum of their constituent parts and if any part of it failed over time, the rest would fail too.

Without realising it he had come up with a perfect idea for his website. Maddie had already begun to link together the threads of other people's stories, and he had seen how effective this was. Now his own site could help to strengthen that of Joy's Acre as well. He got up to fetch a pad of paper and a pen from one of the kitchen drawers and quickly began to jot down his ideas. What he saw in his head might not even be possible, but Maddie would know and if she could get it to work it would look brilliant. As he finished his list he couldn't help but wonder how Isobel was getting on. Would she have found a way to tell her own story?

Turning his attention back to the book, he flicked through a few more pages. Each section focused on a different type of corn dolly – traditional sheaves, fertility symbols, and a third showed more modern designs, which were his least favourite. The last but one section, however, focused on figures, and it was these pages that his fingers lingered over. The designs ranged from the naive to the elaborate, but it was the simple designs which held his attention, and one in particular made him draw the book closer.

It featured a very basic doll, almost stick-like in appearance but with two twisted arms which came together to hold a bouquet in front of a 'skirt' made from splayed-out pieces of straw. The head was a simple oval but a plaited section had been added to give the impression of hair; hair which dangled over the shoulders into two long braids, each finished with a tiny strip meant to resemble a hairband. He looked up suddenly, staring into space.

Earlier that afternoon, just as Isobel had been about to start playing, she had given a flick of her head which sent her ponytail flying over her shoulder. From the first time Tom had met her there had been something about the way she wore her hair which sparked a sense of *déjà vu*, except he hadn't been able to work out what it was that struck him as so familiar. Today though, seeing that particular mannerism, his memories had been triggered yet again, only stronger this time. And now, as the image came back to him one more time, he suddenly remembered where he had seen it before…

All thoughts of corn dollies were pushed aside as he rose quickly from the table and went through into the living room where he kept his computer. He sat down, tapping on the desk impatiently while he waited for it to boot up. His memory wasn't great at the best of times, and he had been a small child when he'd first seen her. No wonder he couldn't remember her name. In any case, the one thing he was certain of was that googling her current name, Isobel Hardcastle, would be unlikely to return any results.

Isobel may have changed her name over recent years, or perhaps, as was more likely, she had simply not given her real name when she booked to stay at the Gardener's Cottage. But the one thing she had been unable to change were her striking looks and her mannerisms. They had been bugging him ever since he met her; those small movements she made which seemed so familiar to him: the way she held her hand to her face, the way she tipped her head to one side when she was speaking, but – most familiar of all – the very effective flick of her head that threw her hair back over her shoulder and away from her violin. She had been doing it ever since she was a child.

First of all he entered her current name into a search engine just in case he was mistaken, but, although this returned information concerning many and varied Isobel Hardcastles, none were his raven-haired musician. He settled himself back in the chair, knowing the information he sought was likely to take some while to find. But Tom was a seasoned night owl, and it mattered little. He had all night if necessary.

His first few searches returned huge amounts of links, all of which he started to follow, clicking deeper and deeper into the well of information, and the first hour slipped by almost without him noticing. Then he tried different search words, trying to narrow the field, marvelling at the number of similar stories, but it was only when he got up to make himself a drink that something else occurred to him. He and Isobel were roughly the same age, and given that he was born in 1985, his eighth birthday would have been in September 1993, and so, allowing for the slight difference in their ages, he needed to search in the timeframe somewhere after 1990, stopping just short of the new millennium.

It took almost another hour before he found what he was looking for, and he read every article he could find, feeling sick to the stomach and hating himself for the invasion of Isobel's privacy. Except that he had to know. If he was to be of any help to her at all, he had to understand the journey she had taken to arrive at Joy's Acre.

And given what he now knew, he understood perfectly why she had changed her name. He could only hazard a guess at what she had been doing in the intervening years since the articles were published – information about her had dwindled away to nothing and, for the rest of the world, her problems had ceased to exist. He closed his eyes and thought about his own agonies over recent times, but these paled into insignificance compared with what she must have been going through. So yes, he now understood perfectly why she would not want anyone to know about her past, but what completely baffled him was why on earth she would want to put herself through all that again.

Chapter 14

Isobel prayed that it wouldn't be Tom at the door when she opened it. Not that he hadn't been helpful, or tactful, or utterly lovely yesterday, but she had still blubbered all over him like a baby. And she really had. She had clung to him like a small child and sobbed her heart out. He had handled the whole thing wonderfully, even managing to take away her embarrassment, but it had still happened, and at some point they would have to mention it again, not least because Isobel still had a massive problem on her hands. However, it was Trixie who met her smile on the doorstep and she welcomed her in, relief flooding over her.

'Is now a good time?' Trixie asked, handing her a covered basket. 'It will keep in the fridge if not, it's only some bread, salad, and a savoury tart. I don't know about you, but I'm finding it hard to face anything heavier with all this heat.'

Isobel lifted the linen covering and looked up at Trixie, a little disconcerted. 'Oh. Have I got to eat all this? I feel like I'm being fattened up for Christmas… Or at the very least spoiled rotten,' she added, realising her comment sounded a little churlish. 'This all looks amazing, but I'm really not sure I'll be able to do it justice.'

It was at that precise moment that her stomach gave an enormous rumble. She put her hand across it. 'On second thoughts, perhaps I will.' She laughed, taking hold of the basket. 'Actually, I don't think I had any breakfast… I slept in until nearly ten o'clock this morning, which is something I never do. There must be something about this place that's getting to me.'

And it was true. She realised when she'd woken that it had been the first night in a very long time that she had slept peacefully.

'Yeah, it'll do that all right… but perhaps you're just beginning to relax. Either that or Joy is working her magic. I'm not entirely sure that's true myself, but Maddie and Clara are convinced she's keeping an eye on us all.'

Isobel frowned. 'But I thought she was—'

'Dead? Yep she is, as a doornail. But apparently that doesn't matter. Actually, I probably shouldn't be so cynical seeing as everything is going so well at the moment. I'd hate to put a jinx on it, and who knows, it could all be true.'

'I'm trying to remember the story from the website,' said Isobel. 'But I think she was a painter, is that right?'

'She was. It was all a bit tragic in the end, as most of her work was destroyed. There are only a handful of her paintings left in existence, and we're lucky enough to have two of them. Seth found one shortly after they moved in here, it came up at auction, and then only recently when we were having a clear-out we found another which had fallen down the back of a dresser.'

She smiled at Isobel. 'It's a long story,' she said. 'You probably don't have time for all this now, but if you're free one day, come over to the main house – the pictures are hanging there and I can tell you all about her… On second thoughts, there's a book about Joy and her husband which was written by one of the villagers when they lived here. Seth won't mind if I lend it to you instead, it tells the story beautifully.'

'I might just do that,' replied Isobel, thinking back to Tom's words of yesterday, the memory also causing her to blush inadvertently. 'Perhaps not today though, I ought to get on really. I had somewhat of a setback yesterday, and I'm still trying to work out if I can salvage anything or whether I'm going to have to start all over again. Trouble is, if I do have to start over I'm not quite sure how I'm going to do it.'

Trixie grinned. 'You and me both. I'm testing recipes at the moment, and there's one that I can't seem to get right whatever I try. I reckon I probably just need to go back to the drawing board.' She eyed the basket still in Isobel's hands. 'Let me know what you think about the tart, won't you? That's a new recipe too, and I'm trying to see which ones are everyone's favourites.'

Isobel felt her heart sinking just a little as she cast about frantically for something to say.

'You're really not very good with food, are you?' said Trixie, leaping into the gap in the conversation that Isobel had left. 'Are you just really fussy? Or is it a weight thing?'

She was scrutinising Isobel, but there wasn't a trace of malice on her face. She was simply interested. It must seem such a strange thing for a cook, to find someone so completely disinterested in food.

'I'm not sure it's really either of those things, just not something I normally bother with. I mean, I eat, obviously, but I've never really given much thought to food before, it's just fuel.'

Trixie seemed satisfied with her answer, although she narrowed her eyes. 'Hmm, well we'll see about that. I shall have to see what I can tempt you with. A few more home-cooked meals and lot more fresh air won't do you any harm. You're far too pale—' She blushed slightly, clearing her throat. 'Oops, there's me going off on one again. What I meant to say is that you work so hard you probably spend far too much time inside. Maybe if you get out and enjoy the sun more, you'll find your appetite picks up.'

Isobel smiled at her blunt, but well-meant, honesty. And she probably had a point, but she was keen to change the subject.

'Have you always been a cook?' she asked, trying to show some interest, just like her therapist told her she should. *People like to be asked about themselves, it's a good way of starting a conversation. And always listen to what is being said to you, the clues are always there, and this will help you to naturally direct where the dialogue goes without it sounding stilted.*

'Goodness no,' replied Trixie. 'This is my first job as a proper cook. But I had to fend for myself from a very early age, so I didn't have a lot of choice – I either learnt how to cook or starved.' She grinned. 'Good job I like it though, isn't it?'

'So, you never had any formal training?'

'Nope. Everything I've learned I've had to teach myself, but maybe that's the best way. You learn from your mistakes, and at least I never had to worry about poisoning anyone else.'

'Until now.'

'True. But so far, so good. And it's brilliant here – like cooking for one big family – and now that the feedback from the farmers' market has been so encouraging, we thought we'd take things a step further. So many people have asked for our recipes that it seemed silly not to give it a go and try and put them together into a proper cookbook. Who knows? It might be a complete flop, but if you don't try you'll never know, will you? I'd much rather try and fail than never have the guts to go for it in the first place.'

Isobel felt something stir inside of her at Trixie's words. How right she was, and on her good days Isobel recognised that feeling well; it was what got her out of bed in the morning. Her problem was that on quite a few mornings, actually more than just a few, the fear of failing yet again was almost overwhelming. She smiled to herself at the coincidence of having landed right in the middle of a place where everyone seemed to be in the throes of some creative process. Of course, it might not be a coincidence at all…

'But that's so exciting! I had no idea that's what you were planning.'

Trixie rolled her eyes. 'I know, we must be mad. We've enough work to keep us going full pelt day and night if we wanted to, and now we're taking on this as well.' She shrugged. 'It wasn't exactly planned, but now that it seems to have fallen into our lap, how can we ignore the possibility?'

Isobel nodded, looked at her watch and then at the basket of food. It was still relatively early and a sudden idea had come to her.

'Actually Trixie, despite my rumbling stomach I think I might take you up on your offer now, if that's okay? Could I come back to the house with you and look at Joy's work? I've had a thought about something, but I promise I won't take up too much of your time.'

Trixie smiled. 'No time like the present, although only on the condition that I get to pick your brains as well.'

★

It was the first time that Isobel had visited the main house. She had knocked at the front door on the day she arrived at Joy's Acre, but had been swiftly whisked away to her cottage and so didn't get to see much beyond the first foot or so of the hallway. Now, though, she noticed the paintings the moment she stepped inside the door. There were two of them, side by side, both very clearly showing images of the gardens and their cottages, and painted in the brightest colours imaginable. There was something innocent about them, she thought. As if an exuberant child had painted them, and yet at the same time Isobel understood how much skill had gone into their execution.

'This is the first,' pointed out Trixie, looking at the slightly smaller of the two paintings. 'See, it shows practically the whole of the garden.'

'But it's hardly changed,' replied Isobel. 'Look, there's my cottage, and I'm sure those are hollyhocks growing in the garden.'

'You're probably right. It's amazing that previous owners never materially changed anything. I mean, it wasn't like it is now – the whole place was pretty rundown – but Seth and Clara have done an amazing job to get the gardens at least looking like they once did. Now we're working on the cottages it won't be long before those too are returned to their former glory. After that, Seth has plans for the rest of the land, and ideally in a few more years it will be a traditional working farm once again.'

Isobel turned her attention to the second picture, peering at it more closely. 'You can really see that Joy loved this place,' she said. 'Her paintings are so… friendly. And it still feels that way today.'

'I'm glad you think so.' Trixie smiled. 'Come on through to the kitchen and I'll get that book for you.'

Isobel followed her through to a warm airy room, dominated in its centre by a large scrubbed pine table, the surface of which was littered with kitchen equipment.

'Have a seat for a minute, I won't be long.'

She chose a chair at the far end, where the table was the clearest, but also where several handwritten pages were stacked alongside a pile of notebooks. The papers were covered in large loopy handwriting, and Isobel picked one up, feeling a sudden pang of hunger again as she read the list of ingredients. She recognised it as a dish that Trixie had served one evening.

'That's my *very possibly* pile,' remarked Trixie, coming back into the room. 'Have a look through and see what you think, particularly if there's anything there that you haven't liked.' She placed the book she was carrying down on the table. 'There you go, a little light bedtime reading. Only make sure you have some tissues at the ready, it's a bit of a weepie.'

Isobel looked up. 'You mentioned it was all a bit tragic, what happened?'

Trixie shook her head. 'Uh-oh, no spoilers,' she said. 'Anyway, what was this idea you had?'

'I'm not sure yet… quite possibly nothing, but I will have a read, thank you.' She picked up another sheet of paper, changing the subject. There were several ideas in her head now, all jostling for attention, but Isobel wanted some time alone with them before she shared what was on her mind. 'Is this the recipe for that chilled soup we had the other day, only I quite liked that.'

It was nearly an hour later by the time Isobel got back to the cottage. Trixie's enthusiasm, not only for food, but seemingly for most things in her life, was infectious, and Isobel could have listened to her for hours. How had she never done this? How had she never mixed with people who could have this effect on her? People who saw life as a thing to be explored and enjoyed, who had dreams and aspirations, but who also managed to achieve these in a balanced way and not with the all-consuming commitment which had enslaved Isobel for her whole life.

Her computer was still on, and a part of her knew that she should sit down and try to work, but the couple of hours she had already spent that morning trying to do exactly that had already proved it was likely to be a waste of time. Her current mood was utterly bizarre, not at all what she was used to feeling, but something was telling her that now was the perfect time to just go with it. She wandered back into the kitchen and plated up the mushroom tart and some of the salad that Trixie had left. Then, carrying it to the sofa, she picked up the book about Joy's Acre, and began to read, her eyes widening more with every page.

★

It took Isobel a lot less time than she had expected to reach the area of woodland Tom had described. From the gate behind her cottage it had seemed so far in the distance, and yet it took only a matter of minutes before she was there. Perhaps it was the day itself that was skewing her sense of time; it was the first in a very long while that she had not kept to a rigid timetable and had simply gone with the flow of life on the farm. Perhaps even more telling was that, instead of picking up her work again this afternoon as she had originally intended, she had simply stretched out on the settee and carried on reading.

Trixie had been right; the story of Joy's Acre was both heart-breaking and heart-warming and, to her surprise, Isobel felt a huge affinity with the artist. Both of them understood the passion behind their art, the driving force to create which took precedence over all else, but which at times seemed to be an affliction rather than a blessed talent. And although Joy had lived during Victorian times, the constraints of society which would have been placed upon Joy during that era felt little different from the confines of Isobel's own life.

The only difference between them was that Joy had been lucky enough to know the warmth of a loving relationship in her life. Joy had been bipolar, but instead of trying to subdue her, her husband had simply brought her to a place where he could love and care for her, at the same time allowing her the creative freedom she so desperately craved. Isobel could understand why Seth and Maddie had both fallen in love with this place. Apart from the stunning position and scenery, there was something indefinable here, and even after such a short space of time, Isobel could feel it at work. She had come to Joy's Acre to escape her surroundings, thinking that this was all she needed to be able to work, but the longer she was here the more she realised that all this had provided was a change of scenery. It was not Isobel's surroundings that had been imprisoning her, but her work itself. It was at once a both liberating and utterly terrifying thought, because without her work, who was she? She would be set adrift, and while that meant she would be free from all the things which had caused her pain in the past, she would also be loosening the ties on the only thing which had ever given her pleasure.

If she were to ever move forward she would have to find a new way to achieve some balance in her life, and from where she was now it seemed an impossible task... or did it? Standing here, in the middle of the field, where all she could feel was the warmth of the sun on her skin, and all she could hear was the gentle rustle of the breeze and the busy hum of insects, it seemed as if almost anything were possible.

They were just into the third week of her stay now, which only gave her a little under a month to finish her piece, or more importantly, as she now realised, to start a new one. The piece of music she had been labouring over simply did not work. Technically, it was very difficult, and like a lot of pieces she had played in the past it would showcase her talent, but there were any number of extremely talented violinists out there. In the past, the only thing that had made her special, setting her aside from the competition, had been her age, and that was no longer a factor. The only thing working in her favour right now was her spectacular fall from grace.

It was much cooler under the shade of the trees and Isobel was grateful for the respite from the heat. The woodland around her was coloured with every shade of green, with just a hint of blue visible through the tops of the trees, and she sat for a moment on a fallen tree trunk recognising the heat of her own thoughts. She took a deep breath and cleared her mind.

The cloistered atmosphere at home did not allow her any room to think and, perhaps subconsciously, she had known that her decision to leave and come to stay at Joy's Acre would allow her to do just that. And now that she had finished reading Joy's story and given herself some space to let it marinate, the seed of an idea planted by Trixie had continued to grow and her thoughts began to tumble faster and faster. There would be much work to be done – it would mean practically starting again from scratch – but simply knowing there was a direction to head in felt like a massive achievement in itself.

She didn't want to think about the other things she would have to attend to as a result of her decision – those were far more difficult than either writing, or playing music – but unless she got this first aspect right there would be nothing to think about in any case. She would have to worry about them later, but for now her new idea must take priority.

Lost in her thoughts, she hadn't realised she was even thinking about Tom until the rumble of her stomach broke the spell. She had been daydreaming; picturing herself playing to him, him listening intently and joining in, adding new rhythms and complementing melodies…

The sudden realisation jolted her and she stood abruptly, thrusting the thoughts away and checking her watch. Her stomach had been absolutely right, it was dinnertime. Even this thought made her smile to herself. She had cut her lunch into tiny pieces before eating it, expecting to have only one or two mouthfuls. Instead, to her surprise, she had devoured the whole savoury tart, shoving forkfuls into her mouth in quick succession. It had been a very long time since she had actually enjoyed her food, and more than that, since she had looked forward to eating a meal. She made her way purposefully back to the cottage.

Chapter 15

Tom was about to head out the door when his phone rang. He swore gently under his breath. He'd wanted to be on the road half an hour ago, but it was turning out to be one of those mornings.

He was just locking his front door, phone jammed between his ear and his shoulder, when one word caught his attention.

'I'm sorry, could you repeat that?' he said.

'Yes. I said I'm looking for a violinist.' The woman's voice sounded extremely anxious.

Tom's heart began to beat a little faster. 'Any particular one?' he asked, only half joking.

There was a long pause. 'Why, how many do you have?' And then a sigh. 'Look, it really doesn't matter, as long as they're competent, and can get here in about an hour and a half.'

Tom took his phone away from his ear and stared at the caller display, but the number meant nothing to him. He frowned. 'I'm sorry, I think I must have missed what you said to start with. Who am I talking to?'

'My name is Sally. Sally Edwards. I've been given your number by Harrington Hall – I gather you're playing for a wedding there in a couple of weeks and they said you might be able to help me.'

Tom let out the breath he was holding as Sally continued. 'I'm one-quarter of Four Play… We're a string quartet who are due to play for Julian and Catherine this afternoon, except our other violinist's husband has just been involved in an accident and she's had to leave suddenly. Perfectly understandable of course, but it's left us utterly adrift. Unless we can find a stand-in there's no way we can play, and I'd hate to let anyone down. You guys are a folk band, aren't you? The wedding coordinator at the hall thought you might be able to help…'

'Well, we are a folk band, but no violinists, I'm afraid…' He began to smile in relief but felt it die on his lips almost immediately as an obvious thought popped into his head. He pushed it one side. 'Or, rather, no competent violinists. I play, but not at the standard you'd require for a string quartet, and I haven't played classical for years.'

'Oh bugger. I thought it was probably too good to be true.'

Tom thought quickly. 'Listen, I can't help you personally, but I do know a few people, you know, friends of friends. How about I make a few calls, and if anyone can help I'll get them to give you a ring straight away.'

That was the best way to go about it, he thought. He hadn't made any promises, hadn't even mentioned Isobel's name, and so if she really couldn't bear to do it there would be no harm done. He would simply ask the question – she would either say yes, or no. He'd better get a move on.

'Thank you, I really appreciate it, you may just save our lives yet.'

Two minutes later Tom was on the road to Joy's Acre.

★

'Tom!' exclaimed Isobel on opening the door to him. 'Is everything okay?'

He looked anxious, but then she hadn't seen him properly for a few days, not since… She dropped her head, not quite able to look him in the eye.

'Everything's fine, but…' He paused for a moment. 'Look, I have a proposition for you,' he said. 'And I can either beat about the bush, or just hit you with it right between the eyes.'

'Okay…' she said slowly, her heart beginning to beat just a tiny bit faster.

'I've just had a phone call from a rather distressed lady who is currently minus a string for her string quartet. Their violinist has just done a bunk and they're due to play at the same wedding venue we're gigging at soon. She was given my name by the wedding coordinator there, who thought I might be able to help.'

'But I didn't think you played classical violin?'

'I don't…'

She took a step backwards, her hand fluttering up to her throat. 'Oh, God, Tom, you didn't!'

He looked instantly stricken. 'No, of course not!' He stepped closer. 'Isobel, I would never…' His voice dropped a little. 'I would never do that to you.' His blue eyes were dark in the hallway, intent on hers.

It was all she could do to hold his look. 'No, I know you wouldn't,' she said eventually, her voice soft. 'But you must have said something. What did you tell her?'

'That you were a world-class violinist and they'd be extraordinarily… No, I just said that I would ask a couple of mates if they knew of anyone. I didn't make any promises, I swear.'

They looked at one another for a few moments. Isobel didn't know what to say. A part of her so desperately wanted to reach out to him, to say something more, but she couldn't. She had enough to think about right now without even more emotions complicating things. It was just that the way he was looking at her…

Tom swallowed. 'So, what do we do now?'

'We?' she replied.

He nodded. 'I wouldn't let you do this by yourself. Whatever you decide is absolutely fine. Say no, if you don't think you can face it, but if you want to give it a go…' He tentatively reached out a hand.

Isobel stared at it as if she had never seen it before, but then lifted her eyes to his. 'I don't think I can play the violin if you're holding my hand,' she said.

Her heart was beating like the clappers, her mouth dry, tongue stuck to the roof of her mouth. She couldn't possibly do this. It was too much, too soon…

Tom cleared his throat. 'I can give you Sally's number if you want to have a chat with her,' he said. 'That's the woman who called me. I guess she'd be able to answer any questions you have. And if it helps at all I'm pretty sure you'll be playing as the guests arrive and during the wedding breakfast. I hate to use the term "background noise", but you know what these things are like; folks are more interested in the food and drink.' He groaned out loud. 'What I meant was that there won't be a huge spotlight shining on you, it won't be anything like the concerts you've been used to.'

She smiled. Despite the rather large hole Tom had just dug for himself, she did understand what he meant and, in all honesty, it was probably true. Whether that made it any better, she didn't know. The seconds were clicking by.

She would have to play again in public some time. She had no choice. It was as inevitable as the passage of time itself. But what would she do if she got there and she couldn't play? Or was actually sick? Right now, that felt like a very real possibility. She looked up at Tom, silently pleading with him to make up her mind for her; she really didn't think she could do it by herself.

His hand stretched forward again, as if he would take her fingers in his. 'Isobel.'

There was a huge weight behind that single word. A whole conversation in fact, but as Isobel read the unsaid words of understanding in his eyes she knew that she would never get a better chance to take this leap. She drew in a slow shaky breath.

'Would you honestly come with me?'

He nodded but remained silent, giving her the time she needed to make up her mind.

She screwed up her face. 'I think I'm going to do this,' she whispered. But then she stood up tall. 'No, I'm *bloody* well going to do it,' she said.

★

Tom had never given much thought to the vehicles he drove before. They merely transported him from A to B, and were always chosen for practicality. He had occasionally thought that should he ever find himself with slightly more money on his hands than he needed to survive, that he might buy something from his wish list instead of making do with whatever was both functional and affordable.

It was with a huge amount of reluctance, therefore, that he opened the door for Isobel to climb into the front of the van. She really deserved something better. It was bad enough that she was quite obviously terrified of what was to come, without having to travel in his dustbin on wheels. He didn't blame her for hanging onto her violin for grim death.

He glanced over at her now, but her expression hadn't altered. He had wondered how best to behave on the journey to the wedding venue. Should he be talkative and animated, hoping that this would distract her from her inner thoughts, or should he be quiet? Respectful of the fact that she might like some time to mentally prepare herself? In the end, Isobel took matters into her own hands.

As soon as she had settled herself in the cab, and fumbled to secure the seatbelt, she reached for the radio's tuning button, pausing for a few seconds each time it found a station, listening to what was on offer, and then moving on. After a few moments, she found a station playing folk music, and turned the volume up to such a level that conversation would have been impossible. Her hands were clasped loosely in her lap, one thumb tapping against the back of the other.

It was a relief even for Tom when the van drew up outside the rear entrance of Harrington Hall and he could kill the engine. He gave a low whistle. Even the back door of the place was a monument to wealth and fine living. He clambered from the driver's side to let Isobel out. They had not spoken one word since leaving Joy's Acre.

She slithered from the passenger seat, holding her violin aloft as if trying to keep it above water, and then stood, unmoving, on the gravel driveway, save for a slight tremor which buzzed through her like an electric current. Her pale skin had taken on an even more ghostly tone, but she was, still, stunning.

'Will I do?' she asked, looking down at the simple, pale blue dress she had changed into before leaving.

He pushed aside the things he hoped he might say to her later, when all this was over.

'You look beautiful,' he said. 'Poised, elegant, confident and assured.' He reached past her and slammed the van door shut, and then, offering his arm for her to take, added, 'Let's go kick some ass!'

★

It was the perfect thing to say, thought Isobel. Tom was determined not to buy into her anxiety and that was just what she needed right now. The reassurance of someone with her, but without them trying to analyse how she was feeling every second, or worse, actually asking her. The warmth of Tom's arm in hers felt nice as they strode across the courtyard. She would try, that was all she could do, and even just being here was a step further than she thought she would ever be able to take again.

Sally had explained their set-up to her on the phone; literally all Isobel needed to bring was herself and her violin. She had quickly run through the repertoire of music they would be playing today, and not surprisingly all of the pieces were familiar to Isobel. In any case, Sally had sounded so grateful and relieved on the phone, she doubted whether she would be held to account for her lack of practice. It was now just before noon, and in an hour's time they would be playing, not only during the reception, as Tom had suggested, but while the wedding ceremony itself was being conducted. She kept telling herself that people would be paying little attention to the music, but she couldn't quite make herself believe it.

Isobel found herself enveloped in a fierce hug as soon as she walked through the door. She only just had time to whisk her violin to one side before it too was crushed.

'Goodness, I hope you're Isobel? I know there can't be too many people around here carrying violins, but all the same, I don't make a habit of hugging complete strangers.' Sally gave a horsey laugh, turning towards Tom. 'Although, in your case I might make an exception.'

Isobel had to smile at the expression on Tom's face. Sally was nearly a foot taller than he was, or maybe it was just that he seemed to have shrunk in her presence. She touched his arm lightly.

'It's okay, Tom, you can get going if you like. I know you've got work you need to be getting on with, and Sally will look after me, I'm sure.'

Sally was nodding vigorously.

Isobel smiled again. 'Go on,' she said. 'Honestly, I'll be fine.' She was trying to make this as easy as possible for him. He had got her this far and now it was up to her. Besides which, if she did lose it completely, she'd really rather it wasn't in front of Tom… again.

'No, I said I'll stay and I meant it,' he said as Sally started backing away, taking Isobel along with her. 'But I'll go and loiter somewhere out of the way for now. I'll catch you later?'

She nodded encouragingly, keeping a smile on her face as he turned and walked back through the door. She felt a tug on her arm.

'I can't tell you how grateful we are,' said Sally. 'And so lucky to have found you. Mary is devastated to be missing it, but at least her husband is okay. They're just waiting for his arm to be plastered now. Come on, we're down this way.'

Isobel trailed after her, along a sumptuous corridor with thick royal blue carpets, and pale lemon walls accented with gilt plasterwork along the dado rail.

'Have you ever been here before?' asked Sally.

'Erm, no.' Isobel was still looking around her. 'I don't really ever come to… places like this.'

'No? Where do you play then?'

Isobel thought of all the things she could say, but they would only invite further comment. 'It's a long story,' she said instead. 'How about you?'

Sally turned and pulled a face. 'No, first time. Always wanted to do a gig here though, it's a fabulous venue.'

They passed through a huge entrance foyer of jaw-dropping grandeur, with one of the largest chandeliers Isobel had ever seen, and carried on through into a room just off to one side. She stopped dead. It was a large space, more duck egg than royal blue this time, but with the same pale walls and heavily gilded panels. At its entrance two enormous urns of flowers stood guard, one either side, spilling over with an array of the deepest pink, purple and white blooms, seemingly of every variety. But it was not these that caught Isobel's attention. Neither was it the swathes of palest blue silk which hung from the ceiling, tied at each corner of the room with a matching bow. Instead, what rooted her feet to the spot were the rows and rows and rows of chairs. There must be well over one hundred, two hundred even. A sudden heat bloomed at the base of her spine.

Once her eyes freed themselves from the seating arrangements she realised that one corner of the room held a raised dais, on which sat four identical chairs, each tied with an elaborate cream bow. Two of the seats were already taken, and the occupants rose to their feet at the sound of Sally's voice.

Isobel couldn't run, and there was nowhere to hide so she extended her hand – the one that wasn't throttling her violin – to Miriam and Annalise.

Yes, it's lovely to meet you too.

No, that's quite all right, I'm happy to help.

Thank you, I bought it from a shop someone recommended.

No, but it's a beautiful setting, isn't it?

She sat down, smiling, willing herself to concentrate. She had to find the place in her head she always went to when she played. If she didn't, she would never be able to make it through…

Someone was talking to her again.

'Now, I think you're familiar with all of these pieces, Isobel, is that right?'

'Yes, but I haven't played some of them in a while.'

This was a really bad idea.

'You'll be wonderful, I know you will… Are there any that you'll have real problems with?'

She shouldn't have come.

'I don't think so. I don't personally like "Ode to Joy", but I guess it's what everyone wants at weddings.'

She would let everyone down.

'Sad, but true. I've played it so many times I have to try and stop myself from yawning halfway through.'

Isobel looked up at the smiling face in front of her. 'Have we even got time to practise?'

Sally looked at her watch and grimaced. 'None, I'm afraid, but don't worry. No one will be listening to us anyway. They'll all be checking out each other's outfits, air kissing, and gushing at one another.' She nodded. 'Honestly, that's what it's like. So we just play. These first three pieces should be enough to get everyone in the room and settled, but if not, we've got the Battishill in reserve.'

She checked to see that Isobel was following what she was saying. 'Keep an eye on the lectern over there,' she added. 'You'll see the registrar come in at some point and go and stand beside it. That's our cue. We finish the piece we're playing, so watch me for the nod on that one, and then we'll be straight into the "Wedding March". The usher on the door will give us a few moments between the two pieces, and will signal when the bride is due to come in. As soon as we get that signal we hit it.'

'Okay, I think I've got that.'

'You're sitting next to me anyway so I can always whisper to you. We obviously don't play during the ceremony, but then once the bride and groom are about to leave, we play them out to the "Allegro Maestoso".' She gave a beaming smile. 'And that's it…! Or at least until we kick off for round two in the main function room for the meal and whatnot. But there we really are just background music. It's very relaxed, honestly.'

The others certainly looked relaxed. The cellist, whose name Isobel had already forgotten, was slurping Coke from a bottle, the other violinist was shrugging her arms out of her hoody, balling it up and stowing it in the bag behind the dais where it couldn't be seen. Sally was already tapping away on her phone, on Twitter probably. *#notlongtogonow*

There was a rushing noise in Isobel's head that wouldn't go away, her palms were slick, and her breath seemed to stick in her throat. She closed her eyes and then wrenched them open again. No, not the dark, that was where it all started. Instead, she looked down at her dress, trying to remember what she had felt when she put it on this morning – standing in her bedroom at Joy's Acre, looking out over the fields, seeing the play of sunlight and shadow, and the look in Tom's eyes when she opened the door to him. Then she felt it.

It was always the same. Like a bubble – there was no other way for Isobel to describe the sensation. It started from somewhere deep in her centre, growing larger, more buoyant, until it seemed to be filling her up from the inside, pressing against her so that her edges became thinner and thinner, as if she were the bubble herself, stretched taut around its outside. And then suddenly her perspective changed and she was inside the bubble. She felt lighter than air, floating gently in the swirling currents around her, shielded from everything that was outside. Here, all was calm and safe, and nothing could touch her.

Her eyes flew open. No! This was wrong. This was not what she needed at all. It was what she had done as a child, what she had been taught to do; to push everything away from her, all the feeling, all the emotion, everything that existed on the outside which she knew could hurt her. And that had been her problem. Now, she needed to live again, to let everything back in. If she didn't, none of it was real, and nothing mattered. And the Isobel who was beginning to find the things that mattered didn't want to ever let them go again.

She could hear the rustle of noise from outside becoming louder as people waited to enter the room, their voices becoming more distinct. Beside her the others began to straighten, and she wriggled in her chair waiting for Sally's cue. She adjusted her music on the stand in front of her, and slowly looked around the room, breathing in the detail, the colour, the scent from the flower garlands. They were about to start. She sensed rather than saw Sally's signal beside her.

'One, two, three, four…'

Lifting her violin to her chin, fingers poised on her bow, she flicked her hair back over her shoulder, and… nothing. She couldn't do it.

Despite everything she had told herself, everything she had been feeling, it hadn't made the slightest bit of difference. Her bow was millimetres from the strings and she knew if she so much as touched them a raucous noise would ring out into the room; her hand was shaking so much. She felt panic rise in her throat, her heart thudding in her chest, as she looked around the room for a way out.

Beside her the others continued to play, but she could see their faces from the corner of her eye, confused and anxious, trying to gain her attention. She shook her head. How could she have been so stupid? She shouldn't have come; it was ridiculous to think that things would change just because she wanted them to. She could feel a swell of emotion rising up, prickling her eyes, the threat of choking sobs becoming more of a possibility with every second. Her eyes swept the room again, searching for somewhere to run to…

And that's when she saw him.

Standing just inside the doorway was Tom. Feet planted, both hands in his pockets, completely relaxed and smiling straight at her. As their eyes locked, he gave the tiniest nod of his head in acknowledgement, and she felt his warmth, like an invisible pair of arms holding her, grounding her so that she could no longer float away, and reconnecting her with everything that she loved, everything that was real. He smiled again, the message in his look clear as somehow her heart began to find its rhythm again. She closed her eyes briefly and when she opened them Tom was still there, unchanged, calm and reassuring. She took a deep breath and let it out, and then another, until she could almost feel their breathing become one. He gave another nod, counting her in…

'One, two, three, four…'

She dipped her head, her eyes still on Tom, and this time, with only the gentlest intake of breath, she let the music pour out of her.

Chapter 16

There was no applause. In fact, there was scarcely any recognition that they had finished playing at all. But Isobel couldn't care less. It was exactly as it should be; the newly married couple had walked back down the aisle amid a sea of smiling faces, accompanied by Handel's 'Allegro Maestoso', and, as the last of the guests had filed out behind them, the four musicians simply laid down their instruments and grinned at one another.

Of Tom, there was no sign. He had slipped out with the other guests, leaving Isobel to quite literally, and quite rightly, face the music, so that she could do so on her own terms. And she did. She pulled it to her, claiming it as her own. It danced inside of her like a small child, exuberant and unashamed, and Isobel let the feeling fill her up, finally chasing away the darkness.

After a few moments three excited faces turned to her.

'Oh my God, that was amazing!'

It was Sally who spoke first, standing up and placing her viola down on her chair before throwing her arms around Isobel.

'I can't thank you enough. You have *so* saved our bacon, and to play like that… bloody hell, I'd hate to hear what you sound like if you *do* practise.' She laughed. 'Or rather I'd *love* to hear what you sound like. Where on earth do you usually play?'

'In the living room at home. I haven't played professionally in years.' She paused, realising as she said the words that the image filling her head was not her living room at home, but her small rented cottage back at Joy's Acre. Any doubts she still had about the decision she had taken only that morning simply melted away.

The second violinist came forward. 'Thank you,' she said simply. 'I don't really know who you are, or where you came from, but I'm so very glad that something saw fit to send you to us today. I don't believe in God, but if I did, I'd say it was a bloody miracle.'

Isobel laughed. 'I think I may well agree with you,' she said. 'I haven't enjoyed myself so much in a very long time.' And then she giggled slightly, the absolute joy she felt inside overflowing. 'I'm probably going to get very emotional now, and incredibly mushy, but I can't thank you enough for letting me play with you. It's been an absolute honour, you are all amazing.' And as if to demonstrate her point she wiped a finger underneath one eye. 'See? I'm a complete wreck now.'

'So am I,' replied Sally, grinning. 'And very, very relieved. Now can we *please* go and find a cup of tea, before I pass out… What a day!'

The four of them gathered up their things, and made their own way up the aisle, chattering as they went. Isobel paused slightly as she reached the door, and turned, taking in the detail of the room for one last time. She had a feeling it would stay with her for many years to come.

It was strange the way that, in the crush of people all standing in the foyer talking excitedly, Isobel could find Tom in a matter of seconds. He was leaning against a wall on the far side, legs casually crossed at the ankles, a drink of something in his hand. As she took a step forward, he did the same, rapidly plonking his glass down on a table, his eyes searching for hers.

She began to weave in and out of the crowd of guests, avoiding excited arm gestures, hands holding glasses of champagne, interrupting conversations, carefully avoiding toes, and murmuring *Excuse me*, and *Thanks*, as she went. When finally she and Tom stood opposite one another, there was just a moment of hesitation before her happiness came gushing out of her and she threw her arms around him in the tightest hug her violin would allow.

'Oh my God, I did it!' she exclaimed, releasing him. She knew her face was shining with excitement. 'I didn't think I was going to be able to at first, but then…' She stopped abruptly, feeling suddenly close to tears. 'I saw you and…'

'And you were brilliant, just brilliant.' He caught hold of her hand. 'Come on, let's find you a drink.'

★

Tom steered Isobel through the foyer and into the main reception room where the wedding breakfast would be taking place. The finishing touches were just being attended to by the hotel staff, but almost immediately the bride and groom would be taking up position ready to welcome their guests in the traditional receiving line, and once everyone was seated, Isobel and the others would be back playing again. There wasn't a huge amount of time. He spotted Sally at the bar straight away, the others having already bagged a table, and he guided Isobel towards them.

Sally turned just as he reached them, a laden tray in her hands. Tom rushed forwards to take it from her.

'Ladies,' he said, 'grab a seat.' He waited until Isobel had sat down, before placing the tray down on the table and pulling out a chair for Sally.

She giggled. 'Goodness, what a gentleman.'

Tom merely smiled. 'I've played at few weddings now, and I know what a bit of a bun fight it can be to get your hands on a drink.' He took the only available empty chair. 'Shall I be mother? Or would you all like me to bugger off, so that you can have a natter?'

Sally leaned forward. 'No, I want you to tell me where you found Isobel, that girl can *play*.'

Tom risked a sideways glance, but Isobel seemed perfectly composed. In fact, she was grinning from ear to ear. He had deliberately whisked her away, not wanting to give her the opportunity to dwell too long on her feelings. She was riding high on a wave of adrenaline right now and he didn't want her to confuse her feelings about today with anything other than her music, whatever he felt about the matter. The important thing was that she concentrate on her playing, and how that made her feel. Even if he hadn't known her history, he would have been able to see how much it meant to her.

He smiled at Sally, beginning to pour out the tea. 'Well, actually Isobel found me really, or rather found us, isn't that right?'

'It seems an extraordinary coincidence, but yes, that's pretty much it,' added Isobel. 'I don't live too far away from here, but I'm trying to finish a composition I've been working on so I rented a holiday cottage for the summer. I thought the peace and quiet might be conducive, but it seems to be a place full of creative endeavour and now I'm getting rather caught up in it.'

Tom pushed a cup of tea across the table. 'It's a place called Joy's Acre,' he added. 'I'm working there at the moment while renovations are taking place. Thatcher by day, folk musician on evenings and weekends. Brilliant timing though, wouldn't you say?'

'The best,' said Sally, with a look to the other two members of the quartet. 'And not just because of today… I don't think I'm speaking out of turn here, but to be honest, Isobel, you coming today couldn't have come at a better time. Our other violinist, Mary, has been struggling to make our bookings over the last six months or so. She has three children and her mother-in-law is very poorly too. Today was a one-off, but I think Mary might actually be quite relieved if we could find someone to take her place on a more permanent basis.' She looked between Tom and Isobel, breaking into a grin at Isobel's stunned expression.

'Would you at least think about it?' she said. 'If you don't live a million miles away, it could be perfect. We travel all over the county, further afield sometimes depending on the booking.'

Tom saw Isobel open her mouth to protest, but then she closed it again. She gave a cautious smile. 'It's difficult at the moment,' she said. 'I'm not sure what I'm going to be doing come the end of the summer. It all rather depends… on how certain other things go, but I will think about it, I promise.'

Sally gave her watch a quick check. 'We might have to take these with us, ladies, we're on again in ten.'

Isobel gave Tom an anxious glance. 'I should have brought my car,' she said, 'then you wouldn't have to hang around. We might be another couple of hours yet, Tom.'

He smiled. 'I don't mind,' he replied, and he really didn't. 'I said I'd stay and stay I will. In any case I might pop and have a word with the wedding planner while I'm here. I needed to do a recce on this place anyway to make sure everything is straight for when we're playing here. No time like the present, as they say.' He leaned back in his chair, sipping his tea slowly. 'So, go on, go have fun.'

★

Tom stood waiting for Isobel. The wedding breakfast was almost over and she had finished playing half an hour ago. Doubtless she would be saying a very fond farewell to the other women in the quartet; perhaps there would even be the first inklings of new friendships among them. He hoped so.

He could see her coming towards him now, her movements slow at first, hampered by the tables and chairs that she had to pick her way through, negotiating waitresses clearing tables, and random small children now let loose from their parents. Then, as she cleared the edge of the tightly packed space, she hurtled across the dance area towards him, her thick plait flying out behind her. Her face shone with the joy of her second performance, but it wasn't only the way she looked that made his heart squeeze just a little more. He could tell the way she was feeling came from somewhere deep inside, as if something had been breached from which there would be no going back.

He wasn't sure he could stand another hug without getting carried away, so was mightily relieved to see that Isobel wasn't going to cross to his side of the table. He was half on his feet, but now sank back down into his chair again, meeting her massive grin with one of his own.

She practically threw herself into the chair, laughing as she did so.

'That was so much fun!' she said, laying her violin on the table. 'But crikey, I'm exhausted. I feel like I've run a marathon.'

'Metaphorically speaking, I think you probably have,' he replied.

She looked up then, acknowledging the truth in his statement. 'And I wasn't even sure if I could still run.'

'It's going to take you a while to stop…' He paused for a moment. 'Or perhaps you might just keep on going…' He took in her expression, still elated, but obviously tired. 'You've certainly been running on nervous energy, that's for sure. Have you had anything to eat since that cup of tea earlier? Or drink?'

Isobel tucked her plait back over her shoulder, and nodded. 'Someone brought us a plate of sandwiches and some pastry things,' she said. 'I think the poor waiter thought Sally was going to eat him alive the way she fell on them, but they were very welcome.'

'Yes, but did you eat any of them?' asked Tom, knowing how little she usually seemed to indulge.

She gave a wry smile. 'One or two… I couldn't manage any more.' She looked around her, brightening again. 'I tell you what I do really fancy right now though.'

Tom raised his eyebrows.

'A bag of crisps, just salted ones.' She licked her lips. 'Those would go down a real treat.'

He got to his feet. 'Coming right up, I'm sure the bar will have some. Would you like a drink to go with them? The sun's over the yard arm?'

But she shook her head vehemently. 'No thanks.'

A few moments later Tom deposited two bags of ready-salted crisps onto the table.

'You're glad you came then?' he asked with a grin.

'Oh, Tom…' she began, her words borne on a sigh. 'You have no idea.' Her eyes searched his. 'I can't thank you enough. This was something I so desperately needed to do, and I never would have—'

Tom held up his hand. 'Ay, none of that. I might have provided the opportunity, Isobel, but make no mistake, what you did today was down to you, and no one else. You screwed your courage to the wall on this one, not me.'

She looked a little disappointed. 'Yes, but just having you with me…' She stopped. 'Well, it certainly made it easier.'

He gave a slight bow. 'Then I'm very pleased and proud to have done so.' Having to keep his distance was killing him.

'Anyway, how have you left things with the girls? You could do a lot worse than take up their offer, even if it's just in the short while.'

She nodded, stuffing crisps into her mouth. 'Mmm.'

He waited until she had finished chewing.

'I said I'd get in touch as soon as I could. But it's difficult, I…' She took another crisp from the packet. 'I don't know what I'm going to be doing. It's not that easy, there are other things…' She trailed off, avoiding his eyes.

He paused for a moment, wondering how much he would be able to get away with asking her. 'So, what are your plans then? Obviously you came to Joy's Acre for the summer to finish the composition you're working on, but what next? There must be an end goal for you?'

'I'm not sure I can answer that.'

'Well I know your music hasn't quite gone the way you wanted it to, but you had a deadline – the least you can do is tell me a little bit about this project you're working on, and what happens when you finish it.'

'No, you misunderstand.' She smiled. 'I'm not being disingenuous, I only meant that I can't answer your question because now I'm actually not sure what happens at the end of my stay. Things *really* haven't gone according to plan.'

'Yes, but what did you originally intend to do?'

She leaned forward, sending her plait over her shoulder. 'Actually,' she whispered, 'I'm not supposed to tell you that either. It's top secret.'

'Yeah, right.' He snorted at her joke, but immediately he did so, he realised that what she was actually doing was laying down a smoke-screen, trying to put him off from asking questions, but like the best secrets, they were more easily camouflaged in plain sight. She wasn't joking at all, and Tom knew exactly what her secret was.

He thought back to the night when he had trawled the Internet looking for information on a young musical prodigy, one he had seen perform as a child and who had mesmerised him with her playing. The woman sitting in front of him now had changed her name and time had ensured she looked nothing like the child he remembered, but the only thing she couldn't change was the quirky way she had of shaking her long thick plait back over her shoulder. It was like her signature.

'You're staging a comeback?' His voice was so quiet he could hardly hear it himself. But Isobel did.

She slowly lowered the crisp she had in her hand, until both hands lay in her lap, lifeless. The colour had all but drained from her face.

'How did you know about that? You're not supposed...'

To his horror, he saw her eyes widen with fear. She stumbled to her feet, the forgotten crisp packet falling to the floor as she caught her chair which rocked backwards violently.

'Isobel, wait!' he shouted, snatching up her violin, but she was already several paces away from him.

She whirled around as he caught up with her, trying to take her arm. She was visibly trembling.

'Tom, take me home... now!'

'Isobel, please.'

'I said... Take. Me. Home.' She spat every syllable at him, before striding off across the room.

Chapter 17

The drive home was one of the most uncomfortable Tom had ever experienced. Isobel refused, point-blank, to even speak to him, but instead sat rigid as a post staring out the windscreen at the road ahead. After a while, he gave up trying to explain and fell silent too, kicking himself for his stupidity.

The minute the car drew up at Joy's Acre, she flung open the door and took off across the yard at a speed he had no chance of keeping up with. By the time he'd managed to clamber from the car and grab her violin she had already disappeared around the side of the house. Tom was pretty sure she would head straight back to the cottage, and that had a very solid front door. If she reached it first there would be no way she would let him in, and his only other course of action would be to stand and shout at her from outside, which was the last thing he wanted to do.

He practically sprinted around the corner of the house, and skidded to a halt in the garden as, mercifully for him, he saw that Isobel had been held up by Maddie, who perhaps had been enjoying a little break in the late afternoon peace and quiet. Although he couldn't hear what was being said, it was obvious from Isobel's mannerisms that she didn't want to talk to Maddie, but never overtly rude, she stopped, and the few moments of conversation they shared were enough to allow him to catch up.

He slowed his pace, waiting until he could see that Isobel was about to move off, and tried to remove the anxious expression he knew was on his face.

'Beautiful afternoon, isn't it?' he remarked, flashing a smile at Maddie as he passed.

He was now only a step or two behind Isobel and reached her just as she pushed open her door. She spun around, struggling to get the door between them, but Tom shot his foot out, wedging it in the gap.

'Don't,' she hissed, holding up a hand to his face. 'Just don't. Whatever you've got to say I don't want to hear it… and get your foot out my door.' Her voice was dangerously low.

'Isobel please, this is ridiculous.' He made a slight backwards motion with his head. 'And for God's sake let me in or you're going to have Maddie on your doorstep as well wanting to know what the hell is going on.' He pushed her violin case in the gap between them, quite prepared to use it as a battering ram if he had to.

She stared at her instrument, and a part of him could see she would love to have snatched it, but instead she held his gaze, dark eyes glittering, and then she shoved the case at him hard and stalked off down the hall.

He closed the door gently behind him and followed her down the hallway. 'At least let me explain.'

'Why should I?' She glared at him. 'I don't want you anywhere near me. You're just like the rest of them.'

That hurt. *The rest of whom?* Whatever Tom was, he really doubted that this was the case. Had today not been proof enough of that? His own anger began to rise.

'Do you want to think about that for a moment? About the last few days in fact, and in particular what happened earlier. You were amazing,

Isobel, you broke through some barrier that has been holding you back for goodness knows how long… and no, you didn't need to tell me that, I worked it out for myself. I thought we were beginning to understand one another. I've shared stuff with you that meant something to me, more than you will probably ever know, and in doing so I've begun to feel better than I have in an awfully long time. So forgive me if I took up the "top secret" invitation that you so very obviously dangled in my face, but I was only trying to help.'

She balked at his words, her mouth opening and closing as she fought to find the right response. 'So how do you know who I am then?' She narrowed her eyes at him. 'Oh, I get it,' she sneered. 'Jesus, I really am stupid… Did my mother send you? Is that what this is all about? You were supposed to get friendly with me, and then once you'd got me to trust you by telling me your little sob story and making me think that we had things in common, you were going to get me to tell you everything I was planning. How did you even find me?' She took another step backwards. 'Dear God, have you been following me?'

Tom stared at her. This was rapidly turning into the script from a rather poor soap opera. *What on earth was Isobel talking about?* He almost laughed until he realised that she was still slowly, almost imperceptibly, backing away from him. She wasn't angry any more, she was scared.

He held up both arms, an age-old gesture to show that he was unarmed and meant no harm, and took a tentative step forward.

'Isobel,' he began, his voice as soft as he could make it. 'I haven't been following you. I haven't been trying to set you up, and to my knowledge I've never even met your mother. I'm a thatcher. I get up early and go to work, I work through into the early evening at which point I go home, have a shower, and if I can stay awake for long enough, read a book for an hour or so. Then I go to bed, get up the next morning and do it all over again. And that's all.' His anger evaporated in an instant as Isobel took in his words, her face beginning to crumple.

'You still didn't answer my question,' she murmured. 'How do you know who I am?'

'Isobel?' He waited until he was sure he had her full attention. 'When I was eight years old my father took me to see you in concert and, over the course of the next four years, I think we attended every appearance you ever made. I pretended to be unaffected by your playing, but in fact your brilliance was the only thing we agreed on. Ever.'

Her hand rose to her mouth as she stood in shocked silence.

'When I first met you, I thought there was something familiar about you, but I only realised who you were the other day when you flicked your hair back over your shoulder just before you started to play for me. Maybe you don't even know you do it, but it's a habit you've had since you were a child, and when I saw that, you may as well have had a neon sign hanging over your head. Of course, it took me a while to work out who you were. As a child the fact that you stopped performing so abruptly meant nothing to me.'

'But it does now?'

There was no point in lying. He would, if he thought he could save Isobel from further hurt, but he knew she would see through him in an instant. 'Yes, I admit I did go looking for information.'

'So now you know everything?'

He nodded gently and the two of them stood in the dim hallway looking at one another. Even the lack of light couldn't prevent him from seeing a slow tear make its way down her cheek. She dashed it away angrily.

'You see? Even after all this time, you see how it makes me feel? Sometimes I think I'm never going to be free from it.'

She turned and walked down the hallway into the kitchen, crossing to the fridge. She took out a dish of something Tom couldn't see and plonked it on the table.

'I'm sorry,' she said. 'You probably haven't eaten anything. But there's some strawberries here if you'd like some. I haven't got any cream or anything, but I think perhaps they're sweet enough to eat on their own, or I've got some sugar if—'

Tom laid a hand on her arm. 'Isobel?'

She sunk onto a chair, dropping her head and clasping both hands together in front of her on the table. Her thumb moved rhythmically back and forth over her wrist as if this tiny movement might provide some comfort.

'I'll make us a drink.'

Neither of them said a word while Tom busied himself making tea, and it was only when he joined her at the table several minutes later that she raised her head at all. He pushed a mug towards her.

'I'm not sure whether this ever helps,' he said. 'But there are certain times in your life when you're prepared to give anything a go.'

She smiled gratefully, clasping her hands around the warm mug, despite the heat of the afternoon.

'I ought to apologise,' she began. 'I was very rude…'

Tom eyed her across the table. 'Possibly,' he said. 'But I spoke without thinking back at the hotel, which was unforgivable, and I'm sorry too. I never meant to upset you… And just for the record, I'm really not a spy…'

Isobel passed a hand over her face. 'That's frankly embarrassing.' She groaned. 'I can't believe I even said that.'

He shrugged. 'You were upset, it happens. I've been called worse, and believe me some of the times I actually deserved it.'

'But not today though.'

'No, not today.' He swivelled his mug around so that the handle was facing him. 'So, what's the deal here, Isobel? I mean, I know what I've read, but I very much doubt that it's the truth, and I'd much rather hear it from your point of view.'

'Oh, I don't know, what's to tell? I'm sure the papers got the gist of it very well. I was a child prodigy. I gave my first solo performance at the age of seven, but by the time another seven years had gone by I was on my way out. At age sixteen I had a nervous breakdown and I quit the music scene for good. To all intents and purposes, I disappeared off the planet. Me and my vast fortune, except that now there's very little left of it and, as being a child prodigy doesn't qualify you for anything else in life, I have no choice but to try to begin working again.'

'Hence the comeback?'

'Yes.'

Tom studied her face. 'Okay,' he said. 'Now try that again, only this time tell me what actually happened. You don't become a child prodigy by accident. Having a nervous breakdown doesn't *just* happen. And people don't disappear for years on end and then suddenly reappear as if nothing had happened in the intervening years.'

Isobel remained silent.

'Okay, then tell me why you looked so scared back in the hallway just now? When you thought I had somehow followed you here to discover your identity. Or perhaps you might like to tell me why you thought your mother had sent me here? Or even why you're terrified that you can't play with any emotion… in fact you never could, could you? Technically brilliant, but cold as ice, that was what the critics said, wasn't it? What a terrible legacy for a sixteen-year-old child…'

'Have you quite finished?' Isobel's lips trembled in a face that was deathly pale, her dark eyes huge by contrast. He could see that she wanted to be angry with him again, to lash out and rip him to shreds with her words, but she also knew he was right.

He held out his hand to her across the table, and was relieved when she gave a rueful smile and tentatively wound her fingers in his.

'Your turn,' he whispered.

'I've spent so many years trying to deny the truth, trying to work out even what the truth was amid all the lies, that sometimes it feels as if I don't even know what it is any more.' She thought for a moment. 'Except here, at Joy's Acre, this is the only truth I have right now.'

'It's as good as any you'll find,' replied Tom.

She nodded. 'I came here because I thought it would be a place where I could forget about everything else and concentrate on the one thing I thought I needed to do, and that was work. Now I realise that the opposite is true. It's not the work I need to concentrate on at all, but all the things I'm trying to forget. And for some reason, Joy's Acre seems to be the place to do that. I've spent most of my adult life under the care of one psychiatrist or another, trying to come to terms with my childhood, and perhaps unwittingly, by coming here I took the first step.'

Isobel gave his hand a squeeze and gently withdrew it, lifting her mug and taking several swallows of tea.

'My childhood was an extraordinarily cold and lonely place, and as an only child I learned very quickly to amuse myself. My mother played the violin and I can only assume that I must have picked it up one day and begun to play in an effort to relieve my boredom. There must have been lessons and practising, and before I knew it I was playing in front of an audience. And for the first time in my life

I heard the sound of appreciation. People were applauding me, and telling me what a wonderful child I was, and the sweetness of that was like a drug I began to crave more and more.'

'I used to watch you at performances and think how glamorous your life must be,' said Tom. 'I used to feel envious of you, and it never once occurred to me what it must actually have been like.'

'My life was planned out for me from the minute I got up, to the minute I went to bed. Everything was carefully controlled, and the more successful I became, the harder I had to work. But it was worth it, just to hear people telling me they loved me, and how beautiful I was.' Isobel scratched her head, frowning. 'I stopped going to school early on and instead had a private tutor who went everywhere with us but, apart from a couple of hours each day, I spent the rest of my time practising. I had no friends, but then I had no need of any, and certainly no time to play with them.'

'So, when did it start to go wrong?'

'It's hard to really pinpoint, but I think it must have been around the age of eleven. I guess my hormones were kicking in because I became very emotional, crying one minute and flying into a rage the next, and I knew it was affecting my playing, even if the audiences didn't seem to notice. And so my parents arranged for a "coach" to come and work with me, a behavioural specialist who taught me to isolate my emotions and totally remove them from my playing, and for a while it worked. I was able to play ever more difficult pieces and the audiences went wild. It became a vicious cycle. The only way I could keep up with the demand for these pieces was by completely locking away anything else I felt and to concentrate only on the technicalities of what I was playing. I was so successful that no one thought of the effect it was having on me.'

'Or they did, but they knew exactly what they were doing…'

Isobel gave a hollow laugh. 'Nothing else mattered just so long as Isobel, the playing machine, carried on… and that was fine until I got a little older and could no longer carry the child prodigy card. I was beginning to be seen and treated like an adult, and certainly compared to them as a violinist, and that's when the first critical reviews began to appear, saying that I was cold and that my playing lacked emotion, and they were right of course.'

A tear dripped off the end of her nose.

'Oh, Isobel…'

'Don't,' she said. 'Please don't. If you're nice to me, I'm going to lose it completely.'

Tom let out a soft breath. 'And what would be the harm in that? You've been treated appallingly in the past, Isobel, by the very people who should have stood up for you, loved you, and cared for you, but you don't have to let that colour your life now. You can be whoever you want to be.'

She shook her head. 'You don't understand,' she said, 'it's not that simple.'

'Only because it's so hard to let go of the past—'

'No, that's not it. You don't understand,' she repeated.

'So tell me,' he said. 'Explain to me why you can't be whoever you want to be now…'

Another tear splashed onto the table, and she sniffed hard. 'Because my life is not my own, Tom. I still belong to them.'

Chapter 18

Isobel winced. It sounded so ridiculous when she said it like that. She was a grown woman for heaven's sake, how could she belong to anyone? And yet she did, and it was so hard to explain what she meant. She didn't really know how it had happened either, the insidious taking over of her life, done so skilfully that she had never really realised it was happening. Except that over the last couple of weeks, and more so in the last couple of days, things were becoming much clearer. And as they became clearer they also became more frightening as Isobel realised the scale of the abuse that had been meted out to her.

Not violence, but abuse took many forms, and in her case it had been hidden under a supposed need to keep her safe, and to look after her. But her liberty and her ability to think for herself had been taken away from her, and that was abuse just as surely as if she had been beaten every day for the last ten years.

'I know what you're thinking,' she began. 'Even I don't know how it happened, how I could let it happen, but that's the trouble with things that creep up on you gradually – it's often hard to see the situation for what it is, because you become so used to it, and you don't know any differently. But you have to understand what it was like when everything came crashing down.'

Tom was being so kind. He was sitting in front of her now wearing an anxious expression, and her hand still rested in his. It tightened gently, and he smiled. 'I'm not here to judge, Isobel,' he said. 'You can say whatever you like.'

'I was only young you see, only sixteen, and although I'd done things and experienced things, had to cope with things most sixteen-year-olds hadn't, I was still emotionally very immature. I didn't have the mental ability to take decisions, or understand the ways of the world financially or legally, and for the first few years after my breakdown it was all I could do to get through each day. Even when things slowly began to get better, in a way it was too late because things had already been put into place and I couldn't see that they needed to change.'

'You must have made a huge amount of money,' said Tom. 'Is that what you're referring to?'

'Partly,' she replied. 'My parents acted as my manager, and yes, you're right, by that stage I was very wealthy. The money from sales of records alone was staggering and given my age it was put into a trust for me. At least some of it was. I still don't know all the details, it happened so long ago. But you have to know that for several years I was in and out of hospital... It started with my nervous breakdown, but by the end I was drinking far too much, and eating far too little... I had my liberty officially taken away from me on more than one occasion as a result. And although it was for my own good, they're terrifying places, Tom – the hospitals, I mean. I became so confused and frightened of being put there again that I would agree with just about anything to prevent it. It meant that my parents' hold over me could tighten even more, and to start with I even welcomed it. It wasn't until much later on when I began to come to terms with things that I realised how wrong this was. But even then, I still wasn't brave enough to change anything. When you're told repeatedly over and over that you're still ill, and that you can't cope by yourself, you begin to believe it.'

'So, what happened to change all that?'

Isobel shuddered. 'I got wise,' she said, feeling the same wave of disgust sweep over her as always whenever she thought about it.

'To put it bluntly, the money began to run out. Whether it had been unwisely spent or mismanaged, I don't know, but we had a huge house and a luxurious way of life, the only problem was that I was no longer earning money to sustain it. My parents had no careers of their own, having long since given those up, and as the conversations began to turn to the subject of my beginning to work again, I realised that I had been the goose that laid the golden egg – the only trouble being of course that I was no longer laying. The worst thing was I also realised that if I was ever going to be able to stand on my own two feet and live my life the way I wanted to, I would need to earn money to support myself, and so I had to go along with my parents' suggestions. It was Catch-22.'

She drew in a long breath and, with a sheepish smile, picked up her mug and drained it, buying herself a little more time. It had been hard enough sharing the details of her past, but in a way it no longer held the fear for her it once had. The future, however, was a very different kettle of fish. That was a very scary place indeed.

'Earlier, you said that I was staging a comeback, and that's why I freaked out, because no one knows about any of this. No one must know for very obvious reasons, but the thought of what I need to do now terrifies me. It's taken me months just to get to this point, to pluck up the courage and leave home. I didn't tell my parents where I was going because they would have only stopped me, and even now they have no idea where I am. When I arrived at Joy's Acre I thought that all I needed to do was work on my music like we'd agreed and everything would be okay. Except that it isn't, it could never be.' She looked up at Tom. 'So, you mustn't tell anyone,' she urged. 'I still don't know what I'm going to do, but no one must know.'

'Isobel, I would never betray your confidence.'

'Over the last little while my parents have been trying to find an opportunity for me to be rediscovered. I've never stopped playing, putting in the same hours of practice pretty much every day, but for the last five years or so I've also begun to write my own music. I even changed my name legally by deed poll so that I could continue unhindered by my past, and eventually, my parents found a promoter who was willing to take me on. He knows the whole story of course, he had to, but even he is bound by a secrecy clause in my contract. I am supposed to be writing an original piece of music that will blow the minds of the music industry, at which point my true identity will be revealed and my comeback will be the massive success my parents have designed it to be.'

She sat back in her chair and sighed. 'So now you understand my predicament,' she added, 'because there is no original piece of music, at least not one that will blow the minds of the industry.'

Tom too had sat back in his chair, and was now watching her with a thoughtful expression on his face. But she couldn't really tell what he was thinking. She didn't know whether he was shocked by what she had told him, or uncomfortable in her presence. Either way it saddened her. She thought back to how she felt earlier, how seeing Tom, feeling his warmth, just before she began to play had meant so much to her, but now she had blown it. She didn't just have baggage, she had a whole wardrobe full of matching suitcases, and no one in their right mind would want to help her carry them. It was quite possible that Tom even thought her stupid in the extreme – a weak and feeble person who deserved exactly what she had got.

The seconds were ticking by and there was still no response from him. Isobel guessed she had her answer. She didn't think she could bear to look at him for much longer, and was just about to leave the table, when he suddenly leaned forward and plucked a strawberry from the bowl in front of them, popping it into his mouth whole.

'Do you know what I think?' he said. 'I think you should tell the lot of them to just sod off.'

At first she thought she hadn't heard him right, but then she took in the sudden grin on his face and realised that she had. It was such an extraordinary change in the mood that the tension in the room popped like an over-inflated balloon, and she giggled; she couldn't help herself.

'I can't do that!' she cried.

'Why not?' he replied, chomping on the fruit in his mouth.

She looked about the room. 'Because… because…' Put like that it certainly seemed hard to think of a reason why. She threw up her hands. 'Well… because I have no money for one. Or very little anyway. And if I did a thing like that there is no way I could go back to live with my parents, so I'd have nowhere to live… Plus of course the rather important fact that I do have a contract to fulfil, and a piece of music to deliver…' She was rather warming to her theme.

'Nuh-uh.' Tom waggled his finger at her. 'Don't you go throwing up huge bloody reasons why you can't tell them to sod off, let's think of some reasons why you can.' He picked up another strawberry. 'Okay, firstly money. Some would say it's a necessity, but it's a very overrated commodity in my opinion, which brings me to your second point; somewhere to live. I believe you're paid up here until the end of August, which is four weeks away, so you have somewhere for now, and after that you can come and stay with me; and don't look at me like that, I have a spare room. This obviously completely negates number one, because you would no longer have any need for money... Now I can see that you want to interrupt, but hold onto those thoughts for just a little while longer until I've at least come up with a cunning plan to address point three.'

He nibbled at the end of the strawberry, watching her over the top of it with an impish grin. 'So... as far as the contract goes, you *have* actually written a piece of music... some music, but, correct me if I'm wrong, it's not the piece of music that you believe is going to set the world alight. So therefore the obvious thing to do would be to write a different piece of music that will, but then I've told you that already.'

She snorted. 'And what if I can't?'

'Then you'll have had a wonderful holiday.'

'And the contract?'

He thought for a moment. 'This guy's an agent, right? So even if you do deliver a piece of music, that's just the start of his work. The only way that *he* will benefit financially from this equation is if he finds a way to make this benefit *you*. At the moment, it's just a speculative punt, and so while everybody hopes that this will lead to a great and glorious future, if he doesn't find a way to make it benefit you, then neither of you have lost anything, and no harm done. That might be a very simplistic way of looking at it, but I wouldn't expect that you have any legal obligation to him at all.'

Isobel's heart almost missed a beat. 'Do you honestly think that's true?'

Tom nodded. 'I honestly do.'

'Right. Well then I guess I want to think about it... but there's no way I can come and stay with you.'

'Why not?'

Isobel stared at Tom. 'Well, because…'

It would be very difficult to tell Tom why not. After all, in all the times they had been together he had never made her feel uncomfortable, in fact, he had acted like the perfect gentleman. But Isobel was well aware that there was truth in the saying no smoke without fire, and if the comments made by Clara and Trixie were anything to go by, Tom was not someone she wanted to get entangled with. She couldn't help liking him, but that didn't mean he wasn't trouble, and staying with him would just be asking for it.

'I'll think about it.' She grinned, not wanting to hurt his feelings, and picked up a strawberry of her own.

For a moment Tom echoed her own smile, but then he grew serious again. 'Listen, Isobel. I know you think I'm being flippant, but I can't begin to imagine the things that you have gone through. And yet, what I see before me now is a beautiful young woman who has an extraordinary talent and, despite everything that has happened to her, still manages to be kind and caring. You have your whole future ahead of you and, perhaps more than anyone, I understand the need for you to prove a point to your parents, and to yourself. But you have to know what you truly want your future to be, and if it's not heading in the direction you want it to, only you can change that.'

She nodded solemnly, recognising the truth of his words. 'I really don't know what to say,' she said. 'I never meant to burden anyone with any of this, but today, the last few days… I don't know, perhaps it's just that I've put some distance between myself and my problems, but Joy's Acre has begun to show me possibilities I never thought I'd have, and now you've shown me that they can be within my grasp after all.' She stared out through the window at the golden late afternoon sun, suddenly feeling tired beyond belief. 'So, what do we do now?' she asked.

Tom followed the direction of her eyes, and inhaled a deep breath. 'I think we both need to eat, rest, and see how we feel in the morning. With any luck the pair of us will feel ready to take on the world, and then that's exactly what we should do.'

Isobel nodded, gratitude flowing over her, and a sudden unexpected anxiety. 'Will I see you in the morning?' she asked.

'You bet,' grinned Tom. 'I'm coming to breakfast.'

Chapter 19

For the first ten minutes or so after he woke up, Tom stared up at the ceiling with a big wide grin on his face. He couldn't help it, he'd never felt this way before. He couldn't remember any of his journey home the night before after leaving Isobel. Instead, it had been quite a surprise to arrive at his cottage and on entering he had sat in the kitchen for quite some time with an equally wide grin on his face. He hadn't thought he would be able to sleep at all, but the moment his head touched the pillow he was out for the count.

This morning his recollection of the previous day, although not quite as vivid, was just as extraordinary. He really shouldn't be smiling though. He wouldn't have wished the things that Isobel had shared with him on anyone, and yet, she had shared them with *him*, and he felt like a giddy school boy. She wasn't the only one whose perception had shifted over the last few days. Suddenly, for the first time in his life, he felt as if he not only knew where he was headed, but that he was headed there for the right reasons.

A check of his clock confirmed just how early it was, but Tom threw back the covers with a sheepish grin and headed for the shower anyway. Judging by the state of him he might well need to make it a cold one.

He hadn't even made it halfway across the yard at Joy's Acre before the front door opened and Maddie came out to meet him. He was surprised to see that her normal cheerful greeting was missing.

'Morning, Mads, is everything all right?'

She gave him a rather fierce look. 'Well I hope so,' she said. 'That may well depend on your answer to my next question. Although I am at least pleased to see that you made it home last night.'

He heaved a sigh. 'Do you even need to ask the question? Given that what you want to ask is whether I had my wicked way with Isobel last night, and you've already had the answer.'

Maddie had the grace to look embarrassed even though there was still a little glint in her eye. 'It's not that, Tom, I…'

'Yes it is. That's exactly what it is.' He felt a knot of resentment tighten in his stomach. He knew he had a bit of a reputation at Joy's Acre, but he had also thought that they knew he had never treated anyone badly, and never would. 'Do you really think so little of me?'

Maddie swallowed. 'That has nothing to do with it, Tom, you know I think the world of you, but Isobel is our *guest*, and more importantly our first guest. It matters a very great deal that she is happy and enjoys her stay and, when I see her like I did yesterday, looking so upset, and with you hot on her tail, what am I supposed to think?'

He glared at her. 'Oh, I don't know… perhaps that I was trying to help rather than automatically think that I was the *cause* of her upset? Thanks a lot, Maddie.'

She blushed. 'I admit, I might have jumped to the wrong con-clusion…' She trailed off, hanging her head. 'I'm sorry. That was incredibly rude of me.'

'Yes, it bloody well was. You're right, Isobel *was* upset, but not because of anything I'd done. In fact, she'd had the most amazing day that came out of nowhere, and spent most of it playing in a string quartet at a wedding. You can ask her about it if you like.' He paused for a moment, trying to calm down. 'Unfortunately though, it brought back some memories of her past that made her angry and, when I tried to talk to her about it, she insisted we come back here.' He gave her a very direct look. 'I also promised I wouldn't discuss it with anyone.'

'No, no, of course not. It's none of my business—'

'No, it isn't. And in case it had escaped your attention, we're both grown adults. I happen to care a great deal about Isobel, and I understand perfectly that she's our guest, but whatever happens between us is our business and no one else's.' He blew out a breath. 'Maddie, Isobel is fine. She loves it here, actually, so you really have nothing to worry about. Ask her, if you don't believe me. Now I'm just on my way over there to have a chat about a couple of things, so do excuse me.'

Maddie held out a hand. 'Tom, I am sorry. I should never have said anything… I was just being overprotective, and interfering…'

He softened slightly at the look on her face. 'You care, Maddie, I get that. Just don't shove it down my throat, okay?'

She nodded.

'I also know that I have a roof to be getting on with, so you needn't worry about that either.' He checked his watch. 'I'll catch you later,' he said, walking away, fully aware that Maddie was still staring after him.

Isobel answered the door so quickly he wondered whether she'd been standing behind it waiting for him, but then he chased the thought from his head. As if.

'Morning!' Her smile was bright as she stood back to let him in. 'Oh,' she faltered. 'Is everything okay?'

Tom nodded. 'Sorry,' he said. 'I've just had my head chewed off by Maddie.'

Isobel frowned. 'Why would she do that?'

It was on the tip of Tom's tongue to tell her, but then he thought better of it. He didn't want to make her feel awkward.

'Just a misunderstanding,' he said. 'Never mind, it's nothing to worry about.' He brightened his face. 'So anyway, what about you? I was about to ask if you'd managed to get any sleep, but I'm guessing that you might have.'

Isobel's face shone. She had on another simple cotton shift dress, hair loose and flowing over her shoulders; everything about her looked more vibrant than he remembered.

'I did. I had the most amazing sleep. I don't think I woke up at all. Mind you, as soon as I was awake, that was it, I had to get up and get going. I'm ridiculously excited.'

'I can see.' Tom laughed. 'But that's okay, in fact it's more than okay. I did wonder how you would be feeling this morning. Whether you would still be positive about things, or if the doubts had begun to creep back in again.'

She shook her head firmly. 'Nope,' she said. 'I feel better than I have in ages—' She stopped suddenly, frowning. 'It's bizarre because nothing has actually changed, but suddenly everything seems so simple, and I'm determined to keep it that way. When I first got up I thought about all the plans I should be making, but then I realised that I don't want to make any at all. I'm just going to enjoy letting things be for a while, and simply see what happens.' She tucked her hair behind her ears. 'But first I'm going to have some breakfast, I'm starving!' She touched his sleeve. 'Come on.'

Tom followed her into the kitchen where he could see that the table was already laid for two. He laid the book he'd been carrying face down next to one of the plates.

'I guessed that Trixie would be up early, and I was right. Although I think I made her jump when she saw me, I was practically lying in wait for her.' She indicated the middle of the table. 'I got what I went for though,' she added. 'When I leave here I'm going to have to get the recipe for these muffins. I can't get enough of them.'

Tom thought about whether he should say anything, but instead he just smiled.

'I don't blame you, they're my favourites too.' He took a seat. 'Actually, if you haven't got anything particular to do this morning, I wondered if you might give me a hand with something?' He waited until she sat down as well. 'Well actually two things?'

'Oh?'

'Although the second thing is more of a question…'

Isobel was already slathering butter onto a muffin. 'Go on,' she said, handing it to him. She pulled apart another of the savoury buns, generously buttering this one too and placing it on her own plate.

'Coffee?'

Tom nodded, licking his lips before he spoke.

'I wondered if you might like another occasion to practise being brave?' he said carefully. 'Although you don't have to give me your answer just yet, you can have a think about it.'

'Which means I'm probably not going to like it.' She took a huge bite of her muffin, amused.

'The wedding we're gigging at is in two weeks' time,' he said, 'and I think you should come and play with us.'

'No.' Isobel's answer was swift and unequivocal, even though delivered through a mouthful of crumbs.

Tom's own muffin paused halfway to his mouth. 'How can you just say no like that? After yesterday?' He wondered if he had offended her in some way.

She smiled. 'Because you play in a folk band and I'm a classical musician.'

He was about to argue when he caught a tiny twinkle in her eye as she chewed her breakfast. He sat back, shaking his head.

'Oh, very funny. Hilarious in fact.' He rolled his eyes. 'I know I'm not worthy to even be in your presence, but despite our lowly status, the lads in the band are really good fun. It'll be a great day.' He pulled a slight face. 'And good practice… you know, for getting back out there again.'

She suddenly sobered. 'I know, Tom, and I will think about it, but, despite how I'm feeling this morning, there is the small matter of a piece of music to be conjured out of thin air, and although I've had one or two ideas, nothing has magically materialised just yet. I do have to be sensible about this, and I just think that my energies might be better spent trying at least to fulfil my contract.'

'And you're sure that's what you want to do? Not just cut your losses and do something else instead?'

She narrowed her eyes. 'What do you mean?'

'Only that if you go ahead and submit a piece of work to this agent of yours, he will then be obligated to do something with it. And knowing your story like he does, you're a performance artist first and foremost, that will be uppermost in his mind. So whatever he does with the music you've produced, at some time you will be expected to perform it, surely? Otherwise what would be the point?'

He paused, thinking, but there wasn't really a way to soften what he had to say next. 'And I'm just concerned that this might not be what you want to do. That it could escalate, and become the very thing you've been trying to leave behind.'

'Yes, but that would be up to me. I don't have to perform to a massed crowd at all, there will be other ways of easing myself back into it.'

Tom shook his head sadly. 'I'd like to think you're right, Isobel. But the only way your agent makes any money is if you make any money, and so it's in his best interest to make you as much money as possible. It might not seem that way at first, but I'd be willing to bet that at some point he'll try to convince you that making your story public is the only way to go. And when that happens, you'll have very little control over what comes next, and the next thing you know you'll be out in front of a massed crowd who the media will already have whipped into a frenzy, and will essentially be baying for your blood.'

She swallowed. 'But you told me I had no obligation to him,' she replied, her voice becoming louder.

'You don't,' he said. 'Until the moment you send him anything… Isobel, I'm not trying to be harsh, simply helping you to see the possibility of things. If you don't want to ever perform again in public, then that's fine, if that's what you really want, but I'm not sure that submitting to this agent will allow that. And if you want to compose, then compose, but do it for you… and no one else.'

He grinned, trying to lighten the mood once more. 'And for God's sake, please come and gig at the wedding with us. They're an ugly bunch of bastards, and I get fed up of looking at the back of Pete's bald head.'

He was relieved to see her smile again. 'I will think about it,' she said, taking another bite of her muffin, 'but no promises. Now what was the other thing you wanted help with?' She directed a look towards the table. 'And what's in that book that you so carefully laid face down?'

He grinned. 'Have you ever made a corn dolly before?'

'I don't even know what one looks like, let alone ever made one.' She pulled a face. 'You have to remember that I've led a very sheltered life. When you practise more than nine hours a day, every day, it doesn't leave time for other hobbies. I have a feeling that I'll be spectacularly crap at most things.'

'Or spectacularly brilliant. Come on, you're a musician, you're hardwired to be creative. I think you might surprise yourself.'

Isobel just laughed. 'We'll see,' she said.

After they had finished their breakfast, and were on to their second cup of coffee, Tom pulled the book towards him.

'I suppose it's my own fault,' he said. 'In that we've given each of the cottages a theme, and the latest one is the Thatcher's Cottage, so... Maddie has in mind a few ideas for decoration which fit with the theme, and one of these includes hanging corn dollies... quite a few by the sound of things.' He opened the book at one of the more simple styles, pulling out the strands of straw he had tucked there. 'Once you get the knack, it's pretty easy really.'

Isobel groaned. 'And, don't tell me, it's getting the knack that's the difficult bit.' She peered at the pictures. 'Go on then, show me.'

Tom got up and moved chairs so that instead of sitting opposite Isobel as he had been, he was now sitting beside her. He shuffled his chair a bit closer. Picking up the strands of straw, he separated them so that he had six in total, arranging them in his fingers to form a set of spokes. He held them out.

'See? Like this.' He passed them to her.

Isobel struggled to even hold them, groaning as she fumbled to keep them all in her grasp. 'This is not going to end well,' she said, 'I can tell.'

'Oh ye of little faith...' He adjusted them in her hands. 'Now, pass the strand closest to you over the next two, going clockwise.'

She giggled. 'What?'

Tom laid his hands on top of hers. They were soft and warm. He gently manoeuvred the finger holding the straw she needed to bend.

'Now twist the whole thing so that the straw you just crossed over is facing you. And bend this one over the next two.' Again, he pressed down her finger. He repeated the movement two more times, each time murmuring the instructions in her ear as he leaned in close. Their bare forearms were touching and he was suddenly aware that every hair was standing on end.

He pulled back slowly, relinquishing her hands. 'I need to go,' he said, with a rueful grin. 'I've got a roof to thatch. But thank you, both for breakfast, and for your help.'

'I'm not sure "help" is exactly the right term to be using. I hope you've got lots of straw, I have a feeling I might need it.'

'I'll drop some off in a bit. But don't worry, you have the whole day to practise.' He stood up and made for the door.

Isobel stared at him.

'So I shall expect to see a heap of wonderful creations later on.' He ducked out into the hallway, popping his head back around the door at the last minute. 'Oh, and have a think about gigging at the wedding with us, won't you? And keep Tuesday free…'

'Tuesday—'

'Yeah. We've been invited for dinner with Kate and Adam. And this time I need *you* to hold *my* hand.'

Chapter 20

Isobel poured herself a glass of lemonade and carried it back out to the bench in the middle of the garden. Half an hour ago she had picked up the book that Tom had given her, and started to look through it. She had even got so far as to pick up several pieces of straw and begin to think how they might go together, before she realised what she was doing. And the thought made her smile.

She was sitting inside. Again. And it seemed to her now, looking back, that pretty much her whole life had been spent inside. She knew from watching films, and reading books, that people of her age always remembered their childhood summers – long afternoons spent playing outside, arms and legs tanned golden brown, and the feeling that there was all the time in the world. Those hazy lazy days of summer, that's what they were called. Unless you were Isobel of course, whose summer days were no different from her winter days, or her spring or autumn days for that matter. There was never any time for playing outside, and the delicious feeling of soft warm air on her skin was something she had little experience of.

Well, today was going to be the day that this all changed. She had picked up the book and the pieces of straw, and carried them outside. And then after a few moments she had gone back inside the house to collect a cushion, and now, she had a drink as well. She was all set.

Opening the book again, she began to leaf through the pages, trying to find the design for the corn dolly that Tom had shown her. It was a simple twisted ring, and she began to read through the instructions. Then she picked up six pieces of straw and read the instructions again, and then one more time, trying to remember how Tom had positioned them for her. She put the whole thing down in her lap and smiled, staring across the garden. She could remember his touch, but not much else.

She pushed the thought away and, trying to concentrate once more, she studied the diagram again, but she couldn't even see how to begin, bending down one straw experimentally and then another before lifting them up again so that she was back to the beginning. It was seemingly impossible to follow. She flicked her hair back over her shoulders and read through the text once more, her tongue stuck between her teeth as her eyes flicked between what she was reading and what she held in her hands. Although she wasn't aware of it, each time she made a bend of the straw she gave a little nod.

After a few minutes she could begin to see a coiled pattern emerge, and it was obvious where she had initially gone wrong once or twice; like a dropped stitch in a piece of knitting. She carried on, bending and twisting, until she had reached the ends of the pieces of straw. In her hands she now held what looked almost like rope, a little raggedy in places, but there was definitely a pattern. She set it down on the bench beside her and picked up another six pieces of straw.

This time, she made sure she got the initial few bends absolutely right, and from then on tried to apply the same amount of force to each bend, pulling the coils tight with each turn, just like she did when she plaited her hair to give a neat braid. A few minutes later she was rewarded with a much better specimen.

She looked at it critically. The walls in the sitting room of the cottage that Tom was currently thatching were whitewashed, the same as hers were, and she could see that the corn dollies would make for very effective decoration. In the book, the corn dollies were tied off with lengths of coloured ribbon, and against the pale wall the contrast would be vivid. However, it was clear that she would need to make something much bigger and more elaborate if it was ever going to be used. Still, she had made a start and was pleased with her efforts.

She picked up the book again, turning the page to see if there was something else she might tackle. Her eye was immediately drawn to an illustration, not of a corn dolly but instead an elaborately woven corn sheaf. Usually made from bread, she had seen these before, often as centrepieces in bakers' windows, or at the harvest festival concerts she had played at. The illustration she was looking at was almost mahogany in colour, with a beautiful shine to it, and full of twists and plaits, made to resemble the ears of wheat. To each side of the centrepiece, also fashioned from bread, were cornucopias, each one spilling over with fruit and flowers. She looked up across the garden, her eyes narrowing as she thought for a moment. She put the book back down and rose from the bench, heading towards the main house.

Her knock at the door brought no reply, and so Isobel walked around to the kitchen window to see if anyone was about. Trixie could clearly be seen inside, but the reason for the unanswered door was also obvious. She held a huge mixing bowl in her arms, and was gently turning over its contents as she danced around the room, her hips gyrating in a distinctly sensuous way. Isobel grinned, reluctant to interrupt her impromptu dancing, but after a few more seconds she began to feel embarrassed by her voyeurism, and waved her own arms wildly in an effort to attract Trixie's attention.

The happy-go-lucky cook was already smiling, but she threw back her head and laughed as she caught sight of Isobel, before putting down the mixing bowl and motioning to the door. She was still laughing as she opened it.

'Caught red-handed,' she giggled, pulling a pair of headphones from her ears. 'That was me trying to be raunchy,' she added, 'but I suspect I just looked a total prat.'

'What were you listening to?' asked Isobel, intrigued.

Trixie blushed a little. 'One of my favourites. Nina Simone's "Feeling Good". Uh, it gets me every time.'

Isobel grinned. 'Great choice,' she said. 'And no, you didn't look like a total prat. My hips do that too whenever I listen to it.'

The two women smiled at one another for a moment before Trixie took a step backwards, ushering Isobel into the hallway.

'Don't tell me, you've come for *more* muffins,' she said.

'Well I could have, easily, but no, not this time. I wanted to ask you something actually, and Maddie too if she's around. I had an idea about something and wondered whether it was a good idea, or a really bad one.'

'Sounds mysterious,' Trixie replied. 'I think I'd better go and fetch Maddie, she's just in the office, I won't be a minute.'

Isobel looked about the kitchen. There was a glorious scent of lemons coming from somewhere, and she crossed to inspect the mixing bowl. It was two-thirds full of cake mixture, and it smelled divine. Isobel would have dearly loved to stick a finger in to sample it. Perhaps as a guest she might be offered the spoon to lick.

'Lemon drizzle,' said Trixie, coming back into the room. 'They're for the farmers' market tomorrow, but I might just be able to keep one back to have with our tea this afternoon.'

'If you don't, there'll be hell to pay,' quipped Maddie, bringing up the rear. 'It's all well and good having the office in the house, but I get subjected to smells like this all day, and it's absolute torture.'

'It must be,' replied Isobel. 'My stomach's rumbling already. Mind you, that seems to be a pretty permanent feature over the last few days.'

She smiled at the two expectant faces in front of her, suddenly remembering that this was their place of work, and they were both probably very busy. It made her feel a little shy.

'I'm sorry to barge in like this, but as I mentioned to Trixie, I've had an idea; something I've seen which I think might be helpful.'

Maddie shot Trixie a glance. 'Go on,' she said, 'we love ideas here.'

Isobel took a deep breath. 'I've had a go at making corn dollies this morning. Tom mentioned how you wanted to use them as decoration in the Thatcher's Cottage. And well... I think they were okay for a first attempt, and I don't mind practising until maybe they're good enough to use, but...' She trailed off as she caught sight of the expression on Maddie's face, and she suddenly realised what she had said. She flushed bright red.

'Oh listen to me, I'm sorry,' she said. 'You must think I'm incredibly rude, and arrogant as well, thinking that I can tell you what to do here, when it's really none of my business.'

It hadn't occurred to her before exactly what she had been doing. But she was staying in a holiday cottage for goodness' sake. She was a guest here, and guests didn't behave like this, almost as if she were one of them. It was just that... she tried to push the thought away, but the sense of belonging that had crept over her was too strong to ignore. She hadn't felt this way in a very long time, that's if she ever had.

But the startled expression on Maddie's face had turned into a rather wary smile. 'Oh, Isobel, please don't apologise. I think my face ran away with me just then, but you surprised me rather, I thought you were up to your ears in work? Tom really didn't have any right to ask for your help with the corn dollies. You should have just said no.'

Isobel fiddled with her ring, twisting it round. Maddie seemed to have got entirely the wrong idea.

'No, it's okay, I'm happy to help. Tom was doing me a favour actually. You see, I have been busy… I probably still should be if the truth were known, but quite unaccountably I find that my plans have changed a little, and until I work out where they're going, I seem to have some time on my hands.' She returned Maddie's smile with a brighter one. 'Which is actually brilliant, but doesn't excuse me from sticking my oar in.'

'Actually, I don't think you've stuck it in yet,' said Trixie. 'And I should warn you about Maddie. One tiny little glimpse of oar, and she'll have the whole boat. Be very careful…'

'Trixie!' said Maddie, pretending to be shocked. 'How could you say such a thing?'

Trixie gave her a sideways glance. 'Very easily,' she said. 'Look at me. One minute I was working in the pub, and just happened to mention that I liked cooking, and then the next minute I'm whisked away here and somehow seem to be doing things I never thought I'd find myself doing.'

Maddie grinned at her. 'And you absolutely hate it, don't you?'

'Absolutely. Every minute of it.' She picked up the mixing bowl and gave it an experimental stir. 'Of course the other way of looking at it, Isobel, is that you're just succumbing to what everybody else does when they arrive at Joy's Acre.'

'But I'm supposed to be a guest,' she protested, laughing. 'If I'm not working, then I should be on holiday, not coming up with an idea to help decorate your cottages.'

Maddie's eyes widened. 'You've had another idea for the cottages?' she said. 'Well, that's different and I demand to know what it is. Trixie, sit this woman down and feed her something, we can't let her escape.'

'Victoria sponge or raspberry and white chocolate muffin?' said Trixie, without skipping a beat.

'Seriously though,' added Maddie. 'I think it's lovely that you're thinking about the cottages here. When they began to take shape, and we knew we would be able to have guests in the not too distant future, we all kind of had a wish that this place would be more than just somewhere to come on holiday. We hoped that our guests would feel at home here and, for however long, perhaps that they were part of our bigger family. It sounds to me, from what you've been saying, that this may well be the case, and I honestly couldn't be happier if it is. I didn't mean to be dismissive of you making the corn dollies for us, it's just that, well, Tom can be very… charismatic, and I was worried you were being coerced into something you didn't want to do.'

Isobel looked between the two women. 'No, it's nothing like that, honestly. I find it hard to explain,' she said. 'But I think it's more like your wish might have come true. I feel so differently about my life since coming here, and I have no idea why that is.'

Trixie hefted a huge dollop of cake mixture out of the bowl and let it gently drop back in. She gave a satisfied nod and put the bowl back on the table. 'So it isn't anything to do with our charming thatcher then?'

'What, Tom?' Isobel stopped suddenly, feeling herself blush. 'Actually, I think it's got quite a lot to do with your charming thatcher. Not in that way,' she was quick to add, 'I'm aware that he's a bit of a—'

'Flirt?'

Isobel smiled. 'Well that's one word for it. But he's been… lovely. A total gentleman and a friend. Nothing more… I wouldn't…' She paused, wondering how best to explain herself, or even whether she should. 'I've been wrestling with one or two problems over my music, and it's really helped having him to talk to about it, that's all.'

Maddie cleared her throat. 'Then that's just perfect, Isobel,' she said. 'But enough about Tom now, I'm dying to hear what this idea of yours is. That's far more exciting.' She gave Isobel a broad smile.

Isobel could hardly remember what she'd come over for. But it was a nice feeling, this standing in the kitchen nattering with two other women.

'Okay, so as I mentioned I had a go at making some corn dollies. But I realised that the trouble with them was that they might be a bit small. Now that's not really a problem, we can just make bigger ones, but as I was looking through the book Tom gave me for more ideas, I came across a photo that gave me an even better one. It was one of those large sheaves of bread, like you see at harvest festival. I think they're only meant to be ornamental, and this one also had two horns of plenty by the side. The main design was pretty intricate on its own, but the horns were also filled with flowers and fruits. It struck me that it would look quite stunning as a centrepiece on the cottage wall.'

'Yes, I've seen those.' Maddie nodded. 'When I was at primary school we used to take one down to the church every year. I think the local bakery always made it. They're almost works of art.'

'The one in the book was hanging on the wall, although it looked a bit dated. I suspect that by today's fashions in interior design it wouldn't stand up to much scrutiny, but in the cottage it might fit in rather nicely.'

'I think it's a brilliant idea,' said Trixie. 'Although I'm not sure that they're actually made of bread, at least the ones hanging on walls wouldn't be. They're more likely to be salt dough, which is even better.'

Maddie shook her head. 'What's that?' she asked. 'It *sounds* like some kind of bread.'

'Well in a way it is, but you wouldn't want to eat it. Essentially, it's just flour, water and salt. You mix it together to make a type of dough which is a bit like modelling clay, and then you just make whatever you want with it. You dry it out really slowly, and then once it's done you can varnish it or paint it, whichever you prefer.'

'And how on earth do you know about that?'

Trixie grinned. 'My mum is a childminder,' she explained. 'Kids love it, and it's really easy to make.'

Isobel frowned. 'But this looked nothing like what a child would make. The photo I saw looked very realistic.'

'Yes, it's just like clay really,' replied Trixie. 'What you get out of it depends on the skill of the person using it. And I've seen some very elaborate and beautiful creations.'

'Are you saying you'd be willing to have a go at making one?' asked Maddie. 'Because if you are, I'll bite your hand off. I don't think either of us have time to do something like that, but I think it's a fantastic idea, and what better than to have it made by our first guest here. It's perfect!'

Isobel could feel a little flush of pleasure building inside her. She had no idea whether she had the skill to turn out anything resembling the photo in the book, but she would have a damn good try.

Trixie beamed at her. 'I'm not sure exactly how you make salt dough,' she said. 'But I could ask my mum. Or better yet, just Google it. I know it's very simple, it's just the proportion of ingredients you need to get right. Speaking of which…' She disappeared through a doorway at the back of the kitchen, returning a few moments later with two bags in her hands.

'There you go… flour, and salt.' She handed the packages to Isobel. 'That's enough to be going on with, but there's plenty more where that came from, just let me know what you need.' She looked at Maddie. 'Actually, I'll be out all day tomorrow at the farmers' market,' she said. 'So if you wanted to use the kitchen here I'm sure that wouldn't be a problem.'

'Would that be all right? I'd hate to mess up the kitchen in the cottage. Oh… not that this is messy—'

Maddie just laughed. 'It sounds like the perfect plan. Of course you'd be welcome over here.' Her gaze wandered over Isobel's shoulder.

Isobel turned around to see Tom walking towards the door. He didn't knock of course, and within seconds was in the room with them. She wasn't sure who was the more surprised, but she was definitely the more embarrassed. She was suddenly very aware of the conversation which had recently taken place, but Tom simply gave a huge grin.

'Isobel!' he exclaimed. 'I didn't know you were over here.'

And despite herself her stomach gave a huge lurch. 'I'm just going actually. I came to talk to Maddie about something…' She trailed off, not sure what else to say as Tom and Maddie stared at one another.

'Well, that makes two of us then. I wonder if we might have a chat?' he said to Maddie.

There was a certain tension in the air and Isobel was suddenly very conscious of outstaying her welcome.

She turned to Trixie, adjusting the packages in her arms. 'I'll be off then,' she said. 'Thanks for these.'

And with that she disappeared out into the hallway before anyone could stop her. Tom had mentioned a misunderstanding between himself and Maddie first thing this morning, and now it very much felt like she was the cause of it. Plus, Maddie had been very quick to judge Tom earlier. The trouble was, that although Isobel also had been very quick to deny that Tom had been the cause of her recent change in behaviour, she was rapidly coming to the conclusion that, in fact, he had everything to do with it.

Chapter 21

It took until Tuesday, but from the minute she woke up, Isobel's fingers were practically itching. She knew from experience that she needed to let ideas brew, to percolate for a little while until things were piping hot, at which point she could pour them out. So she had passed the time reading, working on her salt dough creation, walking the countryside, and playing her violin just for fun. An extraordinary but nonetheless pleasing experience.

Now, though, it was eight thirty, and Isobel was up, showered, full of coffee and scrambled eggs on toast, and ready for a full day's work. *Just like the good old days*, she thought to herself, actually laughing out loud at the irony. It seemed an age since she had last sat at her desk and, although her computer and keyboard felt just as familiar as always, she realised that the person sitting in front of them was very different indeed.

By default, the program she used for composing opened on her last composition, but she clicked it closed without even listening to it. It was tempting, but she knew what it sounded like and hearing it again would not make it any better. It was also part of the old regime. She started a new project and created five individual tracks, naming each of them, and then she took a very deep breath.

Four and a half hours later, when Trixie's knock came at the door, she had the basic melody line for two out of her five characters. It was a good morning's work, but just as important as the number of notes that had been recorded was the feeling that Isobel had made the right decision, and she got up to greet Trixie with a smile rather than a frown at the interruption.

She no longer took her meals alone in her cottage and, after exchanging a few words with Trixie, she followed her outside and into the garden, walking on alone to the main house while Trixie went to fetch Seth and Tom, who were both working on the roof. The kitchen was empty except for Maddie, who was busy cutting a crusty loaf of bread into large slices. She smiled a welcome.

'Grab a seat,' she said. 'I don't suppose the others will be long.' She began to arrange the slices onto a clean board beside her. 'Although I'm glad you're here first… Oh gosh, this is awkward.'

Isobel pulled out a chair and sat down. Maddie sounded quite serious and she wasn't sure what to say.

'It's silly really, because I shouldn't feel embarrassed about asking, but it feels wrong somehow.' She turned around to face Isobel. 'Although you could take it as a compliment…'

'I should just come out with it if I were you.' Isobel laughed. 'The others will be here in a minute and then you'll be stuck.'

Maddie put down the bread-knife and came to join her at the table. 'The thing is that I've had another potential booking for the cottage, but I didn't want to reply before speaking to you first. I know you have it until the end of August, but I can't quite get my head around the fact that you won't be here after then. So I'm just checking really… in case you'd like to stay for longer.'

Isobel was touched. Maddie wasn't trying to be a clever saleswoman, she was obviously sincere in what she said, and her words suddenly lodged themselves in Isobel's brain. What *was* she going to do? The thought of having to leave Joy's Acre was unbearable. Here, everything seemed so simple, as if anything was possible, and all she had to do was reach for it. She couldn't even begin to think about going home, and as for the other things she had to face… Just thinking about them was sending icy cold shivers down her back.

She looked at Maddie's hopeful expression. Everything that Isobel needed was right here, even her music. She could feel the notes inside her head, pressing to be let out, and once they were, others would follow, as sure as night followed day. How could she even think about going anywhere else? The others were coming now, she could hear their voices, but as she sensed her time to respond to Maddie was running out, suddenly one thought arrived in her head with crystal clarity. So strong it actually made her smile. The reason that things seemed so simple at Joy's Acre was because they actually were. And with that, Isobel's mind was made up.

The next minute the kitchen was full. Tom sat beside her, leaning in and gently pressed her shoulder with his. She answered his silent *How are you* question with a beaming smile, which she then extended around the table as Seth and Clara also took their seats.

Trixie took the lid off a pan standing on top of the cooker, releasing a wonderful scent of the summer into the air, like a greenhouse on a hot day, full of concentrated aromas. She began to spoon crimson-coloured soup into bowls, looking around the table as she did so.

'I hope you like this,' she said, 'only we, er, seem to have rather a lot of tomatoes at the moment.' She caught Clara's eye and winked. 'And if anyone hates ratatouille, speak now or forever hold your peace…'

'Or should that be peas…?' put in Tom.

Clara frowned at him. 'No, the peas are perfectly under control, thank you. It's just the courgettes and tomatoes that are being rather, um… exuberant at the moment.'

Seth rested his spoon back in the bowl after taking a mouthful. 'Well, this is gorgeous, Trixie,' he said, 'I certainly wouldn't mind having this again.'

She took her seat. 'Not when you bloody get it for breakfast too, you won't,' she muttered.

The laughter rippled around the table, and Isobel helped herself to a hunk of bread. She would miss this.

After that the conversation flowed, even though everyone was intent on finishing their meal. They all had work to get back to. Seth was the first to leave and although Isobel offered to help with the washing-up, Trixie wouldn't hear of it, and so she and Tom were soon heading back up the path to the cottages. They were just about to enter the gardens when she suddenly remembered what she wanted to say.

'Tom, go on ahead and I'll catch you up. There's something I need to talk to Maddie about. I won't be long.' She retraced her steps back to the main house.

Trixie was still clearing up, but she waved Isobel through to the study where Maddie had already returned to work, standing by a filing cabinet with a pile of papers. She suddenly felt a little shy.

'I just wanted to say,' she began, 'well, thank you really… We got interrupted earlier, when you said about me staying I mean, and the thing is… I would so love to stay, Maddie, but I don't think I can…'

An immediate sense of disappointment hung in the air between them. She carried on.

'So, being sensible, for the sake of your business, I thought I ought to let you know so that you could get back to the person who enquired as soon as possible. I'd hate you to lose the booking.'

Maddie nodded and smiled. It was a grateful smile, but she couldn't hide the regret there too.

Isobel bit her lip. 'But I also wanted you to know how much I'm enjoying being here, in fact, more than that, how much it's meant to me. I might have to leave the cottage at the end of the month but I'm going to be sticking around… somehow… The details aren't quite all there yet, but, I'm hoping…' She trailed off, slightly embarrassed. 'I just wanted you to know.'

They looked at one another for a moment, woman to woman, a silent understanding passing between them. Maddie shoved the pile of papers she was holding onto the top of the filing cabinet. She came forward with her arms outstretched.

'Aw, you daft bat,' she said, enveloping Isobel in hug. She hadn't even had to mention Tom's name.

★

Tom was still waiting on the path by the time she returned to the garden. He looked a little concerned.

'Is everything all right?' he asked, searching her face.

'Oh yes,' smiled Isobel. 'Everything's fine.' She studied him for a moment. 'Are *you* okay?'

He grinned. 'Shitting myself,' he said, and then immediately covered his mouth with his hand. 'Jeez, sorry, that came out a bit wrong. What I meant to say was—'

'A trifle nervous?'

He gave her an apologetic look. 'Something like that.'

She tried hard to stop her grin from showing. 'More polite, but somehow much less eloquent than your first statement.'

'Some would say more so.'

This time she smiled, a warm smile as she held his look. 'Either way, entirely understandable under the circumstances.'

Tom groaned. 'He's just a man for goodness' sake. How can meeting him be such a big deal?'

'Because he's your sister-in-law's new boyfriend, who you care about a great deal. Your sister-in-law, that is. She's been through enough already and you don't want to see her hurt again. Plus, you need to know whether he thinks he's attempting to be a replacement for your brother, or in fact whether he's tactful and sympathetic and wouldn't dream of being anything of the sort. Come to think of it, that also applies to the whole surrogate dad thing too, and uncle for that matter. Tricky business, because he can't be either of those things, so he's got to find some sort of safe middle ground where he's accepted by both you and Lily but without overriding anything that's gone before.'

Tom stared at her. 'Bloody hell, and I thought I was nervous.'

'Just trying to help you understand that he will be having metaphorical kittens as well, which might smooth the way a little. It *is* a big deal, for everyone concerned, and understanding that, perversely, might make it less so.'

'You're amazing, you know that?'

She looked up at him as he suddenly blushed.

'Just trying to help, fair's fair.' And then, embarrassed, as his words reverberated through her brain, she found herself colouring up.

She laughed. 'Right well, I need to get back to work and so do you, so go on, off you go.'

He took a step backwards. 'I'll pick you up at five, is that okay? Kate's serving the meal at six she tells me. Any later than that and I'm a dead man.'

'That's perfect, I'll be ready.'

They had reached the intersection of the paths and Isobel was about to turn towards her own cottage when she suddenly remembered something else.

'Oh, I meant to say… I started work on something new this morning, something which, for the moment at least, feels good, and I was thinking.' She grinned. 'Did you really mean it when you said I should come and play at the wedding with you?'

'Of course!'

'But won't the others mind?'

Tom batted a fly away from his head. 'We've been playing together a long time,' he explained. 'And, well, people come and people go. It's always been a fairly fluid arrangement. In fact, sometimes *I'm* not even sure who's going to show up. There's a core of five of us, but the edges chop and change a little. And that's great, it brings different things to the music, so I know the guys would be up for it.' The fly persisted, and he swatted it again. 'Does this mean that you've had a change of heart? Are you really going to come with us?'

Isobel took a deep breath, and nodded. 'But I don't even know what you play,' she said. 'And there isn't really time to practise.'

Tom gave her a look she couldn't fathom. 'Which is why I took the precaution of making a list, in case you decided to come with us after all.' He fished in the pocket of his jeans, and pulled out a folded piece of paper. 'This is the set list,' he said, handing it to her. 'And I've written the name of the band at the bottom. Just Google us and you'll find our website. All the songs are on there, and I expect you'll know a fair few.' He winked at her. 'Just see what you can do.'

Isobel stared at Tom, a slow smile beginning to spread across her face. 'Now who's being amazing?' she said.

Tom merely grinned.

And then Isobel looked down at the piece of paper, and almost burst out laughing. In large block capitals across the bottom few lines of the page was sprawled the band's name:

Change Your Mind

Chapter 22

Tom might well be nervous about tonight, but Isobel was frankly terrified. It was an occasion that had the potential for disaster to be written all over it in huge neon letters. Not only might Tom and Adam take an instant dislike to one another, but Isobel didn't know Kate or Lily at all well, and she was completely inexperienced in social situations. Despite Kate's friendliness on the one occasion when they had met, tonight felt very different from the informal school concert of a week or so ago.

She dressed with care. Her wardrobe options were limited, but the warmth of the evening made the choice easier, and after drying her hair she decided at the last minute to leave it hanging loose. Coupled with a white shirt dress and sandals, she was happy with her appearance, and she studied herself in the mirror for a few moments. She smiled; nerves were bubbling away inside of her, but there was something else there too. It was a very long time since she had felt excited. It was a weird feeling.

Kate's house was just at the other end of the village and, as Tom had mentioned before, was literally only five minutes away. It scarcely gave them any time to talk on the journey over, or rather Isobel time to chatter inanely and Tom time to listen. And now she was standing on the doorstep next to him, her heart beating like the clappers. He straightened the sleeve of his jacket, a soft blue linen, and then just as she heard the latch being turned he moved his hand to rest lightly in the small of her back. The next moment she was aware of the most gorgeous perfume as Kate caught her in a hug and pulled her inside.

A very excited Lily was practically jumping up and down. Kate laughed.

'Lily, let Isobel get through the door first.' She shooed her daughter down the hallway before turning back towards Isobel. 'I'm sorry,' she whispered, 'but she's desperate to play something for you. She's been practising ever since she found out you're a musician.'

Isobel pulled a face. 'Ouch, sorry. I hope it hasn't been too painful.'

Beside her, Tom gave an exaggerated tut. 'But I'm a musician too,' he said in a deliberately whiny voice.

Kate poked his arm. 'I know, but I meant a *proper* musician.' She took Isobel's arm, grinning. 'Come on,' she said. 'We're in the garden.'

Tom's voice came wafting from behind her. 'See what I have to put up with…'

The garden was beautiful, not large, but bright with colour and the wonderful scent that only a summer's evening could produce, an intoxicating, heady mix that filled the air. Isobel breathed deeply, looking around her, aware of Tom suddenly at her back.

Kate came forward. 'Tom, Isobel… this is Adam.'

Isobel turned to see a figure rising from one of the chairs on the patio to her left, a mop of curly grey hair somewhat of a surprise. In fact, he wasn't what Isobel was expecting at all.

He shook hands with Tom first, a warm two-handed shake, delivered with an accompanying grin. Despite the grey hair they looked about the same age.

'I've heard a lot about you,' he said. 'From Kate of course, although mostly from Lily, I'll admit. So it's really nice to finally meet the man who plays "really jiggy music that makes you want to dance".'

It was perhaps the best opening line that he could have said under the circumstances and, strangely, Isobel felt relief flood through her. Tom laughed.

'That's just the kind of thing that Lily *would* say.' He smiled affectionately at his niece. 'I'm afraid I haven't had the chance to talk to Lily about you though, but if I had, I'm guessing she would probably have said that you wear cool shoes, at least I hope she would.'

He stuck out his foot, which was clad in bright red Converse, identical to the ones Adam was wearing.

'I did think about wearing my best suit, to make a good impression and all that, but seeing as I don't own one, I'll confess I'm pretty much pinning it all on the shoes… It's good to meet you, Tom.'

And then Adam turned towards Isobel, hand outthrust once more.

'And you must be Isobel…The lady for whom Lily is dying to play.' There was a twinkle in his eye that let Isobel know just how much of a treat she was in for. She returned his smile willingly. It was obvious that he and Lily got along brilliantly.

'But you don't play jiggy music, I hear, or did I get that wrong?'

Isobel gave Tom a sideways glance. 'Let's just say that's open to a certain amount of interpretation at the moment. I'm a classical violinist, but I seem to have been led astray over the last couple of weeks.' She cupped a hand around her mouth. 'Don't tell Tom, but I'm even considering a move to the dark side…'

From the angle at which Tom was standing, she couldn't actually see his face clearly, but she could tell he was grinning.

Adam nodded. 'So, I'm guessing that's how you two met?'

'Oh, we're not—'

Isobel stepped forwards, effectively cutting off Tom in mid-sentence.

'I ought to say something poignant like we bonded over our love of Tchaikovsky concertos, but I'm afraid it's not quite as romantic as that.' She gave a bright smile. 'I'm staying for the summer at one of the holiday cottages on the estate where Tom is working. I was supposed to be using the time to finish a project I was working on myself, but instead I found myself intent on murdering both my violin and my career. Tom came to my rescue.' She moved closer, her hand brushing against his. 'Now I'm not sure I'm going home at all.'

Tom's mouth was almost hanging open in surprise and, as she caught Kate's eye, who was standing on their periphery watching Tom closely, it was all she could do to keep from bursting with laughter.

'I'm such a rubbish hostess,' said Kate. 'Nobody has a drink. Now what would everyone like?'

It was the perfect opportunity for Isobel, and moments later she was standing in the kitchen with Kate, ostensibly helping, but instead the two women were trying hard to stop themselves from giggling.

'Oh, you should have seen his face!' exclaimed Kate, turning red. And then she touched Isobel's sleeve. 'I'm so pleased though, I can't tell you. He looked like his birthday and Christmas had come all at once.'

'I probably shouldn't have come out with it quite like that, it was hardly fair. I don't know what came over me, but I've been think-ing about it all afternoon, and Tom was so anxious about meeting Adam, I thought it might… help…' She trailed off, looking rather anxious herself, now that it was beginning to sink in what she had actually done.

Kate gave her a sympathetic smile. 'I think we're all nervous as hell,' she said, 'which is understandable, I guess. It's a big thing – the two of them meeting was never going to be easy. I know what Tom's been through, how he feels about Matt, but he's also very protective of me and Adam is fully aware of that too.'

This time it was Isobel's turn to reach out. 'But you mustn't let the past be the barrier to what could be a wonderful future for all three of you.' She pulled a sheepish face. 'Listen to me, the fountain of all wisdom, just because I've had somewhat of an epiphany myself.'

'They're still very wise words… And for what it's worth, Isobel, I don't know what you've done to Tom over the last few weeks, but he's been happier looking and more relaxed on the last two occasions I've seen him than for a very long time. And judging by the expression on his face just now, he's well aware why…'

Behind her the oven pinged.

'It's only pizzas, I'm afraid,' smiled Kate, 'and a few other bits and pieces. I put Lily on menu-choosing duty because I thought that might be quite a nice idea… but cordon bleu it isn't.' She picked up a tray from behind her. 'I tell you what, if I take these drinks through, would you mind grabbing some knives and forks out of that drawer there, and I'll get the men to lay the table.' She grinned. 'Nothing like a few menial chores to get them bonding.'

'Tom, could you give Isobel a hand for a minute,' called Kate, moving back out into the garden. 'I'm afraid I've put you and Adam on table-laying duty.'

'Oh boo.' Tom smiled at Lily, who was now sitting in a chair, as he was, diligently cleaning her flute.

'Mum, *now* can I play?' she asked.

Isobel flashed Tom a somewhat shy smile as she passed. 'I think we might just have time before dinner,' she said, looking to Kate for confirmation. 'Perfect timing, Lily.'

Half an hour later Isobel began to properly relax. Even though about five minutes ago she had nearly jumped out of her skin as Tom's fingers had found hers underneath the table. Now, they were sitting, little fingers entwined, which was all they could manage without it looking hugely obvious, and trying to eat one-handed. This was fine for her, a right-hander, but for Tom, now having to favour his left hand, it was a little awkward. It was making her want to giggle and she concentrated on what Kate was saying.

Some gentle questioning of both her and Adam had revealed that they had been together since the New Year, and it was obvious, as much from what they didn't say as what they did, that things were already on a serious footing. Isobel hadn't really known what she had been expecting in Adam, but from what Tom had said she doubted he was anything like Matt, the driven and successful banker. Adam was obviously successful, although as yet he had deflected most attempts to talk about himself – not for any particular reason other than he seemed to prefer listening to what everyone else had to say – but he had shown a real interest in Tom's thatching, and was far more knowledgeable about the countryside than she was. His humour sparked the conversation, and Tom, with his equally quick wit, was a perfect foil for him.

Isobel had managed to steal a few looks at him when the conversation was not directed at her, and so far he seemed relaxed and happy to be there. Kate had even mentioned Matt on a couple of occasions, and Tom had seemed happy to talk to her about him. Her life was moving on and Tom looked nothing but pleased for her. Isobel hoped he was realising that it was perfectly okay for him to do the same.

She looked up at the sound of her name, realising that Tom had been talking to her. 'Sorry... I was miles away.'

'I was just explaining to Adam about Joy's Acre. I've never known a place like it, but it's hard to explain what it is about it that makes it feel so special. I was tempted to say it's the people, but that would mean paying you a huge compliment too…' He trailed off with a cheeky grin on his face.

Isobel stuck out her tongue. 'Well it's certainly not the tradesmen,' she said, and then paused for a moment, thinking. 'Actually, I think it is the people… but I think it's the combination of the right people at the right time if you get what I mean. There's such a huge amount of energy there, and that does make sense if you think of the place's history. Back in Victorian times when it was first built, Joy's Acre was a place that brimmed with creative energy, and even though it became unloved and uncared-for for quite a number of years, I don't think that energy ever really goes away.'

Adam nodded. 'It's on a hill, isn't it? I'm not sure why that makes any difference, but it does. I'm a keen walker, and I've done up hill, and down dale all over the country, but there's no feeling on earth like when you're standing on top of a hill.'

'Do you know I've never really thought about that,' Isobel replied. 'But I think maybe you're right. Whatever it is, it certainly seems to affect the people there, but then they're very special people too, so that has to play a part. Everyone that works there has their own creative talent. Tom's friend, Seth, who owns Joy's Acre, is physically creative, he likes to build things, a bit like Tom, I suppose. And his partner, Maddie, doesn't make things as such, but she has the most extraordinary creative vision. It was more down to her than anybody that Joy's Acre became what it is today.'

She paused to take another slice of pizza. 'Then there's Clara, who I think might just be the earth mother herself; she has a way of nurturing everything around her, not just plants, but people too. And Trixie is the most amazing cook, she's even got me drooling and I'd always been a bit take it or leave it when it came to food, but her and Clara's creativity just keeps growing and growing. They've even started another small business now.'

'And let's not forget your own creative endeavours,' said Tom.

Isobel raised her eyes to the ceiling. 'Oh yes, they've even got me at it now too. I've found myself making corn dollies and salt dough decorations which, if you'd told me three weeks ago I'd be doing, I'd have laughed hysterically.'

She caught sight of the expression on Adam's face. 'Sorry, I'm rambling now. But you kind of have to see it to believe it.'

Adam leaned forward across the table. 'You carry on,' he said. 'I love it when people ramble, that's where the best stories come from.'

Isobel grinned. 'But aren't I boring you?' she asked.

'Not at all. Stories are my stock in trade.' He smiled at the unspoken query in her eyes. 'I'm a documentary filmmaker,' he said.

Chapter 23

They practically fell through the front door of the cottage, laughing.

'Tom, if you ask me one more time if I'm okay, I swear I will batter you senseless with the nearest blunt object.'

And just to illustrate her point even further she looked around her for something to wield.

He threw up his hands in defence. 'Okay, okay!' He laughed. 'I'm just not sure I actually believe you.'

Isobel grinned. 'I know, weird, isn't it? I should be panic-stricken at the very least, but I'm really, really not.' She was already walking down the hallway. 'Although, poor man, talk about how to stop a conversation dead. I felt for Adam. It was all going so well, and then, boom!'

Tom was looking at her, now that they were in the kitchen. 'I thought you handled it really well though.'

Isobel sighed. 'The only thing I could do was come clean. I mean, if the almighty gap in the conversation wasn't obvious enough, my sharp intake of breath and jaw hanging open would have been. I couldn't possibly have covered that up, anything less than the truth would have looked utterly contrived. And I didn't want anything to ruin what really had been a lovely evening. He would have fretted endlessly that he had said the wrong thing for some reason, and whatever excuse we made up would never have convinced him otherwise. He'd have gone on forever not knowing what he'd done. That's not the start I wanted for you both.'

Tom gave her a look which made her stomach flip over. 'But what about the risk?'

Isobel couldn't quite believe how she did feel. She had asked herself the same question over and over in the car on the way home, thinking that somehow she was being delusional. But every time she asked the question, she came up with the same answer.

'Do you know, I actually feel relieved. I feel as if a weight has been lifted off my shoulders. So what if my story gets out? Tom, it's old news. It happened to me years ago, and like the monster under the bed I let it grow and grow until there was no room for it under the bed any more and I let it fill my life as well. Yeah, people might be interested for a few days, or a few weeks, but seeing as I'm not going to be making a comeback any time soon, what does it matter? *I* won't be news, and what's the point of dredging up something that was reported to death at the time? You've seen the articles, you know what happened back then… but that's where it belongs.'

He nodded, an unfathomable expression on his face. 'You really are amazing, you know that?'

She ignored the bait. It was important that Tom knew how she felt, without them getting… distracted.

'Besides, I actually believe what Adam said; that he has never, and will never be interested in making documentaries about stories like mine, and I don't think he's lying. So who else is ever going to find out? Chances are it's no one.'

'I know Kate won't say anything.'

'There you go then.'

'So, do you think he meant what he said about Joy's Acre then as well?'

Isobel scratched her nose as a stray hair tickled her face. 'That I'm not sure about. I think, despite how things turned out, he still felt a bit self-conscious about what he'd said and that perhaps he was trying to be the perfect guest. He was undoubtedly interested in Joy's Acre, but I think more from a conversational point of view, and that by the time he gets back to his office in the morning, embroiled in the one hundred and one projects he probably has on the go, he won't give Joy's Acre a second thought.'

She looked at Tom for a moment, and then turned and picked up the kettle, crossing to the sink to fill it.

'So, anyway. I'm not sure you answered my question in the car either. What did you think about Adam? Do you feel happier about things now that you've met him?'

'That wouldn't be you changing the subject, would it?'

'Possibly,' Isobel admitted.

'Well then, yeah, I feel good,' said Tom. 'And I didn't expect to like Adam quite as much as I do. He's not what I thought Kate would ever go for, but I'm happy that she has. He seems a genuinely nice guy.'

'And...?'

She could sense rather than see a huge intake of breath.

'I feel as if he's given me back two people I care about a great deal, and I never thought I'd have that.'

'Kate and Lily, you mean? How so?'

'Matt's gone, I know that. And nothing is ever going to bring him back. But it's weird... His memory haunted me so much it stopped me from focusing on the good stuff, on the people left behind. It got so that I dreaded seeing them, because all they did was represent what I had lost, and I forgot that *they* were still very much alive. Now, though, I can see a future for us all, and that includes remembering Matt as we should, as a part of our lives rather than trying to shut it out. And Lily and Kate are a part of my life too, I know that now.' He looked up at her. 'I probably have you to thank for how I feel.'

Isobel focused on his face. 'Well I don't see how. What have I done?'

'Been brave enough to talk about the one thing I couldn't, the thing that everyone else avoided but that you hit me with right between the eyes. The very thing of course that I needed to talk about.'

'Don't attribute that to bravery, I—'

'Why ever not, when you're probably the bravest person I know.'

She threw him a sideways glance. 'Yeah, right.'

'I mean it. Not many people could have overcome the things you have.'

There it was again, that distracting look in his eye.

'So, did you mean it when you said that you were going to stay at Joy's Acre?'

She set the kettle to boil. 'Well, I can't stay here... I don't have enough money, and I—' She stopped as he took a step closer. 'Thought perhaps—'

'That you might have my spare room?'

She looked up at him. 'Yes...'

'Or my not-so-spare room...'

'Yes...' *Oh God*.

Seconds later she was in his arms, his lips against hers, his hands buried somewhere in her hair, and she had absolutely no idea where *she* was.

★

It could easily have been her heart beating, except that the noise seemed to be coming from outside of her body, an altogether different rhythm.

Whatever it was, it was insistent. Reluctantly she began to pull away. She had no idea what the time was, but it must be quite late.

'I'll go,' said Tom, motioning towards the door. He grinned. 'It's probably Maddie, wanting to know whether I'm about to have my wicked way with you.'

'Well then,' replied Isobel, skipping out of his reach. 'I shall be able to tell her myself that, yes, you are…'

She pulled open the door, fully expecting to see a smiling face on the other side, and surprised to see it was Seth and not Maddie after all. And then she stopped dead.

'Hello, Isobel.'

It took only a second for her world to turn upside down as the blood rushed from her head and the horizon tilted alarmingly. She would have fallen had Tom's arms not materialised from nowhere. There was a strange anguished mewling noise coming from somewhere and then she realised that it was her.

'Mum!'

'I'm sorry, Tom,' said Seth, 'but she said it was urgent, and I—'

'I've come for my daughter. I'm taking her home.'

Isobel trembled violently. She was aware of Tom moving swiftly to her side and then his hands were holding her face, forcing her to look in his eyes.

'It's okay, Isobel, it's okay.' He took a step past her. 'Well Isobel doesn't look like she wants to go, so I don't think that's going to be happening. I have no idea what's going on here, but you certainly were not invited in, so on that basis, Seth, perhaps you could show her out.'

'Don't get involved with things you don't understand,' said her mother, narrowing her eyes and peering at Tom. 'Ah, I see… You'll be the reason why Isobel has decided to behave in such a ridiculous fashion. Well I'm sorry to disappoint you, young man, but Isobel has obviously told you a pack of lies about herself. She's a very sick girl and can't possibly stay here, she needs to be at home. Where she can be loved and cared for properly.'

The colour drained from Tom's face. He looked utterly distraught, and anger suddenly flared inside of Isobel, the adrenaline surge giving her back her voice.

'I'm only going to say this one more time, Mum. I made it quite clear that I wasn't coming home when I spoke to you on the phone, and nothing about that statement has changed. In fact, you can take this as notice that I have now officially left home so don't waste any more breath. I don't care what you say any more, I'm not interested.'

'Oh, you might think you have all the answers, but you're forgetting one simple thing. You have no money and nowhere to live. You can't stay here forever, can you?'

Isobel had argued with her mum plenty of times over the years, but whenever they did, it always came back to the same thing, and as soon as her mum played the trump card, Isobel would know she had lost – but not this time.

'No, Mother, I can't. But there are other places to live, apart from just here or with you. And it's funny how as soon as you begin to think you can have a future, you suddenly find one stretching out ahead of you.'

'Oh pathetic…' Her mum's voice was dripping with disdain as she took in the pair of them standing firm on the doorstep. 'How much more predictable can you get? A beautiful girl with a tragic past… and you think you'll be the one to save her. Well, how noble indeed. You know nothing about my daughter, nothing at all, and yet you've obviously swallowed all her lies in your desperate rush to get her into bed. I bet she hasn't told you *everything*.'

Tom took a step forward. 'I know everything there is to know, and you're right, your daughter is probably the most beautiful woman I've ever met,' he said, his voice dropping by almost an octave. 'She is also one of the kindest, the bravest, most generous, and talented people I have ever been lucky enough to know… despite her upbringing. Now I'm only going to say this once. You are on private property, and certainly not welcome here at this time. Are you going to leave now, or do we have to call the police?'

Seth took his mobile phone from his pocket.

'Oh, tawdry threats now, is it?' She drew herself up. 'Right, well I was trying to make this easier for you, Isobel. But now you've forced me to come out and say the very thing I was trying to protect you from.' She put her hand to her forehead. 'It's bad enough…'

Isobel looked at Tom, faltering for a second. What did she mean? 'Mum?'

'I didn't want to have to tell you like this…'

She could feel Tom's arm tightening around her.

'I'm sorry, Isobel, but your father has had a massive stroke. He's in intensive care… and, I'm afraid, not expected to last the night.'

Chapter 24

'Shit,' said Tom, looking at Maddie. 'Shit, shit, shit.'

'I'm so sorry, Tom, but I'm not sure what else we can do.'

'I should have followed them… or gone with her at the very least. Not just let her drive off with that… psychopath!'

'Tom, you don't know that. Just because you didn't like what you've been told before, you can't go jumping to conclusions. For all you know her mum was telling the truth about Isobel's father. In fact, I'm sure she was. It's an outrageous lie to have told otherwise.'

'Yeah,' muttered Tom. 'Now you're getting it…' He rubbed at his forehead, frowning. 'Anyway, what do you mean, just because I didn't like what I've been told before? By whom? Isobel… or her mum?'

Maddie remained silent.

Tom glared at her. 'I don't bloody believe you…! You saw what Isobel was like when she first came here – uptight as hell, pale, wouldn't eat, wouldn't say boo to a goose. All that stuff she told me… she was *not* making it up. Why the hell would she?'

'Tom, I didn't mean—'

'And you of all people should know what it feels like to have lies made up about you…' He broke off suddenly, sagging into a chair and putting his head in his hands. 'Christ, Mads, I'm sorry, I didn't mean…' He was close to tears.

Maddie leaned over and put an arm around his shoulders. 'We'll keep looking,' she said. 'Just because it doesn't look as if she has any social media accounts doesn't mean she doesn't exist. There'll be a trace of her somewhere, we'll find her. Besides, all her stuff is still here, Tom, she'll have to come back for it sometime… or someone will.'

She paused for a moment. 'And I need to apologise, Tom. I let my worries about this place get in the way of our friendship and that was inexcusable. I should never have doubted that what you and Isobel shared was something special.' She squeezed his shoulder. 'I'll do everything I can to help you find her.'

He looked up at her gratefully. 'Thanks, Maddie,' he said, only just managing to get the words out.

'And thinking about it logically… if what her mother said was true then it's quite possible that Isobel has just lost her father. Whatever their relationship, she'll be in shock and grieving. But, you're not going anywhere, she knows that. And she'll come back to you when she's ready.'

Tom blinked hard. He knew Maddie was trying to help, but the problem was that he didn't believe a word Isobel's mother had said, and nothing would convince him otherwise. He'd been so bloody stupid. Why hadn't he asked Isobel for her address at the very least? He knew she didn't want to go home, and yet he'd done nothing to stop her being taken back. And now she was gone. And had been for three days.

There was an insistent ping from the computer beside him, and he got to his feet wearily. He'd taken enough of Maddie's time already and she had work to do. So did he for that matter, but the thought of climbing back up onto the roof again so that he could stare at Isobel's cottage all day wasn't one he relished. He'd go and grab a bite to eat and then see. Perhaps he might knock off early and go to the pub.

The others were all in the kitchen when he arrived, tucking into a plateful of sandwiches. Trixie jumped up as soon as he entered and crossed to the coffee pot.

'Sit down, Tom, I'll get you a drink.'

He smiled gratefully. He hadn't said a word to any of them about Isobel; he didn't need to. Seth and Maddie had filled them in, and whatever they had thought of his attitude towards love and romance before, it had ceased to matter. It was now that counted, and Tom was one of them; they were on his side.

He took a seat in between Seth and Clara and half-heartedly helped himself to some lunch, smiling at Trixie as his drink was gently placed beside him. The sandwich was halfway to his mouth when Maddie came flying down the hall. His heart leaped into his mouth as he looked up eagerly.

'You'll never guess what just happened!' she exclaimed, and then her face fell as she realised that the news she was bringing was not of the kind that Tom was so obviously waiting for. She mouthed *Sorry* at him.

Seth looked up. 'Don't you just hate it when people say things like that? Of course we're never going to guess, Maddie. Put us out of our misery before you wet yourself.' Ordinarily, everyone would have laughed at that, but not today.

She still stuck her tongue out at him though. 'Rude.' But then she stared directly at Tom, sobering. 'Oh, Tom… this is really good news, except now…'

'Spit it out, Maddie.'

'Well, I've just had an email from some chap who makes documentaries. Apparently, he had dinner earlier in the week with, and I quote, a delightful young lady who spoke very eloquently about Joy's Acre. So much so that he was sufficiently moved to find out more.'

Trixie had just lifted her drink to her lips to take a sip and her hand jerked so violently that its contents slopped alarmingly against the rim, only just managing to cling onto the inside.

'What does that mean?' she asked.

'It means, Trixie, that this chap – Adam is his name – wants to come and find out a little more about us with a view to possibly making a film about life at Joy's Acre.' She gave Tom a sideways glance, trying to restrain her enthusiasm. 'Do you want to fill us in a bit?'

'Not much to tell really. You all know Isobel and I had dinner with my sister-in-law the other day. Adam is her new man, and we got chatting, that's all.' He stopped. 'Actually, that's not all… Isobel got chatting, very eloquently as it happens, about falling in love with this place. How when she came here things in her life were very different to how they are now. How she loves all of you, the history of the place, the energy here, all the creativity… how that's made her feel.' He put his sandwich back down. 'And she didn't even know Adam was a film director, but she said it all anyway. She should be here telling you all about it, not me.'

'Oh, Tom…' Clara laid her hand over his.

Seth picked up a stray piece of tomato from his plate. 'Well, whether you realised it or not at the time, Tom, both Isobel, and you as well I would imagine, obviously made quite an impression.' He dipped his head at them. 'We probably ought not to get too excited about this,' he nodded at Trixie who was visibly squirming in her seat, 'at least not yet anyway. Not until we know what his intentions are. But it could provide the most wonderful opportunity for us, I don't need to tell anybody that.'

He looked across to Maddie, who was still standing by the door. 'What does he want to do? We could send him some information.'

Maddie grinned. 'I think it's moved on a little from there,' she said. 'He's spent quite some time this morning looking at everything on all the websites, and has even followed up some of the references to the history of Joy's Acre, particularly Joy herself and her paintings. He says he's seen enough to want to pursue it, and has asked if he can come here and meet with us all.'

The sound of Seth's coughing was loud in the silent room. 'So, when does he want to come?'

'On Sunday.' She looked at Tom. 'He's away the rest of the week on another project, but will be back at the weekend, and on Sunday he's planning to spend the day with Tom's sister-in-law. He'd have to check with her of course, but it struck him that, provided it was okay with everyone else, it might make for the perfect opportunity.'

'Oh my God…' said Clara, voicing what everybody else was thinking. 'I'm not normally here on Sunday of course but…'

Trixie touched a hand to her hair. 'Maybe it's time for a change,' she said. 'I'm not sure I'd want to be seen on television with bright pink hair.'

'Let's not get too carried away,' said Seth. He was trying hard to be the voice of reason, but Tom could see he was just as excited as everybody else. 'What about you, Tom? Can you be here? It wouldn't seem to make much sense if you weren't.'

Tom glanced across at Maddie. 'I'm playing at that wedding Saturday night,' he said. 'And it will be a late one.'

'Well, yes but surely—'

'And, like I said, Isobel should be here. It's all down to her, how can any of this happen without her?'

He stared down at the remains of his lunch, but it was all too much. He lurched to his feet, heading for the door, praying that Maddie would move because he really didn't want to have to push past her.

'Tom!' she called after him.

'It's okay, Maddie, let him go…'

★

He shouldn't have, he knew that. But then the minute he walked out of the door at Joy's Acre he already knew he was going to come here, and it was pointless trying to reason with himself. He was definitely in no mood for listening. The off-licence was on his way home, and kept very convenient opening hours, and even though the choice of whiskies on offer was very good, he couldn't have cared less about that either.

He drank the first glass straight down.

Chapter 25

The light was far too bright, but somehow Tom didn't think that was what had woken him. He pushed his head down further into the pillow and resolutely shut his eyes. It didn't make the pain any better but at least with his eyes closed there was marginally less to think about.

For a couple more minutes he actually thought he might make it back to sleep, but then it came again, a nagging sensation that there was something not quite right. He lifted his head once more, trying to make sense of what his brain was trying to tell him, and then sat up cautiously, groaning as pulses of pain shot through his head. He could smell bacon…

It took several minutes clinging to the edge of the bed before he felt sufficiently stable to stand, and quite a few more before the heaving sensation in his stomach subsided enough to allow him to move. He peeled his tongue away from the roof of his mouth and looked around for something to drink. Something that wasn't whisky.

Now that he was verging on being properly awake, the smell of bacon was not the only thing that was out of the ordinary. He could definitely hear voices. He looked at the clock on his bedside table. It was nine in the morning. What the hell was going on?

He reached the bedroom door, and peered out onto the landing, even more confused when he opened it and realised that he recognised the sound of Clara laughing. He crept down the stairs.

'Jesus, Tom, would you go and put some clothes on? I can't cope with that this early in the morning.' Clara was standing behind his ironing board, with what looked suspiciously like one of his shirts laid out flat on the top. She set the iron down and moved out from behind it, crossing to the kitchen table where she took a couple of items from a pile of neatly folded clothing.

'I'm not sure I could cope with that at *any* time…'

Tom's head swivelled to see Trixie by the cooker. At least that solved the mystery of the bacon. His stomach lurched.

'Right, put these on.' Clara thrust a tee shirt and pair of jeans at him. 'And then come and sit down.'

He looked around the room in astonishment, and then at the clothes being held out for him, realising belatedly that he was standing in his boxer shorts, and nothing else…

'What have you done to my kitchen?' he managed. His voice sounded weird, even to him.

'Cleaned,' said Clara, matter-of-factly. 'And tidied, and washed and ironed. Thrown all your rubbish away, and poured the rest of the whisky down the sink.'

'And opened the windows,' added Trixie. 'Don't forget that. It smelled like someone had died in here.' She gave him a very direct look. 'Now go on, get dressed. Your breakfast is nearly ready.'

He stared at her. 'Trixie, I really don't think I could…'

'Clothes,' she said. 'Put them on?' The tone in her voice brooked no argument. He did as he was told.

She rolled her eyes. 'I think we meant for you to go somewhere else and put them on, but… never mind. At least it's better than all that flesh.' She turned back to the cooker. 'You can sit down now.'

He felt slightly happier being seated if he were honest, but he was still having huge trouble trying to keep up. He cradled his head in both hands, running his fingers through his hair.

'Ladies…' he began. 'I realise I'm not at my best. But would one of you kindly explain what is going on?'

Clara whisked the shirt off the ironing board, and buttoned it up over a hanger that was dangling from the door frame.

'Well, it's really very simple. Trixie and I are your fairy godmothers for this morning, because in case you haven't realised, it's Saturday.'

He looked at her blankly.

'Saturday? The day of the wedding… The wedding you're playing at, in just over four hours?'

'Oh, shit…'

'Exactly…'

'How can it possibly be Saturday, it's only…' He struggled to count off the days he'd been at home, but he couldn't get much beyond Thursday.

Trixie placed a groaning plate of food in front of him. Sausages, bacon, mushrooms, fried egg and tomatoes.

'There you go,' she said. 'Eat that, no arguments mind. I don't care whether you feel sick. I'm an ex-barmaid don't forget, I've seen it all, and heard all the excuses. You need food inside you, end of.'

★

It was now half past ten, and Tom was again sitting at the kitchen table, only this time, he was showered, shaved, properly dressed, and just about to drink another cup of coffee.

'Better?' Trixie sank into the chair beside him, an altogether softer smile on her face.

He was amazed to find that he did feel much better.

'You two make quite a team,' he smiled ruefully. 'And I'm sorry… for being such a pain in the arse.'

Trixie leaned across, nudging his arm. 'It's okay, it's allowed, under the circumstances…'

Clara came and joined them at the table. 'We've missed you the last couple of days, you know.' She gave Trixie a pointed look. 'But you know that Adam is coming tomorrow, don't you? It's all been arranged.'

Tom didn't know for definite, but he had guessed as much. 'It's a great opportunity,' he said. 'And it has to go ahead, I know that.' He inhaled and then let his breath back out slowly. 'It was just too much, you know; having it all come about because of Isobel, and then knowing that she wouldn't be around to see it. It didn't seem right. It doesn't seem right.'

'And you've still heard nothing from her?' asked Clara.

'Of course he hasn't. He wouldn't have got himself into such a state if he had, would he?' replied Trixie.

'No, I guess not… It's early days though, Tom. Don't give up hope yet. She's obviously going through a difficult time, and I'm sure she'll be in touch when she can.'

Tom gave them both a grateful smile. 'You're both being very kind, but it's ridiculous, I know that. We hardly know one another… For goodness' sake, we shared one kiss, and that's all, and I'm acting like some love-sick teenager. I don't know what's the matter with me.'

'Yup, you've certainly got it bad,' said Clara. 'I've never seen you like this, that's for sure…' She gave him a warm smile. 'But do you know something? I really rather like this version of you. The one that cares about someone else more than they care about themselves. The one that isn't afraid of talking about how they really feel. And the one who for the first time in their life has discovered what it means to fall in love…'

He opened his mouth to argue and then closed it again, staring at her. He swallowed a mouthful of coffee, and then checked the clock on the wall. And finally, he made eye contact with both Clara and Trixie, who were grinning at him like Cheshire cats.

'So, what do I do now?'

'You drink your coffee, and then you go and get your things because Seth will be here in about ten minutes. You get all your gear together, and let him drive you to the wedding where you will play beautiful music and help a young couple to celebrate their marriage. And then you start to take one day at a time because that's all you can do. And put your trust in fate, of course, because if it's meant to be, it will be…'

★

'Are you sure you're up for this, Tom? You still don't look great to be honest.'

Tom grimaced, acknowledging the truth in Seth's words. 'I can't let these people down,' he said. 'Or the guys in the band. I'll be fine. And, sadly, having gone on one or two benders in the past, I don't feel as bad as I might have otherwise.'

They had just turned into the huge wide gates of the wedding venue and were making their way up the sweeping drive. It seemed incomprehensible that he had been here with Isobel only a matter of a week or so ago. So much had happened since then.

'And you really didn't have to drive me, Seth, I would have been okay.'

Seth checked his mirror. 'You may well be still over the limit, there's no point in taking chances.'

'Yeah, but now you've got to hang around for me to finish and then bring the van back. These things don't always have a set finishing time, you know. I really don't know how late I'm going to be.'

'No, I know,' replied Seth, bringing the van to a halt by the rear door of the hotel, almost exactly where Tom had brought Isobel before. 'But then again I could always leave the van here and get a lift home with Maddie.'

Tom nodded automatically, before realising what Seth had actually said. He looked around the car park, sure enough spying Maddie's sleek sports car in one corner.

'Well now I feel really bad, having you drag Maddie over here as well. I'm sorry, Seth. I've made a total bollocks of this, haven't I?'

Seth didn't reply, but merely slid out of the driver's seat. 'Right, come on, I'll give you a hand with your gear.'

★

The blokes in the band were a great bunch, but like most blokes in a band they smoked, drank, and were not afraid of a ribald comment or two. That was why Tom liked them. They were decent, uncomplicated, ordinary people, and hugely talented with a mass of creative energy that was highly infectious. But give them an inch, and they could sometimes take a mile, and given they were expecting to meet Isobel today, Tom really didn't think he could deal with their banter.

He was just about to make up some excuse and let them know she wouldn't be coming when he felt the weight of a hand on his arm. It was Ginger, the oldest member of the band, and a good friend.

'That's tough luck, mate,' he said, with a look to Seth, who had just deposited an accordion at the edge of the stage. 'We've been told about Isobel,' he added, 'so you needn't worry; you'll get no trouble from any of us today. An' I've threatened to thump anyone who does.'

Seth straightened, looking a little sheepish. 'I thought it best to explain,' he said. 'I wasn't sure you'd be able to cope otherwise.'

Tom dragged in a breath. He was grateful, but it still hurt. 'Cheers, Ginger,' he said. 'We'll just play, okay. And I'll try not to let anyone down.'

The big man nodded, and went off with Seth to bring in the rest of the gear. With Maddie helping as well, it wasn't long before the equipment was set up, and reluctantly Tom picked up his banjo. There were plenty of wedding guests milling around now, and they were going to want to hear some sort of music soon. He plucked a string, listening to see if the note was in tune before adjusting it slightly. He checked his watch – there was only twenty minutes to go before they were on.

He had no idea how he was going to get through this. His head was feeling better than it had done first thing, but his shoulders were tight and there was a dull throb at the back of his eyes. It wouldn't take much for a full-blown headache to erupt again. He rubbed a hand across his face and concentrated on his task.

At first he didn't notice. Amid the jumble of other instruments being tuned, it was hard to make out any individual sound, but gradually the notes wormed their way into his brain. It wasn't that they were wrong, simply that they were coming from the wrong instrument. He looked up at the rest of the band, but they were all engrossed in what they were doing. He turned back to his banjo, but then looked up again sharply. Someone was tuning a violin…

His head swivelled sharply to his right, eliciting a jab of pain, but he didn't care. Because, standing just a little distance away, leaning up against a table, was Isobel.

As soon as their eyes met she broke into a run, her violin held out to one side. Seconds later, his hand was buried somewhere in her hair as he pulled her to him, breathing in the very scent of her. She was trembling as he kissed her, but after a few moments she audibly took a deep breath, and he could feel her lips begin to curve upwards into a smile as she very slowly drew away. She sniffed, pulling herself up to the tallest she could be so she could look him directly in the eye.

'One of these days I'm going to do that when I'm *not* holding a violin in my hands.'

Tom looked down at it, and then very gently took it from her, one hand still resting against her shoulders, and then, without even looking, he thrust it into the hands of the person standing next to him.

'I'm sorry,' he said, 'but would you mind holding this for me, just for a moment. There's something the lady needs to do, and she requires both hands.'

And then Isobel kissed him. Properly this time.

He pulled away, laughing, as Seth and Maddie both materialised by his side. 'You bastards,' he said, grinning. 'Every single one of you was in on this, weren't you?'

'Of course!' exclaimed Seth. 'Although to be fair, we didn't know anything about it until Isobel came banging on the door at eight o'clock this morning, asking for your address.'

'Well, we couldn't let her see you in a less than perfect state, could we? So operation Clara and Trixie was put into place to sort you out, while Isobel and I did some serious wardrobe raiding.'

Tom grinned, looking at Isobel. 'I like your boots.'

She stuck her foot out. 'Aren't they beauties? I'm not sure Trixie's ever getting these back.' The sparkly silver Doc Martens flashed in the light. 'And the dress belongs to Maddie,' she said shyly.

She was wearing a midnight blue velvet dress with a fitted bodice and a full tulle skirt which fell to just below her knees. She looked utterly perfect.

'Well I couldn't turn up in any old thing, could I? And believe me it would have been any old thing. It had to be something special, something that would exactly voice how I'm feeling. And on reflection this seemed like the perfect outfit in which to kick ass.' She paused for a moment, touching her fingers to the sumptuous dark material. 'Because, boy, do I intend to.'

'Ahem...'

There was an amused clearing of a throat from behind him, which Tom ignored the first time, until it sounded again even louder. He pulled away from Isobel, laughing.

'I might have known... you lot knew she was coming too, didn't you?' He groaned, turning back to a grinning Isobel.

'Gentlemen,' he said. 'May I present Isobel Hardcastle.'

Ginger came forward. 'Aye,' he said, grinning, 'I thought it might be.'

He held out his hand. 'Ginger Rogers,' he said.

Isobel flicked a glance to Tom. It was a common reaction. He laughed. 'It's okay, that really is his name.'

'Well, it isn't, of course, not really, but I've been called as much for so long I can't even remember what my real name is any more. I'm pleased to meet you.'

Isobel stared at his red curly hair and bushy beard. 'Ginger,' she said. 'I like it.'

He took her slender hand in his huge paw and kissed it gently. 'Now, don't you take any messing from any of these boys here, today... especially, this one.' He broke off, eyeing Tom. 'But if you do, just let me know, and I'll come and sort them out.'

Isobel laughed, looking around her. 'I'll remember that.'

Tom turned to the others. 'And this here is Jack, respectable, married, an *accountant* for goodness' sake. Then we have "Yolo", though it's spelled "I-o-l-o", as he's Welsh, but never mind, and lastly that's Pete, whose claim to fame is that he once shared a taxi with Hugh Grant.'

'It's lovely to meet you, all of you.'

'I think the pleasure's all ours,' replied Jack, giving Isobel her violin back, and Tom a direct stare, his eyebrows raised. 'You sly old devil,' he said.

Ginger gave his fellow band member a gentle punch on the arm. 'Oi, leave him be. The poor man's been through enough…'

Tom rolled his eyes. 'Right, come on, one of you lot go and get some drinks, we're on in ten minutes or so. Let's see if we can't get some of these people up on their feet.'

He took Isobel's arm, steering her gently to one side for a moment. 'You look happy,' he said. 'Still gorgeous, of course, but I didn't expect to see you looking happy. Are you okay?'

Isobel's eyes began to glisten. 'I feel amazing,' she said. 'I can't tell you now, there isn't time, but this really is the first day of the rest of my life, Tom. And I'm here, with you, that's all that matters.'

'But your father—'

'Is fine…' She gave a quick shake of her head. 'I'll explain later, but everything is fine. Perfect.'

'Then I'm glad,' he said. 'I truly am.' He took hold of both of her hands. 'And are you ready for this? It's going to be different, that's for sure.'

'I have absolutely no idea,' she replied. 'At the moment my head is buzzing so much I can hardly think straight, but I'm going to give it my best shot.'

'Right between the eyes,' he said. 'Let's knock 'em dead.'

And she did.

Chapter 26

Tom wasn't quite sure how Isobel was still going, and he suspected that she would sleep very, very well tonight. He almost laughed out loud at the thought, because there was a certain part of his anatomy which sincerely hoped that neither of them would get any sleep. He was sitting watching her from a supposedly comfortable chair which had been provided for them so that they could rest in between sessions, and he had never been more proud of anyone in his life.

Watching Isobel chat to the band now he could see that they were hanging on her every word, and it occurred to him that this afternoon had been such a success because every single one of them had been vying for the best band member accolade, and had played accordingly. Whatever their motives, and he wasn't naive enough to think that these were entirely innocent, he knew that it was mostly to make Isobel feel welcome, and he found it rather touching that they had all made such an effort.

The music they played, by its very nature, was open to interpretation, and improvisation. They jammed it up, looking to see where they could add or embellish, and they had played together for so long that they each knew each other's strengths and weaknesses, and could watch each other for the changes and signals that were almost unconscious between them. He had really hoped that Isobel would find her place among them. And then he smiled to himself; who was he kidding? He'd wanted Isobel to shine, to be an ethereal star among mere mortals. He'd wanted to shout at them all: *She kissed me, she kissed me.*

They had played their hearts out and, although it had taken Isobel a couple of numbers to really feel confident about joining in, from then on she had played up a storm. By some miracle – or, in Isobel's case, the enormous commitment she had to the things she cared about – she had managed to learn nearly all of the songs from their set list. And for those that she didn't know, she simply jumped in when she could.

Now, they were having a breather between the evening sessions. At just gone eight o'clock, the marquee where they were playing for the night was heaving with people of all ages. The band had been fed and watered, and so far they had played one set, easing folks in more gently, until they'd had time to get one or two drinks inside of them, and loosen up a little. This was when Tom loved playing the most. The band would ramp it up from now on, and Tom took a particular pride in knowing that before too long they would have everyone up on the dance floor.

He smiled as he saw Isobel walking back towards him. She had a particularly cheesy grin on her face.

'And what have you been up to?' he asked.

She plonked herself down on a chair beside him. 'Never you mind,' she said, tapping the side of her nose. 'Just sorting out a little something for later.' She gave him her best *butter wouldn't melt* look. 'So don't ask me, because I'm not going to tell you.' She fanned her face. 'Blimey, it's boiling in here.'

Tom had already rolled up his sleeves a while ago. 'It is, and it's going to get worse. Marquees are a bugger for that in the summer. Still, at least they've had the sense to put us near the back flaps. We can open those if you like before we get going again. And another drink wouldn't go amiss, would you like one?'

'Please.' She nodded. 'Just water would be great.'

He looked at her for a moment, wondering how she would take his next question. 'Isobel, can I ask you something?' He saw the assent in her eyes. 'Admittedly we haven't known each other that long, but I've never seen you drink anything other than tea, coffee, or soft drinks. Do you never have anything stronger?'

Her hands were held loosely in her lap, and she looked down at them now. 'Tom, I've been there and done that. I even still have some of my identity wristbands from the hospital to prove it. Drinking can give you a wonderful place to hide, but after a while you forget you're still behind the curtains. I decided a while ago that if no one else was going to come and find me, I'd better find myself.' She chewed at the edge of her lip. 'And actually, it's a bit like cleaning windows, you never see anything good through dirty ones.'

Tom nodded slowly, there was nothing more to say. He smiled his acceptance of everything that Isobel had ever been.

'Water it is then,' he said.

He touched a hand to the top of her hair as he rose to go and join the queue at the bar. He'd been thinking about his own drinking for a little while now, and although the last few days had seen him spectacularly fall off the wagon, he knew without doubt that he had been on his last bender. Not one single drop of alcohol had passed his lips during the day, nor would it. He was seeing things clearly for the first time in what felt like forever, and he didn't want anything to blur his vision. From the minute Tom had seen Isobel standing tuning her violin, he knew that today would be a day he wanted to remember every single second of.

'Excuse me?'

He looked up into a smiling face beside him.

'Sorry, I can see you have your hands full.' The lady beside him at the bar looked apologetic. 'I just wondered if you had a business card, that's all.'

Tom had just taken possession of two glasses and two bottles of water, and would have put them down had the space he'd just vacated not immediately been filled by three other people. He grimaced, holding out one of the bottles.

'Would you mind holding one, sorry. I can fish a card out for you then.'

'Oh, of course. Here, let me take the other one as well, and then you'll have both hands free.' She took both bottles. 'I hope you don't mind me nabbing you like this, but I don't want my husband to see. He's got a big birthday coming up later this year and I've been wondering about having a band play at the party the family are throwing for him.'

Tom gave her his best enthusiastic grin. He always made sure he carried cards with him whenever they played. It was how they got most of their business.

'I don't mind in the slightest,' he said, pulling his wallet free from his pocket, and extracting a card. 'There you go.' He took one of the bottles back so that she could take it.

'Oh, you're local. Even better. Do you get very booked up? His birthday's quite close to Christmas.'

'I'd have to check,' said Tom in his best non-committal voice, knowing full well that they were free. 'Tell you what, if you want to drop me an email in the next day or two, we can hopefully get something sorted for you. Are you folk fans?'

'Oh yes.' She nodded vigorously. 'And you're very good, especially that young violinist you have. My husband's taken quite a shine to her.' She gave a nervous laugh. 'Mind you, when you look like that…'

Tom didn't have the heart to tell her that Isobel wasn't a normal part of the band's line-up. Besides, who knew? Maybe by then she might be…

'Well, thank you, I'll hope to hear from you then.' He eyed his other bottle of water.

'Oh, yes,' she laughed. 'Sorry, you'll be wanting that, won't you?' She passed it to him, her attention already back on the business card in her hand. 'I'll definitely be in touch. Thanks again… Tom.' She looked up and smiled before turning and threading her way back through the throng of people.

Tom stared after her, grinning. All things considered the day was turning out better than he could ever have expected.

He arrived back at his seat to find Isobel deep in conversation with Ginger. The pair sprang apart like repelling magnets the minute they saw him, which Ginger found hugely funny. He snorted with laughter, desperately trying to keep a straight face, and then, realising how futile this was, gave in.

'Ay, lassie, we've been rumbled…' he spluttered, laying on a thick Scottish accent, which he did remarkably well.

Isobel too looked like she was fit to burst. 'Sorry, Tom,' she said, tapping her nose again. 'We were just discussing tactics.' She grinned at Ginger. 'I think we're done though, aren't we?'

'I reckon we are.' And with that he stood up, winking at Tom.

'I don't suppose you're going to tell me what any of that was about, are you?'

She grinned. 'Nope,' she said, getting to her feet. 'Come on, time to go.' She held out her hand, and Tom had no choice but to take it, allowing himself to be towed back up to their stage area.

'Right, lads,' said Ginger the minute they were all settled. 'What say we take no prisoners? I want every last Dick and Harry up on the floor. Isobel reckons she's got this, and if she's game, then so am I.'

There were enthusiastic nods all round. Tom felt decidedly like the last person to get the joke.

'Okay,' he said slowly, looking at Ginger. 'What are we talking?'

The others in the band all looked at one another, amused expressions on their faces, but no one said a thing. Tom waited, letting the seconds click by, but still no explanation was forthcoming.

'Anyone want to give me a clue?'

Jack took a slight step forward. 'My wedding?' he said. 'We played it then… or rather it played us…'

Tom wracked his brains, trying to think back, and then all of a sudden it came to him.

'Dear God,' he said. 'You're not serious?'

'Oh, we are, Tom, we really are,' grinned Ginger. 'You might want to take a drink before we go.'

Isobel took up her violin, and beamed at Tom. 'What could possibly go wrong?' she said.

Tom reached down for the accordion on the chair behind him, and settled it comfortably around him. He flexed his fingers experimentally, and took a deep breath.

'Ginger, you're a dead man,' he said.

The corpse in question took a step forward and switched on the mike that stood front and centre stage.

'Ladies and gentlemen,' he said, pausing for a moment until he had everyone's attention. 'Time to turn up the heat a little now. Hang onto whatever you can find... I give you... "The Parson's Farewell".' He gave a showman-like bow, before turning to the band. 'A one, a two... a one, two, three, four...'

Isobel's bow flew over her strings as the opening notes of the fastest song they ever played rang out. And that was just the start of it; from then on in, it got faster and faster...

Tom hardly stopped for breath, his eyes fixed on the group as they all followed Isobel's lead. She was merciless, elbow flying, fingers flying, hair flying, one silver boot tapping out a maniacal rhythm on the floor, but they each held their own... just. She slowed them down before the end, giving them all a moment to breathe before the dizzying finale Tom knew was coming. She was looking at them all in turn, just as they were looking at her, and with a slight nod, and a huge grin, he saw her bow draw back to its full length before she was off again, repeating the chorus one last time, a fast, crashing, fury of perfect noise that was utterly exhilarating.

And then it was over. There was a pause of perhaps a second or two but no more, before noise of a different kind filled his head, only this time the noise came from the guests. The applause was thunderous, intermingled with whoops and cheers, and the odd shout of *Again!* He had never heard anything like it. Tom slapped his hand against Isobel's in a resounding high-five, as all around him faces beamed. They had nailed it. They had bloody nailed it.

He almost missed the signal that Isobel gave Ginger and was about to say something when he realised that both Jack and Iolo were watching her as well. Confused, he shook his head at her, but she simply grinned, walking forward towards the mike.

'Did you like that?' she asked. Another roar went up, and she gave the room a thumbs up. 'It's not an easy song to play, especially if you're the accordion player, so while Tom has a rest, *I'd* like to play you something a little different.' She turned slightly so that she was practically facing him. 'It's from an original piece of music I've written which is simply called "Joy's Acre"…'

The hairs began to rise on the back of Tom's neck.

'… It's actually a place, and one that has become very special to me, for all sorts of reasons, none more so than the man currently looking rather shocked to my right. Ladies and gentlemen, get your breath back, and grab a partner, because, yes, this is a love song… Tom, this one's for you…'

Chapter 27

It was the brightest, most beautiful day Isobel had ever seen. The birds were singing and the sky was full of the lightest, fluffiest clouds... *Dear God*, she thought to herself as she drew open the curtains, *would you listen to me, I sound like Doris Day...*

She smiled as she looked out across the fields which led away from Joy's Acre, down the slope of the hill and towards the village. They did indeed look stunning in the morning sunshine, although given Isobel's mood she could have found beauty in a concrete wall today.

Since she had woken, a little after five, she had re-lived all the moments from yesterday over and over in her head. She examined them critically, as she did with most things in her life, and fully expected to find that she had been looking at them through rose-tinted glasses. It came as a huge and wonderful surprise therefore to realise that every single memory she had of the day was honest and true. Her feelings this morning were just as they had been.

There had been so much during the day that brought joy and, although at times Isobel had been so nervous she felt as if she could barely play a single note, as the day had turned to night, her fears had simply evaporated and it had been hard to even remember that they had been there in the first place. By the time their final set of the evening had come around, Isobel knew that she had finally shed the remnants of her old skin, and in its place was something shiny and new. And throughout all of her transformation, Tom had been by her side.

She turned to look back at him now, still fast asleep, one arm lying protectively over the side of the bed she had just vacated. They had slept that way for most of the night, or at least for the few hours that had remained of it, and Isobel had added it to her, admittedly still small, but growing list of things she had done for the first time. In fact, yesterday had been a day of firsts from beginning to end; the first time she knew she was in love, the first time she had played in a band, the first time she had worn sparkly silver boots and not cared one jot if people stared at her, and the first time she had ever seen a man cry.

The piece of music she had started to compose at Joy's Acre had been finished over the last few days, just as Tom had said it would, in a mad tumbling rush, that poured from her with a speed that she had trouble keeping up with. Even so, her idea to test the water with it at the wedding had only been vague in the extreme, but once she had thought of it, it was one of the few things that had kept her going. Then of course she had got chatting to Ginger and finally realised it could be a real possibility. She had only mentioned it in response to a question about what she was currently working on, but he had been so interested in the concept that his suggestion to play a part of it had been immediate. And as soon as he mentioned it she knew exactly what part she would play…

She didn't think it was a moment either Tom or her would ever forget. From the minute she started to play until her bow sounded the final note, she saw every emotion pass across Tom's face. He was deeply moved, but it was his realisation of what it had meant to Isobel that brought tears to his eyes. In the four and a half minutes that it took her, she discovered she had always had the ability to play as if her soul was laying itself bare, it had just taken a very special person to give her a reason to do so. It had come as almost as much of a surprise to Isobel herself, and for a second she had faltered in her playing, just slightly. No one listening had even noticed, apart from Tom, that was, and as the tears sprang to his eyes, she knew she would play that way from now on. Always.

She checked her watch. Despite the momentous events of yesterday, today was also a day that would hopefully be remembered by all at Joy's Acre. She had no doubt that Maddie and Seth would have made copious preparations for Adam's visit in her and Tom's absence yesterday and would be totally organised for his arrival. It was time for Isobel and Tom to get moving. There were things both of them would need to attend to and they wanted the day to be a success as much as anyone.

There were many and numerous ways in which she could wake him, and pretty much all of them brought a slight blush to her cheeks, but it was now approaching eight o'clock, which at Joy's Acre would mean the day was already very much underway. As Adam was due to arrive at ten, it was quite possible that there would be a knock at her door sometime soon. Under the circumstances perhaps the sound of the kettle boiling might be the safest way to ensure that Tom got up and about.

First on her own list of things to do was to go and find Seth. He would be busy, they all would, but she needed to get him on his own if her last little surprise was going to work. Going downstairs, she crossed to the window to see if she could spot anyone outside, but the garden was deserted. She knew Trixie would be hard at work in the kitchen, no doubt whipping up something tempting in the cake department, but the others could be anywhere. She wandered through to the kitchen, suddenly desperate for a cup of tea.

There was groan from behind her just as the kettle was coming to the boil.

'I am definitely too old for this shit…'

Isobel whirled around to find Tom standing in his shirt sleeves, rubbing a hand over his face.

'Oh, I don't know,' she replied, eyebrows arched. 'I think you performed very well last night…' She let the sentence dangle.

Tom caught the glint in her eye and broke into a broad grin. 'Why thank you, ma'am. Glad to be of service.'

'Well, don't thank me, I'm sure the rest of the band were very grateful…'

Tom's face fell. 'Oh, I rather hoped you meant—' And then he stopped suddenly, realising he'd been totally played.

'Isobel Hardcastle, you are quite without shame.'

She giggled. 'I know… great, isn't it?' She dropped her head then, suddenly feeling shy. 'Morning,' she said, looking up through her lashes.

Tom's arms went around her a second later. 'Isn't it though?' he murmured into her neck. 'Quite possibly the best one ever.' He kissed her gently on the forehead. 'Everything okay?'

'Oh yes,' she breathed. 'Everything's fine…' She pulled away slightly so that she could look at him better. 'I don't quite know what to say, Tom,' she began. 'I want to thank you, but that sounds rather trite, given what's happened over the last day or so… You've given me so much, and I—'

Tom put a finger on her lips. 'No need,' he said. 'I think we understand each other perfectly.'

And it was true, thought Isobel. There really was no need to explain. She had never felt more certain about anything in her life before.

'I'm not quite sure what we do though,' she said. 'About us, I mean, and here… what we say…'

'I wouldn't imagine we'll need to say anything,' replied Tom. 'If yesterday's mercy mission didn't spell out exactly how things are between us, then Maddie has probably had the binoculars trained on us since we got home last night…'

The thought hadn't even occurred to Isobel. 'Probably… It's not going to make it awkward for you, is it?'

Tom cocked his head at her. 'I think their response showed clearly enough how everyone here feels about things, don't you? I would say we very much have their blessing, Isobel. Not that it's needed, but then that's always been the way of things at Joy's Acre. We're all in this together, and you're as much a part of that now as any of us.'

'Today should be about Maddie and Seth, and Joy's Acre though, don't you think? There's plenty of time for us.'

'So I need to go and cancel the Red Arrows' flypast complete with skywriting then?'

Isobel tipped her head on one side. 'Hmm, maybe rearrange it for tomorrow…? Nice idea though.'

'I thought so,' Tom replied. 'Seriously though, I think you're right about today. And it's very tactful of you if I may say so, generous too. I'll obviously drag you off into the bushes the minute no one's looking though.'

'I would expect nothing less.' She held Tom's gaze for a moment longer. They really did understand each perfectly. 'Right, cup of tea next, and then bagsy me first for the shower.'

★

Isobel finally rooted Seth out in the barn. He was standing in the middle of the huge empty space staring up at the rafters.

'Penny for them?' she said.

'How many have you got?' came the reply.

'Oh… not that many actually.' She walked over to meet him. 'I've not really ever looked in here before, not properly.'

He smiled in reply. 'It's better than it was. A lot better. I've repointed all the brickwork, which is a massive job in itself, but some days the space just seems… I don't know, overwhelming.'

She followed his gaze up to the ceiling. 'There's no massive hurry for it though, is there, not for the moment?'

'No, none at all really, in the grand scheme of things. I just thought I'd pop in here for a bit, that was all, before Adam arrives. I was enjoying a little daydreaming… wondering what we could do if we had an injection of cash.'

'From a TV company perhaps?'

He grinned at her. 'Something like that…' He drew in a breath. 'Anyway, what can I do for you? You're looking very well this morning…'

She blushed. 'I have a favour to ask actually. I need a bit of help, well from you and Tom, but I don't want to ask Maddie. Could you just come over to the Thatcher's Cottage for a minute, and I can explain?

Seth gave her a quizzical look but led the way out of the barn anyway.

'The thing is, it's a bit of a surprise for Maddie, well you as well, but more so for her, I think. I'm not really sure what the plan of action is for today, but I thought that Adam would probably be given a guided tour at some point. So once we're done, would it be possible to keep her out of the cottage until then?'

'Well, I can try… but she's gone into major organisational mode as you might expect…'

They had reached the cottage door. 'There's a lot riding on this for all of you, isn't there?'

'I'm trying hard not to think of it that way. After all, a week ago, none of this had happened, and we were all perfectly happy, going about our business, knowing that we'd get there in the end...'

'But it has happened, Seth.'

'I know... but the chances of anything coming of Adam's visit are tiny. I don't want to fall into the trap of pinning all our hopes on this, and then being massively disappointed when nothing comes of it. It could sour everything we have here.'

'You'd feel like you'd all failed, when in fact nothing could be further from the truth.'

Seth looked at her as if a lightbulb had just gone on in his head. 'Yes,' he said. 'That's it exactly.' He ran a hand through his hair. 'Perhaps I could get you to remind me of this conversation if it does all go pear-shaped.'

'I'd be happy to,' replied Isobel. 'Although I'm sincerely hoping I won't need to.'

Isobel motioned for Seth to go on ahead of her. She wanted him to walk into the living room first, and was dying to see his reaction.

★

It seemed like only five minutes later that they were all gathered in the kitchen. Seth had gone to wait for Adam, so that he could be escorted inside, and now they were all loitering in a state of high agitation, waiting for his arrival.

Maddie had given Isobel an enormous hug as she entered the room, followed immediately by Trixie and Clara.

'Now the day is perfect,' said Maddie. 'It wouldn't have been right without you.' She gave a joyous smile. 'Or without you, Tom. I can't tell you how pleased I am for you both, how pleased we all are. Even though it was a bit of a shock to have Isobel come banging on the door yesterday, in so many ways the timing couldn't have been better.'

Isobel drew away from Clara's embrace. 'I'm only sorry it was so last minute.' She glanced at Tom. 'I had quite a few things to put into place at home, and it meant cutting it rather fine, but the end result was more than I could ever have wished for.'

Maddie nodded, giving her a sympathetic smile. 'I hope you don't mind, Isobel, but Tom has told us what you've been through... not the whole story, that's between the two of you, but enough to know we needed to help. And Tom was so upset, not even knowing where you'd gone. We were all so scared we'd never see you again.'

An involuntary shiver ran through Isobel. 'When I saw my mother on the doorstep, I honestly thought it was all over, but you know, it was the very fact that she had come here that gave me the strength to do what I've done. She'd invaded the one place that was mine, where I had felt myself come alive again, and I was determined not to let her take that away from me.'

'But your father's illness?'

'She made it up. I had to go with her when I heard that, I couldn't take the risk that it wasn't true. But in the end that was her downfall. Even I never thought she would stoop that low. And in doing so she gave me all the ammunition I needed to finally put my past behind me. I've consulted a solicitor, and although it might take some time to sort out my affairs, ultimately they will be *my* affairs, and no one else's. I am free to do whatever I please.'

'So how did your mother find you in the end? I still don't understand how that came about.'

'A stroke of luck on her part. A neighbour attended the wedding where I played in the string quartet. She bumped into my mother and mentioned it, that's all. It didn't take long to make a few phone calls and find out the name of the quartet and from there to find out where I was. I'd mentioned where I was staying you see, never giving it a second thought.' She felt Tom's hand slip into hers. 'But I will never, ever be going back home—' She stopped, correcting herself. 'Be going back to that place again.'

'And of course,' added Trixie, 'now that I've found someone else who shares my love of sparkly boots, we're not going to let you.'

The emotion in the room was palpable, and Isobel, who had been taught to hide hers all her life, embraced it, wiping her eyes and grinning at her sudden ability to cry happy tears.

It was Isobel who spotted Adam first. Closest to the window she had the best view of the yard and gave an excited squeal, making everyone jump, and within seconds it seemed they were all shaking hands.

Adam greeted her and Tom warmly and almost as soon as the introductions were performed he sat at the table, firing up his laptop. He told everyone at least three times that they should relax, and that today was meant to be very informal, but of course no one took the slightest bit of notice, and sat nervously waiting for him to speak. Isobel leaned up against the sink, one hand brushing against Tom's and the other fiddling with a button on her dress.

'So I guess I should explain how this all works before we go too much further, and then if you want to go ahead we can get down to practicalities before we both make a final decision.' He glanced up fleetingly in between clicks on the keyboard.

There was complete silence in the room. Tom looked at Isobel, and Clara stared at Maddie. Maddie frowned at Seth, who in turn threw a perplexed look back to Tom. No one wanted to be the one to ask the question, until Seth suddenly cleared his throat.

Becoming aware of the expectant atmosphere filling the room, Adam looked up. 'Is that okay?'

Seth nodded. 'It's fine… but, perhaps I've missed something here… when you say *final decision*, what does that mean exactly? Sorry, that probably sounds like a really stupid thing to ask.'

'No, not at all, it's only that I want you to be sure before agreeing to go ahead with the filming. I'll be honest, for me, today is really just about confirming what are fairly sound assumptions about this place but, although we obviously try and limit disruption, there will be some, I can't pretend there won't be. You need to be certain that you're happy with everything that will be involved.' He smiled, looking around the table.

Isobel saw a quick glance flick between Seth and Maddie.

'No, I'm sorry,' continued Seth. 'I'm still missing something. I thought today was just a bit of a chat, fact-finding, that kind of thing. Except you're making it sound like you have plans in place…'

Adam stopped fiddling with his laptop, and gave Seth his full attention. Then he turned his gaze on Maddie, who was smiling, but clearly confused.

'But didn't the email from Petra explain everything?'

Maddie shook her head slightly. 'Who's Petra?'

'My secretary, she's the one who—' He took in Maddie's blank expression. 'You didn't get the email, did you…? I don't believe it…' He sighed, closing his eyes for a second. 'I'm so sorry, she's just about to go on maternity leave, and… well, let's just say her mind is on other things.' He groaned slightly. 'You must think I'm totally deranged.'

Seth grinned. 'I was beginning to think I was.'

Adam pushed his laptop to one side. 'Right, well I'd better start at the beginning then.' He took his glasses off, and rubbed one eye before replacing them.

'My company has been commissioned to make a series of eight, one-hour films, focusing on four small rural businesses – so two hours essentially for each business – and these will be aired seasonally next year. We've just finished filming our spring slot, but I'm looking for a business to focus on for next summer... and from what I've seen and heard I'm pretty certain that Joy's Acre fits the bill. I've been scouting out a few possibilities, but to be honest, none of them were really what I had in mind, so meeting Isobel and Tom last week was like a sign from the heavens... I couldn't quite believe how easily it was all falling into my lap. You'd be perfect for defining the very essence of everything that's great about the summer.'

He paused for a moment to look around the room. 'A romantic back story with Joy and her paintings, an idyllic holiday setting, beautiful gardens, home-grown and -cooked food, traditional craftsmanship and, of course, at its heart, huge entrepreneurial skill which has brought it all together. People absolutely love this stuff.'

No one said a word.

'And you're a new business too, so even better.'

It was Trixie who caved first, giving a small excited squeak which she tried to smother only to have it explode from its confinement in a strangled squawk.

'Holy cow!' she yelled, grinning at Isobel, and then the room began tumbling with questions as everybody wanted to know how this had come about.

'Oh my bleepin' God!' she exclaimed.

Adam grinned. 'Now you're getting it,' he said. He looked over at Maddie, who was staring at Seth, a look that Isobel recognised well. It was the way she looked at Tom.

'I have to say, Maddie, that were it not for your website, I might not have bumped Joy's Acre quite so high up the list. Isobel and Tom did a very good job of piquing my interest, but that's rather an occupational hazard, and often when I do a little digging, things fall flat. Only not in this case. Everything I saw on the site just seemed to draw me in deeper and deeper.' He angled his laptop around so that she could see it. 'This, for example, would work very well as a concept on film too. I love the whole scrapbooking idea. Please tell me you haven't lied about any of this…'

'I haven't lied about any of it,' said Maddie, in a deadpan voice, looking frankly stunned.

Adam laughed, a deep throaty chuckle. 'I tell you what. I can see you're all finding this a little hard to take in. Why don't we go for a wander and I'll let you guys do the talking.' He made to pull his chair back from the table, and waited for everyone else to do the same. 'And don't be shy. I want nervous ramblings, passionate ravings, seemingly mindless chatter, it all helps build a picture and, believe it or not, some of the best gems come from when people think they're either boring me or have an excruciatingly bad case of verbal diarrhoea. Shall we go?'

Chapter 28

There was a mad scramble as everyone got to their feet, with Maddie and Seth leading the way. Isobel hung back, noticing that Tom had done the same. He'd made no obvious point of it by being overtly chivalrous and ushering Clara and Trixie on ahead of him, but the soft kiss that found its way onto her lips as they reached the doorway made the point very nicely indeed.

Joy's Acre was looking its absolute best. The gardens were flooded with sunlight and painted with every colour of the rainbow. Not only that, but the vegetable garden was burgeoning with produce. Everywhere you looked nature was showing off her bountiful best, helped of course by Clara's ever green fingers.

'Oh my goodness,' said Adam, walking forwards into the middle of it. 'I had no idea. You get absolutely no sense of this from the house, do you?' He turned to Clara. 'And this is all your handiwork, yes?'

She nodded, shy, but with a proud grin on her face. 'Mostly. But Seth and Trixie help out too.'

Seth took a step forward. 'We water stuff, Adam, or occasionally do other piddling little jobs. This is absolutely all down to Clara.'

'Well, I've never seen anything quite like this.' He spun around, trying to take it all in. 'And how long will it look like this, Clara? I can't believe it will get any better.'

'Oh, a few more weeks yet. It looks particularly lovely at the moment because some of the showiest flowers are out right now. But things come and things go, and there's always something to take their place. Everything has its time in a garden, but from the quietest darkest days to the loudest and most flamboyant, there is something of worth to be found in it all.'

Adam stared at her. 'I think that's quite possibly the nicest way of looking at life I've ever heard.'

Clara blushed furiously under his gaze but she caught Trixie's eye and grinned.

'I'm just thinking of filming times, you see. I don't want to miss any of this, so I think we need to look at this aspect with some urgency, particularly as I'd imagine it impacts quite heavily on the produce and cooking side of things. You must feel like a kid in a sweet shop right now, Trixie?'

'I'm totally spoilt for choice: strawberries, potatoes, beans, spinach, gooseberries, peas, rocket, celery, redcurrants, beetroot, courgettes…' She broke off, laughing. 'Do I need to go on?'

Adam was still gazing around the garden. 'Amazing. And I need to see this cookbook too before I go. I saw some of the recipes on the website, and you're going to sell these at the local markets, is that right?'

'Well, it's only a hand-bound thing, but yes, that's the idea.'

'Doesn't matter,' replied Adam. 'It's still a brilliant example of the way in which Joy's Acre connects with the local community. Don't let me forget, will you?'

Trixie shook her head. 'No bloody way.'

'So now I ought to look at the buildings themselves. Seth, can you talk me through their renovation, and then I want to get a close look at your thatching, Tom. I was intrigued by your website too, the whole thing with the bread and the straw being a by-product of that industry. You know, that had never actually occurred to me – how closely the two were related.'

Tom's eyes sought out Isobel's as he acknowledged Adam's compliment.

Seth pointed towards the cottage Tom had been working on. 'Let's go inside first, and you can see where we're up to.'

He led the way across the garden. 'The cottages are obviously Victorian, and it was important that we kept the whole site as true to its heritage as possible. It was Maddie actually who came up with the idea of having a theme for each of the cottages and then furnishing them accordingly. So Isobel is staying in the Gardener's Cottage, and this next one will be the Thatcher's Cottage. Then after that the Blacksmith's and finally the Woodcutter's. The basic structures were still relatively sound, but needed re-thatching of course, and then we've stripped out the insides to provide a blank canvas for whatever we can salvage, reclaim or generally reinvent to provide for in the way of furniture and decor.'

'And you've managed to successfully marry these with modern fittings as well?'

'Hmm, a tricky one,' replied Seth. 'But we knew that while visitors might like to stay in a traditional cottage they would certainly not like original Victorian plumbing, so no, we've had to compromise in those areas, simply to get folks interested in staying here, but, well, hopefully you'll see for yourself if that has worked when you see where Isobel is staying. For now, have a look at what's still work in progress.'

He invited Adam to enter the cottage first, stepping back so that Maddie could follow immediately after. He turned and gave Isobel a swift thumbs up as he did so, which no one noticed, apart from her and Tom. She really hoped she'd got it right…

Fortunately, she didn't have to wait that long to find out. It was the first thing Adam noticed.

'Stunning,' he said simply as he walked in the living room.

Her heart gave a small leap of pride, because she had to agree with him. It had exceeded all her expectations.

Maddie's mouth hung open. 'Oh…' was all she could manage. But then she turned to Isobel, her eyes shining. 'When did you do this? It's beautiful… and perfect, just perfect.' She flung both arms around her, hugging her tight. 'I can't thank you enough.'

Adam was looking between the two of them. He was quick to catch on. 'You made this, Isobel?'

Hung on the whitewashed wall in front of them, perfectly centred, was the salt dough wheat sheaf she had made. It was the colour of warm bread fresh from the oven, with a rich smooth sheen to it. Not only that, but to each side was a cornucopia which overflowed with fruits and vegetables, each one carefully crafted until they were almost exact replicas of the real thing, painted and varnished. They provided just the right touch of colour without detracting from the intricacy of the centrepiece.

'I wanted to give back something to Joy's Acre, in return for all it's given me,' said Isobel, biting her lip slightly in embarrassment. 'It seemed the right thing to do.'

Maddie hugged her again, and then so did Tom, surprising her with a kiss full on the lips, just a quick one before returning to stand back beside Seth, but it was enough.

Seth slung an arm around Tom's shoulders. 'Completely and utterly perfect in every way.' And Isobel wasn't entirely sure to what he was referring.

'And that's not all she's done either,' remarked Tom, looking not unlike the Cheshire cat. 'Go on, Isobel, tell everyone.'

Isobel could feel her future beckoning. A violinist who had fallen in love with a place so much she had written a piece of music about it, just as Joy herself all those years ago had painted her love for her home on canvas.

'I've written some music,' she began, unsure how to continue. She could see Maddie and Seth exchanging glances with Adam, as was everyone else. 'I could play it to you, if you want me to… a bit later on.'

'What kind of music?' asked Adam immediately.

'A story, if you like. About a place I've come to love very much, and the people who live there.'

Maddie looked at Seth for confirmation. 'I'm sorry, Adam, but I think we've got to hear this now, it's way too exciting to wait. We can always come back here after…'

Isobel was torn. In a few minutes, once they had finished inside the cottage, they would move outside and it would be Tom's turn to shine. His chance to showcase all his hard work that had provided, and would provide, each and every one of the cottages here with their crowning glory. He deserved this as much as anyone, and she so desperately wanted Adam to see his talent. She looked hesitantly across to him, but he was standing, just as he had at the first wedding she had played at, in the very moment before she had struck the first note; feet planted, a soft smile on his face and love and encouragement in his eyes. He gave her the slightest of nods, blowing her a kiss.

'This just gets better and better,' murmured Adam. 'Go on, Isobel,' he said, 'lead the way.'

Her heart was in her mouth as she opened the cottage door and stepped outside. She never dreamed she would be doing this again quite so soon.

'Come on,' whispered Tom, holding out a hand for her to take.

Together they walked across to the cottage that she would always think of as hers and went through into the living room. She picked up her violin, which lay where it always had since she arrived, and moved to stand against the far wall, waiting until everyone had settled round her.

'You'll have to bear with me,' she said, 'because this is all very new to me too. I haven't had much chance to practise.'

Then she lifted the instrument, and gave one final flick of her head, sending her hair flying back over her shoulder, before tucking her violin under her chin. She readied her bow.

'This is from an original piece of music I've written,' she said. '"Joy's Acre".'

She closed her eyes, and everything that Isobel had become poured out onto her strings, sending all her emotion, love and profound joy soaring around the room.

Lost in the music, she only just heard Adam's voice sound quietly after a few moments. 'I think we may have found the perfect score for the documentary, don't you?'

Isobel smiled at Tom and continued to play, and as the notes rang out though the open windows of the little cottage on the hill and out into the summer air, Isobel knew that her journey was far from over, in fact, it was only just beginning.

A Letter from Emma

Thank you so much for your company throughout *Summer at the Little Cottage on the Hill.* If this was your first visit to Joy's Acre, I hope it's a place you have come to love as much as I have. If you'd like to stay updated on what's coming next then please sign up to my newsletter here:

www.bookouture.com/emma-davies

Of course, Seth, Maddie, Tom, Trixie and Clara first began to tell their story in *The Little Cottage on the Hill,* and I have loved seeing them grow and develop individually as I've written each successive book. I never know quite how they're going to turn out, and as characters they have managed to surprise me on more than one occasion, but I hope you'll join them again as autumn and winter both bring new challenges, romance, and a few tough times as well. As with any community, life isn't always plain sailing, but with a little love, hope and friendship, plus copious amounts of cake of course, many a storm can be weathered, and it's been an absolute joy to spend a year in their lives. I hope you think so too.

One of the things I love about being a writer is when readers take the time to get in touch, it really makes my day. The easiest way to do this is by finding me on Twitter and Facebook, or you could also pop by my website, where you can read about my love of Pringles among other things…

I hope to see you again very soon, and in the meantime, if you've enjoyed your visit to Joy's Acre, I would really appreciate a few minutes of your time to leave a review or post on social media. Even a recommendation to anyone who'll listen at the hairdresser's is very much appreciated!

Until next time,
Love Emma x

@EmDaviesAuthor

www.facebook.com/emmadaviesauthor

www.emmadaviesauthor.com

Acknowledgements

Music can be defined as the art of sound in time... that which expresses ideas and emotions in significant form through elements of rhythm, melody, harmony and colour, but however you define it, it is an extraordinarily powerful thing. It does indeed transcend time, and stays with us and is a part of us throughout our lives. In fact, hearing is the last of our senses to leave us before we die.

I wouldn't class myself as a musical person at all; I don't play any instruments for example, but music has always been there as the back beat of my life. For me, like books, music has the most wonderful ability to conjure up images, to transport me to new places or even to invoke memories of past times and places, and so for me personally the writing of this book has taken me on a huge journey of my own.

It took me a while to truly understand Isobel, and I so desperately wanted to tell her story in the right way, so huge thanks are due to my editor Jessie Botterill at Bookouture for helping me to shape her and her story in the best way possible.

And lastly, to musicians everywhere, a huge debt of gratitude is due. Not only have you inspired me, but you bring an immense gift to the world, and I couldn't imagine ever being without it.

Made in United States
North Haven, CT
28 July 2022